DEATH SONG

Jørgen Brekke

TRANSLATED BY STEVEN T. MURRAY

PAN BOOKS

First published in Norway 2012 by Gyldendal Norsk Forlag
First English language edition published in the USA 2015 as *Dreamless*
by St. Martin's Press 175 Fifth Avenue, New York, N.Y. 10010

First published in the UK in paperback 2015 by Pan Books
an imprint of Pan Macmillan
20 New Wharf Road, London N1 9RR
Associated companies throughout the world
www.panmacmillan.com

ISBN 978-1-4472-2274-3

Copyright © 2012 by Jørgen Brekke
Translation copyright © 2015 by Steven T. Murray

The right of Jørgen Brekke to be identified as the
author of this work has been asserted by him in accordance
with the Copyright, Designs and Patents Act 1988.

1 3 5 7 9 8 6 4 2

A CIP catalogue record for this book is available from the British Library.

Printed and bound by CPI Group (UK) Ltd, Croydon, CR0 4YY

Visit **www.panmacmillan.com** to read more about all our books
and to buy them. You will also find features, author interviews and
news of any author events, and you can sign up for e-newsletters so
that you're always first to hear about our new releases.

To Karl, for all the songs

Little Charles, sleep sweetly in peace,
Soon enough you must wake,
Soon enough see our evil time
And taste its gall.
The world is an island of sorrow
As soon as you breathe you must die
And stay behind as earth.

—Carl Michael Bellman

PROLOGUE

A *fly balanced* on the edge of the blade, its wings tucked in.

How did it do that?

If he turned the ax and brought it down on the chopping block, he'd cleave the insect in two. If it stayed there, of course. But they never did, those flies. They didn't stay in one place. Not like he did. Sitting at the piano every day, his father standing behind him, holding a stick that he'd been given by a conductor who was more famous than he was. The stick stung the boy's fingers.

I make mistakes when I play because I don't have the music in my fingers like he does, thought the boy.

He liked reading the musical scores. They conjured up pictures and figures, secrets written in a language that he only partially understood. He never let his father watch when he read the scores. That would encourage his father's dreams, give him hope and make him even more cruel.

His fingers. The ax. The fly.

He blew at it, and it took off buzzing toward the rafters. Then he turned the ax. If he spread his fingers he could see the cuts that had been made in the chopping block. His right hand lay on the uneven surface. He was left-handed and didn't want to lose any fingers he might need. So he aimed for the little finger and ring finger on his right hand. They were the two least important. It was essential to strike in the right place, not too far up, not too far down. If he chopped off only a little stump, that wouldn't be enough. He mustered all of his attention.

The ax whistled through the air and struck just under the middle joint of the two fingers. The sound reached his brain before the pain did. Crunching, like the sound of his mother slicing carrots. Then a silent movie began rolling. Two fingers shot up in separate arcs from the chopping block and landed on the damp garage floor. They were like rubber, bouncing away before coming to a halt. Only when they stopped moving did he notice the burning heat in his hand.

Then he heard his father outside.

"If you quit fooling around and really try to play this time, you can come back inside."

The garage door opened.

His father stood there, motionless, staring at him. At first his face was flat and stiff, like a marble bust. Then he screamed.

His father understood what he'd done.

In the silence after the scream, the big man collapsed. But the boy remained standing there quite calmly, listening to the blood dripping onto the floor. Rhythmically, as if striking the keys of a piano. Music was finally pouring from his fingers.

The fingers. The drops of blood. The floor.

At last those terrible hours at the piano were over.

PART I

I

Stockholm, 1767

Christian Wingmark moved his eyes from the dice he was holding to the fly on the watchmaker's forehead. It was moving slowly, counterclockwise. Between them towered stacks of coins. More than 107 *riksdaler*. The only thing that mattered. When he threw the three dice, any count above nine would win him the whole pot. Only the gaming board could offer the prospect of a better life to a troubadour and rogue like him, who otherwise lived a vile and foul-smelling existence.

There were many men seated around the table, but he focused only on the royal watchmaker, from whom time had run away. Jean Fredman's face was slack, as if he'd already been defeated. At one time he'd been in charge of the clock on the cathedral, responsible for time in the capital of the realm; he'd been a gentleman among the most honorable of men. Ballads had been sung about him in those days. But who would sing about him now? Wingmark had no idea whether it was the loss of his workshop, his obsession with gambling, or a thirst for strong spirits that first had toppled the watchmaker, but he'd lost both his wits and all sense of decorum and no longer knew even what time it was. Mad dreams had kept him at the gaming table lately, and his hands had grown so accustomed to raising a goblet that soon they'd be able to do little else.

He and Wingmark were the only ones left vying for the pot. A watchmaker who could already see Charon beckoning from the rushing river, and a young troubadour who might have found his muse.

"Yesterday I wrote the ballad that will make me rich and famous one day," he said loudly to the assembled players, noticing that his hands had stopped trembling. "All I need is this pot. It will more than cover the printing costs."

No one spoke. He was filled with trepidation and anticipation.

"Oh, shut up and throw the damned dice!" shouted one of the men crowded around the table.

A pot this big had never been seen before at the inn called the Golden Peace, and all the other customers had gathered around the two men who were fighting for it. Everyone was impatient to see the outcome.

"No, let's hear more about this ballad," said a man with a deep voice.

It was the innkeeper who spoke, a red-nosed man with a talent for music who had mastered the French horn, flute, lyre, oboe, bassoon, clarinet, bass violin, and harp. He also dabbled in playing kettledrums in addition to running the inn. He was seated at the table with the other men, although he'd been knocked out of the game several rounds earlier.

Wingmark glanced at the innkeeper, then ran his hand over his forehead and wiped the sweat on his trousers.

"If you do have a song that might truly bring fame and honor to an idler like you, we'd like to hear it," said the innkeeper, a dangerous glint in his eye. Everyone at the table, even the pitiful watchmaker, bellowed with laughter. They didn't believe him. But that was of no consequence. One day they would all see him for what he was.

Wingmark didn't utter a word until the laughter had subsided. Then he said, "Tonight I prefer to let the dice speak on my behalf." He looked at poor Fredman, who immediately stopped snickering.

"Well said. So throw the dice," replied the merry innkeeper.

His heart stood still. He looked at the dice as they rolled back and forth on his clammy palm. He clicked his tongue, stamped his feet in time to an inner melody, and took one last gulp from his goblet. Then time stood still as well. It was as if Fredman had sucked all of time into his fevered chest. Wingmark's hand began to move. It hovered at the edge of the table. The spectators all leaned forward, as if they might see the numbers on the dice in advance. Then he sketched an arc in the air. The dice flew from his hand, and he felt like he'd thrown tiny bits of himself across the tabletop. He fixed his eyes on only one of the dice, the one that landed last. For an instant, it teetered between five and one, but then fell with the one showing.

He shut his eyes to think. *I need at least nine from the two dice that I haven't dared to look at. Am I to fail after all?* Then he opened his eyes and stared at Fredman. Wingmark realized that the watchmaker had already looked, and he was seeing the face of a vanquished man. Quickly he glanced down. All three dice were on the table, and one of them showed a one. The two others showed five. At that instant he fell forward and felt his forehead strike the table with a thud. A marvelous new melody filled his head.

In a daze, he stood up and held his arms high.

A tempered cheer spread through the premises, and he realized that most of the customers must have been siding with the watchmaker. But what did that matter? It didn't make his sense of intoxication any less. Tonight he would buy a drink for all of them. Tomorrow he could go to the printer.

Then a roar came from the entrance and everyone turned toward the sound. A stout man stood in the doorway. Around six foot two, he was dressed like a gentleman, and Wingmark knew that a gentleman he was.

Two days ago, the troubadour had written a ballad for Sir Erik's eldest daughter, who was about to be married. He'd used the payment to buy his way into this game. Now he was the only one who understood why a furious man was standing in the entryway to the Golden Peace. The man was Sir Erik's most trusted servant. The ballad had not found favor with the highborn lord. Something in the song must have offended him. Could it have been the comparison between Sir Erik's daughter and Aphrodite? Or was it the impudent Bible parodies that Wingmark had woven into the song, which he himself had found so amusing?

"Where is that cursed trickster?" bellowed the man in the doorway.

Everyone stepped aside, understanding that this had to do with Wingmark. He'd just won the biggest pot in the history of the Golden Peace. Nobody won that sort of fortune without paying a price.

With three angry strides the stout fellow arrived at the table.

"Aha! So here you are. You call yourself a poet, but really you're nothing more than a charlatan whose only talent is the ability to offend all that is good and noble." The well-dressed gentleman looked at him with scorn. "But why am I wasting my words on you?"

Wingmark noticed that he was holding a rapier in one hand. From his belt he drew out another. This weapon he tossed on the table, scattering the silver and copper coins in all directions.

Wingmark stared, bewitched at the sword and the money that would buy him a way out of debt and misfortune. But what would buy his way out of this dilemma?

"Take the sword or leave it! Either way, I'm going to end your life, you miserable worm."

Wingmark grabbed the sword from the table.

"Perhaps you are right," he said. "The ballad was not one of my best. But I assume that a gentleman such as yourself would wish to settle this dispute outdoors, am I right?" He pointed toward the door.

"If you wish. It makes no difference to me where you begin your journey to hell." He motioned for Wingmark to lead the way.

For a brief moment the troubadour considered whether he might stuff a few coins in his pocket without his adversary noticing, but he saw that the money was lost. Now it was a matter of saving his life.

Slowly he walked out of the inn, holding the sword. Behind him came Sir Erik's man, with all the customers from the Golden Peace in tow. Once outside, he bowed to his opponent and took up the proper stance as he glanced around. Then he threw the sword to the ground and turned on his heel. With his back turned, he dropped his trousers around his knees and bent forward, exposing his pale backside.

"Here you have my honest opinion of your Sir Erik's daughter. Give him my greetings," he said and then turned again to face his challenger.

The man was momentarily stunned, his mouth falling open. Then he raised his sword.

Wingmark thumbed his nose at him and heard the laughter swell from the crowd that had gathered. Then he took off running. He shoved his way between two half-drunk spectators and broke free from the throng. After taking two steps forward, he stumbled on a loose cobblestone and fell to his knees, but he quickly got back on his feet before anyone managed to stop him. Then he sped off in earnest, and no one could catch him. He ran inside the wretched garret he had rented to fetch his lute, his notebook, and a much too meager cache of money.

After that, Wingmark disappeared from Stockholm for good. He knew what he had done. No one insulted Sir Erik or his daughter or his servant without paying a price. If he ever set foot in the city again, he was a dead man.

He found a little-used bridle path and followed it away from the city, heading in a northwesterly direction. Only a few times did he turn to look back at Stockholm. It was a beautiful city, filled with dreams and songs. The narrow lanes might seem perfect for dancing during the long summer nights. But in the winter they were cold and filled with snow. He'd spent his best and worst years there. Watched his youth disappear. In spite of years of misery, trouble with women, and drunkenness, he remembered that his real name was not Christian Wingmark, and that he'd learned to play his first lute in a different city, in another country, where he had once been happy.

When he could no longer see the city behind him, he was surrounded by forest on all sides, and he had acquired the company of countless flies. Their early appearance this spring was a torment. People said that it was because of the unusually warm temperatures at night. But right now the flies didn't bother him. He listened to their buzzing and imagined it was a melody.

Then he began to compose a new ballad.

2

Grälmakar Löfberg was not really his name; it was just something he called himself. He was being buffeted by a gusty wind coming from the street, so he stopped. It was an unreliable wind, constantly shifting. Through the trees he could see the Ludvig Daaes Gate as snowflakes blew past the streetlights like swarms of soundless insects in the night. The cars had disappeared, leaving Trondheim in silence. The gusts slowly subsided, and few thoughts crossed his mind. Only the memory of a dream. It was weeks ago that he'd dreamed of anything at all, but old dreams still whirled in his thoughts like withered leaves. He'd met the devil over on Nonnegata, right outside the kiosk where he went every day to buy his cigarettes.

Satan was a polite man with a black coat and a hollow gaze.

"Have you finally come to get me?" Löfberg asked.

"No," said the devil gloomily. "You've been here a long time."

When he asked what that meant, he received no reply. Only after awaking did he understand the meaning: Hell is having to keep doing what you've always done.

Slowly he allowed this phantom of a dream to disappear into the dark of night. He took the music box out of his pocket and wound it up. The music began as soon as he let go of the key. He turned around, took two steps back, and set the music box on top of her. That was when he heard footsteps on the deserted street.

It felt like the wind was following her, poking her in the back the whole way, as if the icy gusts were trying to hurry her through her nightly walk, back to the bed where she should have been with her snoring husband. For once, Evy Saupstad hadn't fallen asleep before he started his loud sawing, and then it was too late. Now she was paying for how soundly she'd slept on the plane home from Tenerife. She envied her husband, who had waited until they got home to sleep. At the corner of Ludvig Daaes Gate and Bernhard Getz' Gate, in the Rosenborg district where she lived, she stopped to let her dog do his business.

She looked at her watch. It was three-thirty in the morning. She was glad she was still on vacation for a few days yet, so she could sleep late.

Her side of the street was lined with trees. This green oasis in the neighborhood was a wooded hill that rose steeply for several hundred yards.

She was about to straighten up when she heard the melody. It came from somewhere among the trees. A slow, rolling tune, bright and clear. She walked toward the music.

She was less than ten steps from the street when she saw something in the pale shimmer that filtered through the bare wintry branches of the trees. It was a lovely little thing, a cylinder-shaped box with a ballerina twirling on the lid as the music played. The ballerina seemed to be trying to shake off the snow that had settled on her hair. As soon as Evy Saupstad caught sight of the music box, it abruptly stopped. Silence descended over the trees, and she thought about how quiet it was at this time of night. The lonely hours. If someone really wanted to be alone in a city like Trondheim, this was the time to go outside.

The dog started barking, and that was when she saw it. The music box was not sitting on the ground. The snow had spread a white blanket over the figure underneath, a lifeless human body. As she moved closer, she saw that the snow was red near the neck. Blood had gushed out of the slit throat and congealed in the cold. A metallic smell wafted past her nose, then disappeared with the snowflakes and the wind gusting past.

Evy couldn't help gasping. She looked around anxiously. Footprints led away from the corpse and into the woods before veering toward the entrance to a motorcycle club. The driveway to the club was approximately fifty yards farther along Ludvig Daaes Gate, toward Rosenborg School. The footprints were starting to disappear under the snow. She turned on her heel and ran the few yards out of the woods. The dog stopped barking as soon as they reached the street. The little creature made her feel safer, even though she realized that a one-year-old miniature dachshund would be no match for the monster who was responsible for what she'd just seen.

Then she pulled out her cell phone and called the police.

He headed toward the bomb shelter. He could see her from where he was standing. She leaned down to pet the dog, and fortunately it stopped barking. He couldn't stand the barking. It made his head spin. He took a deep breath.

The woman took a cell phone out of her pocket and tapped in a number.

He stood and watched as she talked. He could hear the shrill tone of her voice but not the words she said. His footprints were starting to be erased from the ground, but the body had been found before it vanished completely under the mantle of white. Did it matter? He took a roundabout way back to the car and then drove home, to the yellowish brown ceiling over the bed and the hours of sleepless agitation.

3

Chief Inspector Odd Singsaker realized that he'd been too pessimistic when he bought a new bed after his divorce. For some reason he'd assumed he'd be sleeping alone for the rest of his life, so he'd chosen a single bed. It was relatively wide for just one person, but much too narrow to share it with someone else, especially an American homicide detective who slept like a restless snake. This was intolerable if the intention of spending time in bed was to sleep, which was occasionally the case.

It was 2:00 A.M. He'd been awakened by Felicia's hand on his shoulder. He moved it away, placing it carefully on the duvet. He lay there, listening to her breathing as he thought about the dream that he'd been yanked out of. He'd been arguing with her, the sort of stupid argument that happens only in a dream. He told her that he never listened to music, at least not if he could help it. This had made her unaccountably upset, and she had threatened to leave him and go back to the States. What could he possibly say to that? His clothes were suddenly soaking wet. Sweat dripped from his shirt-sleeves.

At exactly that moment Felicia had put her hand on his shoulder and he'd awakened. Relieved. As much because she was not going anywhere as because he was not sweating. His skin felt refreshingly dry. He wondered if this dream held some hidden meaning, but he couldn't decide what it might be. Long ago, he had admitted to Felicia that he hated music, and she had merely laughed when he explained that music disturbed his thoughts.

"Does that mean that you need to be thinking all the time?" she had asked.

"Yes, I think I do," he'd replied.

He stared into the dark. Next to him, Felicia turned over, smacking her lips.

I'm afraid of losing her, he thought. That was what the dream meant, nothing more. It was his fear of being abandoned. The thing was that he didn't yet fully understand why Felicia Stone had stayed in Trondheim after the events of last fall. Why had she chosen him?

It took a long time for him to fall asleep again. And when he did, he was awakened by the phone ringing. He grabbed it from the nightstand.

The alarm clock told him it was 4:03. For a moment he lay still, staring at the bright little display of his cell phone, which was trembling like a lemming in his hand. He saw the name of his boss, Gro Brattberg, who was the head of the Violent Crimes division of the Trondheim police.

Thirty minutes later, Odd Singsaker was standing outside in the snowstorm on Ludvig Daaes Gate, suddenly aware that he was still wearing his pajama top under his coat. The process of getting dressed had gone a bit too swiftly for a distracted chief inspector this morning. Strangely enough, these pajamas were the last Christmas present that he'd gotten from his ex-wife, Anniken, before they'd separated. They were made of heavy flannel and were warm under his winter clothes. He fastened the top button of his coat, hoping that Grongstad, the crime tech who was now approaching from the grove, wouldn't notice the pajama collar sticking up. Slowly and methodically a team of white-clad techs worked among the trees. They seemed to almost merge with the falling snow as they muttered to one another. The surrounding area had already been secured by uniformed officers.

Grongstad was a self-possessed man who seldom wasted words, never bothering Singsaker or the other detectives with anything they didn't need to hear. But at the moment he was unusually upset.

"This fucking snowstorm!" he said. "It's contaminating the whole crime scene. All the good footprints are gone. Such rotten luck that it's snowing tonight."

"It often snows this time of year," said Singsaker drily.

"But why tonight? It's so rare to have such a fresh crime scene. The body is still warm. And then everything is ruined by the heaviest snowfall of the year."

"Look at the bright side. If that woman hadn't been out walking her dog in the middle of the night, we probably wouldn't have found anything at all until spring. I'm sure you'll find something." Then Singsaker added, "But maybe you've already found something?"

"Well, yes," Grongstad replied. "As a matter of fact, a couple of things have caught my attention." Now he was back in his usual mode. "The footprints have been totally wrecked as far as providing us with any evidence, but they haven't been completely erased. I'm guessing that we're talking about a size eight and a half shoe or larger, which makes it highly likely that our perp is a man. We can see where he came from and in which direction he left. It looks like he made a few circuits of the grove before he moved on. What's interesting is that it seems he entered the grove from the street, where we're standing, and then left by way of the motorcycle club." Grongstad pointed toward an opening in the trees about ten yards away from where they stood.

Singsaker was trying hard to get his brain working. It took him a lot longer to wake up in the morning since he'd had brain surgery a year ago.

"So that means he didn't go back to a parked car," he said.

"Exactly. Of course he could have arrived by car, but as you point out, he may not have parked it at the edge of the woods, which would seem to be the natural thing to do if you wanted to dump a body."

"I'm not sure the words *natural* and *dump a body* really belong in the same sentence, Grongstad," said Singsaker. "But I get what you mean."

"The theory that he arrived on foot is supported by the tire tracks. Or rather, the lack of them. A couple of vehicles have driven by here in the past few hours, and their tracks have also been nearly covered by the snow. But there is no indication that anyone pulled over and parked here around the time that the footprints were made in the woods. If anyone had been trying not to draw attention to themselves, it would have been most natural to pull into the driveway to the motorcycle club, since it's partially hidden from the road. But there aren't any tire tracks. Not even old ones. So, we're not able to ascertain anything definite based on the snow-covered footprints. We don't even know whether the same person made all the prints. It looks like the perp wandered around in the area. Plus, we have the footprints from our witness. She entered at about the same spot as the perp, and then exited the same way she'd come in. It's possible that a third person could have been on the scene as well."

"So theoretically the victim could have come here alone or even with the murderer, and then been killed right here?"

"It's possible. But in that case, it happened quickly and without much of a fight. So far we haven't found anything in the blood spatter that can tell us much. They've also been largely wrecked by the snow, and we've found only small amounts of blood around her throat. The blood could have come from the fatal blow, but it's also possible that he cut her throat afterward."

"Wait a minute, Grongstad. What do you mean, 'afterward'?" Singsaker suddenly shivered. He was reminded of a case he'd investigated last fall, the so-called Palimpsest murders. Several flayed corpses had been involved.

"He removed something from inside her throat. At first we thought he'd simply slashed her neck. But then we found this." Grongstad opened the briefcase at his feet and took out a plastic bag. Inside was a short pipe-shaped lump of cartilage. Someone had cut it to bits. "We think this is her larynx," Grongstad went on, "or what's left of it. Looks like he removed something else. But this is Kittelsen's domain, of course."

"Kittelsen. Right," said Singsaker absentmindedly, pausing to think and chew gently on his tongue. Kittelsen worked in the main lab in the Department of Pathology and Medical Genetics at St. Olav Hospital. He was one of Norway's grumpiest forensic doctors, but also one of the most meticulous.

"I'm sure Kittelsen will be able to tell us what happened here," he said. "But not why. What do you make of it all, Grongstad?"

"I'm not sure. We also found this music box. It was on the victim's stomach. That was why the witness discovered the body. If it hadn't been playing a tune, she would have walked right past, and the body would now be lying under two feet of snow. Was this a blunder, or was it deliberate? And what does the music box have to do with it?" Grongstad took it out of the briefcase.

Singsaker studied the little ballerina, noticing at once that this was no cheap mass-produced figure. Her hair looked like genuine human hair, and her facial features had been hand-painted, giving the doll personality. A tiny, shy, and yet haughty-looking woman.

"I've never heard this tune before," said Grongstad, winding up the music box. "Do you know it?"

He let go of the key, and the two policemen listened to the melody in silence. Finally, Singsaker shrugged.

"You know me and music, Grongstad," he said, smiling apologetically.

4

He was asleep and back in the woods. It was the same night. The body was still lying at his feet.

The heavens had cleared. He could see the huge moon. Clouds scudded past, and for one bizarre moment, it felt as if they were the ones standing still as the moon tumbled out of control across the sky. He felt as small as a snowflake. At first he thought it was a cloud formation. But it wasn't. It was a man. He was moving across the sky with a big rolled-up sheet of paper in his hands. And it might be the ballad he was holding. It was almost certainly the ballad. The man's face was in shadow beneath a dark hood.

And behind him came the man with the violin.

Then came the men carrying the coffin.

He could hear the melody, the music they were marching to. Step by step by step they traversed the sky. Giants bearing a burden on their shoulders, keeping pace, moving slowly, like time itself. Father is inside that coffin, he thought.

Then he awoke and stared up at the filthy ceiling. He lay there with a nagging feeling that the dream should have lasted longer.

But what does it matter? he thought. I dreamed. For the first time in weeks, I dreamed. But it wasn't her song that had made him fall asleep. The song hadn't worked the way he'd expected.

It was 6:45. Strictly speaking, it was early, but Singsaker was no longer struggling to wake up. He felt strangely clearheaded, even though he hadn't yet had his daily shot of aquavit. Or maybe that was precisely the reason.

They were assembled in the conference room of the Violent Crimes and Sexual Assault team of the Trondheim police, with as much coffee as they'd been able to scrounge up. With them was the head of the department, Gro Brattberg. Also present was Inspector Thorvald Jensen, the only colleague Singsaker ever socialized with. He did his best to share Jensen's enthusiasm for hunting and ice bathing, but in his heart he knew that it was really his colleague's inner calm that appealed to him most. Jensen reminded Singsaker of who he himself might have been if his mind could have been toned down a notch, if he hadn't had the brain surgery, didn't indulge himself with a shot of aquavit every morning, and hadn't gotten divorced, only to fall in love with a young American woman. In short, if he was not the person he was, he could have been Jensen. Singsaker wondered if that wasn't, in fact, a good basis for a friendship. Jensen was rocking his chair back and forth, his hands clasped on his stomach, as he fixed his sleepy eyes on the ceiling. Next to him sat Mona Gran. She was the youngest of the detectives in the unit. Grongstad and Singsaker sat at either end of the table. The meeting began with the two of them, since they'd been at the crime scene.

Grongstad went first, meticulous as always. Singsaker had little to add except to pose a few questions related to what Grongstad had told them. In his opinion, they needed to clarify three things: How had the killer and the victim arrived at the scene of the crime, and how had the murderer left? Was it possible to come up with any motive for the murder, based on the evidence discovered so far? Most noteworthy was the music box, which looked like an antique, and the fact that the victim's larynx had been cut out. But the last question was the most important: Who was the victim?

Brattberg started in after Singsaker finished. "Our first priority has to be identifying this woman without a throat."

Singsaker appreciated Brattberg's precise descriptions, which were often specific and thought-provoking. The woman without a throat, he thought to himself. That means something. There's something significant about that. No one in the room disagreed with the priorities of the head of the Violent Crimes team. They all knew that in most homicide cases, the killer has some sort of connection to the victim, and so the more they found out about the deceased, the closer they would conceivably get to the perpetrator.

"Gran, I want you to go through all the missing person reports. From the whole country. Look at the most recent first and then work your way back," said Brattberg.

Mona Gran nodded and made a note in her iPad.

"Singsaker, you need to find out more about the music box. Where's it from? Is it old? Where was it made? And what about the tune it plays? I'd say that music museum at Ringve Manor would be the place to start. Don't they have a good collection of music boxes out there?"

"Jonas Røed," said Gran. "Talk to Jonas Røed. He's probably the foremost expert on music boxes in Norway. He works at the museum."

Everyone turned to look at their young colleague, impressed. She shrugged.

"I go out to Ringve a lot. The best museum in the city, in my opinion," she explained. "Singsaker, you'll like Røed. A real nerd and kind of reserved. But he knows everything about musical instruments."

Singsaker wondered why that would be a reason to like someone, but he didn't voice his puzzlement.

"Jensen, have a talk with Kittelsen as soon as he has anything to tell us. Has the body been delivered to him yet?" Brattberg looked from Jensen to Grongstad.

"It was taken over to the St. Olav lab half an hour ago, but if I know Kittelsen, you won't get anything out of him until he's had his coffee break. Which is at noon," said the crime tech.

Everyone chuckled. They were all familiar with Kittelsen and his moods.

"From what I saw," Grongstad went on, "it wouldn't surprise me if he says that she was severely beaten before she was killed. Her body was covered in bruises. But as I mentioned to Singsaker earlier, it's unlikely that it happened where she was found."

"So you think she was moved there after she was dead?"

"It's too early to say for sure. Although I do think that her throat was cut in the woods. So the question is, What killed her? The beating, which came first, or the knife, which came later?"

"We need to get Kittelsen to move quickly on this," Brattberg said without much hope. "In the meantime, the rest of us have to get to work and start collecting information. It's going to be a busy day."

The meeting was over. Gro Brattberg handled things clearly and in a straightforward way. And that boosted everyone's confidence. Singsaker felt a mild headache fade almost before he noticed it. None of them wanted another chaotic investigation like the one they'd been through while investigating the grisly murders the previous fall.

Singsaker happened to know quite a bit about Ringve Manor. As he drove out to Lade, he refreshed his memory, in case it would prove to be useful to the case.

The manor had been separated from the Lade estate in the

seventeenth century. It had had numerous different owners and had undergone several phases of construction. Like most people who lived in Trondheim, Singsaker associated the estate most closely with Victoria Bachke and the museum.

In 1919, the young Victoria, then twenty-one years old, visited Ringve for the first time. Several months later she married the owner of the estate, Christian Ancker Bachke. She and her husband then made plans for the founding of Ringve Museum, although their vision was not realized until after Christian's death. A museum honoring the naval hero Peter Wessel Tordenskiold was first established in 1950. Two years later the present-day museum opened, devoted to musical instruments, based on the extensive and diverse collection owned by the Bachkes. Ringve is today Norway's National Museum for Musical Instruments, and the collection includes approximately two thousand audio exhibits. It was also the country's only professional workshop for conserving instruments.

Singsaker trudged across the cobblestone courtyard between the nicely restored mansions. Ringve did seem like the right place to start. The woman without a throat, he thought. Maybe that was significant; maybe it wasn't. The killer had removed the human body's own musical instrument and replaced it with a mechanical one: the music box. It was possible that everything he knew about Ringve was just filler in his brain. He often wondered why his memory loss from the brain tumor operation a year ago hadn't erased any of the the haphazard knowledge he had. An absurd and yet frightening thought occurred to him. What if those random thoughts were the ones that fed the tumors?

Then he went inside and asked to see Jonas Røed.

"Well, this is certainly interesting. A music box made with remarkable skill. We rarely ever see one of such good quality. Especially not with such an exquisite ballerina on the lid."

Jonas Røed's voice was slightly shrill and intense. It sounded like an untuned instrument that Singsaker had never heard before, but one that could undoubtedly be found in the museum. Røed gestured vigorously with one hand as he talked, emphasizing his words. His hair was equally energetic and oddly enough matched his last name, Norwegian for "red." His hair was cut short in back, and in front his bangs partially obscuring his eyes. Singsaker wasn't quite sure what to make of this man. Like anyone with a passion for something the detective didn't understand, Røed seemed inscrutable.

"So it's not an ordinary music box?" he asked.

Singsaker looked at the back of Røed's T-shirt as he bent over the instrument in the cramped office out in the barn. It was an old, faded Metallica concert shirt with a list of the cities they'd played during a tour in the 1990s. The T-shirt, once black, had now faded to gray.

"No, it's definitely not ordinary." Røed had opened the music box and used a loupe to examine the cylinder inside. "Somebody changed the cylinder recently," he said.

"What does that mean?"

"A music box consists of three main components. First, the comb, which is usually made of finely tuned metal teeth, although some music boxes have strings. Player pianos, for example. Each tooth vibrates at a certain frequency and produces a specific tone. So they can only play the tones of the particular number of teeth. This music box can play both major and minor notes. To strike the teeth, the music box usually has a set of pins that are affixed to cylinders or drums, which can be permanently attached or sometimes are removable. The pins move toward the teeth, and that's how the music is produced. Finally, something has to make the pins move. In the case of some music boxes, this is done manually, by turning a crank. On others, such as this one, a spring has to be wound. The tune that it plays is programmed onto the cylinder, while the musical scale is in the teeth. I believe that the music box and teeth, which appear to be original, are old. But the cylinder has recently been replaced with one that's homemade. And it was done by an amateur, judging by the soldering. But whoever put it in the music box knew what he was doing."

"Would you say that he had a good knowledge of music?"

"Yes, absolutely," said Røed.

"A musician?"

"There are many ways to become a music expert. Music can be seen purely theoretically. Some people compare music to mathematics. Making a new tune for a music box requires some theoretical expertise in music. But it doesn't necessarily mean that you have to know how to play an instrument. Because that also demands dexterity and talent."

"So theoretically somebody who isn't a musician could have done it?"

"That's for you to figure out. I can only tell you about the mechanical device. In terms of the container itself, I'm almost positive it was made in Europe, most likely in Sainte-Croix, Switzerland, which was the major manufacturing site for music boxes and clocks. In my opinion, it was made sometime in the early 1800s. There is no maker's mark, which wasn't unusual prior to the industrial age. This would be a real collector's item if the cylinder had been original. But I'd guess that it's not one of a kind, even though I've never seen this exact model before. Music boxes like this were sold as toys to children of wealthy families here in Norway, and you can still find similar ones stored away in attics."

"What about the tune it plays?"

"Quite a melancholy tune, in the minor key. It makes me think of a rather sad lullaby. I've never heard this particular melody before. But it's suitable for a music box, which has a sound all its own. I love tunes played in the minor key on old music boxes with plenty of resonance, like this one. Those fragile, sad tones seem to fill the whole room. Doesn't it sound almost magical?"

Jonas Røed let the music box play the whole song, and Singsaker had to admit that it gave him goose bumps.

"Isn't it odd that you don't recognize the song?" he asked.

"Why do you say that?" replied Røed.

"Because this is what you work with. I'd guess you've listened to hundreds of music boxes, and have a keen interest in all kinds of music."

He couldn't help glancing again at Røed's T-shirt.

"You're right. But that may be the point. Perhaps whoever replaced the cylinder did it because he couldn't find an original music box with this obscure tune. If you want to find out more about it, there are other people who know a lot more about music than I do."

"Could you suggest a few names?"

"If this is really a lullaby, I'd talk to Professor Jan Høybråten at the Institute for Music at NTNU. He's the foremost expert on our Nordic ballad tradition."

Singsaker thanked Røed, who handed the music box back, giving the device an odd look as he did so. Singsaker couldn't decipher what that look meant. Maybe Røed would have liked to keep it for a while to study it further.

Mona Gran turned down the volume of the music she was listening to through her earbuds. She seldom asked herself whether it was appropriate for a policewoman to be listening to death metal, and she hadn't shared her taste in music with everyone in the department. Jensen knew about her music taste, and he used to tease her by giving her the sign of the horns. She marveled at how childish men could be. One day she had asked Jensen if he knew what that sign meant if made behind the back of an Italian.

"No clue," he replied.

"It means his wife is being unfaithful." Then she had stood behind his back and held up the little finger and index finger on her right hand as she laughed. After that, she lectured him about the different meanings the sign had had in history. Did he know it had once been used as protection against evil spirits, much like the way Catholics used the sign of the cross?

After that, Jensen stopped teasing her.

Singsaker, on the other hand, had no idea what sort of music she listened to. He just thought she was the nicest young woman in the department. And that actually might be true. But she couldn't figure him out. He treated her like he was her father, and she let him, maybe even enjoyed it. She didn't feel the need to keep her musical tastes secret; it was just something they'd never discussed. She suspected he might not even know what death metal was.

Music helped her concentrate. She needed all the help she could get, now that the real work was about to start. It was ten-thirty in the morning, and the Trondheim police still hadn't received a report of anyone who had gone missing during the past twenty-four hours. That wasn't necessarily significant, since it could take a while before people were actually missed. The woman they were trying to identify might have lived alone. Or maybe she was a student with few friends in town. She might have met the killer on her way home from a late-night party, and her friends might think that she was still sleeping it off in someone else's bed. But the police couldn't sit and wait for someone to discover that she hadn't come home. Gro Brattberg had decided to release a description of the woman. But it wasn't a particularly distinctive description: dark blond hair, blue eyes, average height, somewhere between twenty and thirty, attractive but without any distinguishing marks. Most likely this would bring in too many tips and a ton of extra work. But this was often what helped them solve a case. Breakthroughs in an investigation seldom came from flashes of brilliance; instead, they came from the methodical and thorough examination of a seemingly endless string of unrelated information.

While they waited for tips to come in, Gran had to consider the possibility that the victim might have come from somewhere else, or that she might have been missing for a long time.

Every year, more than a thousand people were reported missing in the various police districts in Norway. Most were young, like this victim. They usually disappeared from some kind of institution and turned up in crime-riddled areas, especially in the big cities. Only rarely was a missing person found murdered, like this woman without a throat.

Gran studied the photo that Grongstad had given her, trying to come up with key words to send to other police districts, and to use in a search of the databases. Her first search attempt was not successful. There were too many hits. She stared at the small grainy pictures of young women, wondering what had happened to all of them. None of them bore any resemblance to their corpse.

She turned her music up and leaned back in her chair. Either we get lucky and find a match soon, she thought, or else this is going to take a really long time. She stretched her back and then closed her eyes and let her thoughts drift. As she sat there, one hand had come to rest on her stomach, just below her navel. This had become a habit of hers. Maybe she was hoping that her hands had healing powers that she wasn't aware of. She was twenty-seven years old, and several months had passed since her worst suspicions had been confirmed. They'd been trying for two years to have a baby, but she'd gotten her period each month, like clockwork. So it hadn't been a shock to learn that something was wrong. She was the one with the problem—constricted Fallopian tubes from an infection that she never knew she had. After more attempts and tests, the doctor had reached the conclusion that it might not be impossible for her to conceive naturally, although it was very unlikely, and that she was a good candidate for IVF. Two days ago she'd received a referral to the fertility clinic at St. Olav Hospital.

Mona Gran smiled. She took out her earbuds and began making calls.

"Professor Høybråten?"

Singsaker cleared his throat. He'd knocked on the office door and heard someone tell him to come in. But the older gentleman hadn't looked up when the door opened, nor when Singsaker went over to the desk where the man was sitting. He was leaning so far over that it almost looked as if he were asleep.

"Professor Høybråten?" Singsaker repeated.

Only then did the man react. He sat up straight and stared at the detective, his gaze both distant and piercing. It was obvious that he'd been deeply immersed in his own thoughts, and that he wasn't pleased by this interruption.

"Excuse me," he said. "How may I help you?"

Jan Høybråten was older than Singsaker. His white hair stuck out in all directions. He would have been retired if he'd been anything other than a professor.

"My name is Odd Singsaker. I'm from the police. We're investigating a murder that was committed last night in the Rosenborg district."

He assumed that Høybråten wouldn't have heard about the murder, since the news had been released too late to be included in the morning edition of the paper. The professor didn't seem like someone who got his news online, or listened to the radio while he worked.

"Yes, one of my colleagues told me about it," he said, as if he'd read Singsaker's mind. "But what does it have to do with me?"

Singsaker tried to determine whether it was surprise or something else he heard in the man's voice. Annoyance? Nervousness? He wasn't sure. An old man's voice could be so capricious.

"I'm here to ask for your help with a specific detail of the case," he said. "Your expert advice."

He took out the music box and wound it up.

"This was found near the body, and we have no idea what the tune is."

Then he let go of the key and set the mechanical device on the professor's desk.

Høybråten listened to the melody. Halfway through he closed his eyes, looking as if he were trying hard to concentrate. When the notes finally stopped, he opened his eyes and shook his head.

"No, strangely enough, I've never heard it," he said.

"And that surprises you?"

"Yes, it does. There's something oddly familiar about the melody. But I'm positive I've never heard it before. A minor key in six/eight time, slow tempo. Mostly likely a lullaby. It could be a ballad by Bellman. But it's not."

"Bellman?"

"Yes. Carl Michael Bellman. You don't know who he is?"

"I've heard his name. A Swedish composer, right?"

"The greatest of all ballad composers. He lived in Stockholm in the 1700s."

Høybråten looked at Singsaker, his expression no longer remote. He seemed to consider whether he should launch into a lengthy lecture about the Swedish musician, but apparently he realized it would be casting pearls before swine.

"I'm giving a concert of Bellman's ballads at the Ringve Museum next week" was all he said.

"Really? You're going to sing?"

The professor didn't answer for a moment, as if deciding how to respond.

"No, unfortunately, I no longer sing. I'm afraid my vocal cords aren't what they used to be. Nodules. I'm an old man now."

Again Singsaker sensed there were emotions behind the professor's words that were not being conveyed by his tone of voice.

"It's a small group of specially selected girls from the Nidaros Cathedral girls choir," the professor went on. "I'll be directing. Actually, I was just sitting here going over the repertoire when you came in. But to get back to the matter at hand: This is not a Bellman ballad. I have no idea who might have written it."

"Do you think it could be a Nordic lullaby?" asked Singsaker.

"I can't claim to be familiar with every lullaby ever written. And much of the folk music that was composed here in the north before the 1800s has been lost, quite simply because it was never written down. So it's possible. Could you play it one more time?"

Singsaker wound up the music box again while the professor got out pencil and paper. This time he made notes as the music played. By the time the song was over, he had a sequence of notes on the page.

"I'll do some research for you," he said. "If I find anything, I'll get in touch."

Singsaker nodded and picked up the music box. As he left the office, the professor got up and went over to open the window as he fumbled for a pack of cigarettes in his pocket. Many of the employees at the university were still fighting the no-smoking regulations.

Singsaker got into his car, which was parked in the big lot outside the university area on Dragvoll. Parts of the city's university were located out here in the country, near what had previously been a farm. From the parking lot there was a magnificent view of the city.

He searched his pockets for his notebook and found it at last. Then he put it on his lap and let his finger glide over the black leather

33

cover. It was a Moleskine notebook, a welcome-back gift from his colleagues in the department, given to him last summer after his brain surgery. He'd always used this type of notebook, so it was an especially thoughtful gift. Yet it had taken him a long time to start using this one. At first he didn't know why. But after a while he'd realized that jotting down notes now meant something different from what it had in the past. It was the same as realizing that his memory was not the same as before the operation, and it that might never be the same. That was something he had to accept. He'd become a forgetful man who could no longer get by without a notebook. But as soon as he became reconciled to this fact, his relationship to his notebook had changed. Only then did he understand what a wonderful gift it was. He'd started calling the notebook "the better half of my brain," and he didn't use it just for police work. He also jotted down notes about everything in his personal life that he thought was important to remember.

He turned to the last page he'd written on. He was surprised that he'd made love to Felicia twice last night. Could that be correct? He smiled and felt an urge to drive home and see her. But instead, he took a pencil stub out of his breast pocket and wrote, *"Høybråten seemed nervous. Why?"*

At 1:05 P.M. the phone rang in Mona Gran's office.

"Hi, Officer Jonas Borten here. I'm phoning from Greenland," he said. Then he added, without a trace of humor, "The police department in the Greenland district of Oslo. I'm at work."

"How can I help you?" asked Gran.

Borten didn't reply for a moment, as if caught off guard by her willingness to help.

"I'm calling because I think I can help you," he said finally.

"That sounds good. We could use some help."

"It's regarding the murder victim you found last night. I might have something for you."

"Yes? What is it?" she said, trying to hide her impatience.

"We don't have any new missing person reports that match your description, but something made me think about a case I worked on a few weeks back. I think it was the address that caught my attention. When I was a kid I lived in Bakkaunet, not far from Kuhaugen, so I know the area well. Ludvig Daaes Gate was on my way to school. And that's one of the reasons why I remember the case. We got a missing person report about three weeks ago. A woman from Oslo. She shared an apartment with another woman, who filed the report. But after only twenty-four hours, the missing woman called her friend from the train station in Trondheim and said she was on her way to meet a former lover who had moved there. We dropped the case, but just to make sure, I did a search on this lover of hers. He lived not far from Kuhaugen, and it turned out that the purportedly missing woman had previously filed a police report charging him with domestic violence. A stabbing. I didn't give any more thought to the matter. Just another thoughtless young woman going back to her abusive lover, and there was nothing we could do about that. But then I hear about this homicide, and it happens close to the place where her lover lives, and there's a knife involved, and the description fits the woman, so I thought that—"

"The description also fits about ten thousand other Norwegian women of the same age," Gran said, interrupting. "But we can't leave any stone unturned. Do you have a photo of this woman?"

"Yes, that's exactly what I have. Of course, this could just be a shot in the dark, but that's what happens so often. We shoot and shoot until we finally hit the mark. Give me your e-mail address, and I'll send over the picture right now."

She gave him the address.

Then she put down the phone.

Two minutes later she clicked on the e-mail that he'd sent. A picture popped up on her screen. It showed a smiling young woman wearing a little too much makeup.

"Jabba the Hutt," Gran muttered to herself. "It's her."

5

When the entire investigative team gathered at two-thirty that afternoon, everyone had the feeling that a lot had happened since they'd last met. The victim had now been identified—her name was Silje Rolfsen. She was twenty-three years old and had been living in Oslo, where she worked in a clothing store. In early January she'd come to Trondheim to visit her ex-boyfriend Jonny Olin, and after that no one had heard from her except for the one phone call she'd made from the train station. Her friends in Oslo and her family had all assumed that she was staying with this Olin guy during the three weeks she'd been gone.

"The first thing we need to determine is whether she was, in fact, staying with him," said Brattberg between bites of a jelly doughnut.

Singsaker had never understood how Brattberg could have such bad eating habits. Not that his were much better, since the aquavit and herring that he had for breakfast were often the most nutritious part of what he ate over the course of a day. But that suited the sort of person he was, while Brattberg was an entirely different type. He didn't know anyone more disciplined than she was. Siri Holm, a librarian and one of his friends, had once told him that all good detectives had to have a weakness, something that held them back. This was a theory that Holm had derived from the crime novels she was always reading, but he thought there might be some truth to the idea. If Brattberg was a champion at solving crimes, then pastries had to be her Achilles' heel.

Jensen was the first to respond. "I'll bet she was staying with him the whole time. The first week everything was probably hunky-dory, but the next week things went south. He started yelling about trivial things, maybe slapping her around. The third week all hell broke loose, and he completely lost control."

"And cut her larynx out and left her in the woods with a music box on her chest?" asked Gran, interrupting him.

Singsaker glanced at her, impressed. He was the only one who knew Jensen well enough to know that young women made him terribly self-conscious. Not that he'd ever admit to it. But this was only something that Singsaker had noticed after years of working with him, conducting interrogations and interviews, and carrying out investigations. Jensen was a nature lover, hunter, and ice bather with a solid marriage, but young women just made him nervous. And even though Jensen could laugh and joke with Gran, Singsaker was convinced that she also made him uneasy. The sort of comment she had just made would have a strong effect on his friend. Yet she was absolutely right. There was something about this case that went beyond a simple crime of passion.

"And it isn't just any ordinary old music box," said Singsaker. "It's rare, and old, and in its original condition it could have been worth a lot of money, if the owner hadn't made alterations. Someone replaced the cylinder so that it now plays a tune, probably a lullaby, that even a professor of music history couldn't identify."

"Do you think the killer composed the tune himself?" asked Gran.

"Well, that's a possibility we do need to consider. If he did, then we're dealing with a very talented person, because according to both the curator at Ringve and Professor Høybråten, the melody is extremely appealing. Another possibility, which is equally likely, is that we're dealing with a lullaby from the olden days that has been forgotten until now."

"But why a lullaby?" Brattberg interjected. "Something tells me that the type of tune is significant. Was he trying to soothe the victim to death?"

"If it's really a lullaby, that's one potential theory," said Singsaker. "Potential and odd."

"I think we're making a mistake if we discount the boyfriend," said Jensen. "We don't know what he's thinking. But you're right; this is no ordinary murder. And after trying to get through all morning, I finally spoke to Kittelsen."

"Not a bad day's work," said Singsaker caustically. Everyone knew that the jibe was aimed at Kittelsen, not Jensen.

"He took a look at the larynx," Jensen went on. "And what he told me, in brief, is that the vocal cords were removed. They're gone."

"So you think the killer took the victim's vocal cords with him?" asked Singsaker, clearing his throat as he attempted to feel his own.

"It appears so."

"Has anyone noticed the strange symmetry here?" asked Gran. Her voice had a calming effect on the uneasy mood in the room. "He took what we as human beings use to produce sound. At the same time, he leaves behind an instrument with the body. And it's ironic that the sound from the music box was the reason the body was discovered."

"Do any of you think the killer did this deliberately?" asked Brattberg.

"It's not likely," said Jensen. "The murder was committed in the middle of the night, the wooded area was a good hiding place, and if the snow had done its job, the body would have remained undiscovered for a long time. Everything points to careful planning."

"In that case, we're dealing with a killer who made a mistake. Or maybe it was so important for him to play that particular tune that he didn't care if he ended up getting caught."

No one had any counterarguments to Brattberg's theory.

"But I think we need to put some of these speculations aside for a while," she went on. "Let's start with the facts. We know that Silje Rolfsen came to Trondheim a little less than three weeks ago to visit her boyfriend, Jonny Olin. So we need to start with him."

Once again Brattberg had cut right through to the heart of the matter, as only she could do. Music boxes and missing vocal cords are unusual factors in a homicide case, thought Singsaker, but violent ex-boyfriends are not.

Singsaker would have liked to go along to pay a visit to Jonny Olin, but he had an appointment that he couldn't change. So the task was assigned to Jensen and Gran, while he got in his car right after the meeting and sped over to St. Olav Hospital. He arrived ten minutes late for his scheduled appointment with Dr. Nordraak.

The memory test went well. Dr. Nordraak usually worked with alcohol-related psychoses. Conducting these memory tests was another of his fields of expertise. Today he hadn't been any more arrogant or conceited than normal, and he'd only made a few brief comments about how Singsaker had been late, as usual.

Now they were going to go over the results.

"You're definitely on the mend," said Nordraak, leaning back in what looked like an IKEA desk chair in his cramped office. His designer tie was visible under his white coat. He looked as if he felt he was too important for such spartan surroundings. Singsaker had never visited Nordraak at his office in the Østmarka Hospital, but he'd heard rumors of antelope-head trophies on the walls.

"And what exactly do you mean by 'on the mend'?"

"That you're still going to forget certain details, that you'll have brief periods when you lose focus and your thoughts seem to float, as you describe it. But it will be within normal parameters."

"I'm just starting a major investigation."

"Then you should be glad that you don't have to do all the work by yourself. You'll be able to contribute. As you know, the symptoms that we're talking about are not uncommon for someone your age, even without having brain surgery. They won't prevent you from doing your job. You should just concentrate on doing whatever you're good at."

And what am I good at? thought Singsaker as he stood up. The answer he came up with was vague. I'm good at thinking, he decided. With or without a perfect memory.

"Are you aware that many of the symptoms you're experiencing are common among creative people? Artists and scientists? The problem is that you have too many things in your head at the same time. Your brain has trouble sorting them out."

"So if I brood less, my memory will improve? Is that what you're saying?"

"Perhaps. But it's not that simple. I don't think you can stop brooding just like that. That's an integral part of your injury. But, as I said, you should focus on what you're good at."

Singsaker thanked the doctor, thinking that this was the first time he'd seen Nordraak's human side. He'd always thought the doctor was all form and no content. But now he actually felt reassured by what he'd heard. Furthermore, he thought that if a status-conscious careerist like Dr. Nordraak could put him in a good mood, there might be hope for the human race after all.

Back at the department, Brattberg gave Singsaker a brief rundown.

Jonny Olin had been cooperative and had agreed to come to the station for an interview with Jensen and Gran. He was now sitting in one of the interview rooms along with the two officers. He claimed he had talked to Silje Rolfsen only a couple of times on the phone in the past few months. Singsaker rolled his eyes and went to get himself a cup of coffee.

The man stood in the front hall, sniffing the air. For some reason this was something he always did. He didn't know what he was trying to smell. Could it be his mother? That penetrating odor of tobacco and old textiles that had left this house long ago?

The new owner had painted the entryway, and installed a new wardrobe with a sliding door. He noticed only a faint scent of acrylic paint before he went inside the house, which hadn't changed much since he and his mother had lived there years ago. He was now renting the house, after having sold it immediately after his mother's death. No one knew that he had leased it, not even his wife Anna. Here he could go about his business in peace.

He went into the kitchen and sat down, immediately thinking about the dream he'd had the previous night, about the man and the funeral procession in the sky. He thought about his father, long dead. With his shotgun in his mouth, drenching the wall behind the marital bed with blood. He knew his father's suicide had had something to do with him, with the fact that he'd chopped off his fingers so that he could never play for his father again. His mother had put him in a suit and taken him to the funeral. The whole ceremony had seemed empty and absurd. A meaningless event, a shadow of something real. The words were hollow, and he hadn't cried. Now he knew that his dream was about the real funeral. There was true sorrow in every step the giants had taken across the sky, and they had carried the coffin with the weight of the world on their shoulders. When he woke up, he'd hoped that this was the dream he'd been seeking for so long and that from now on he'd be able to sleep peacefully. But he feared his hope would be in vain, that he'd been given only one night of peace, and that once again he was going to be hurled back into sleeplessness. Gradually, these dreamless nights would transform into nightmares. The killing had not been enough. It was the wrong woman, the wrong voice. He needed someone younger, purer, compliant. He knew whom he needed.

Fortunately he had another music box. It was heart-shaped, covered with blue velvet, and on the lid was a singer wearing a white cutaway, vest, and silk scarf. It was the second of his mother's two music boxes. Now he carefully took it apart.

On the cylinder was the thin copper plate with the pins that plucked the teeth on the comb to produce the music. Again he replaced the plate and pins with one that he'd made himself. He spent a long time on the task. When he was done, he cleared away all the tools, the pincers, soldering iron, magnifying glass, and rubber mallet. He stowed them away in a kitchen drawer. Then he sat down in front of the music box, which was on the table.

He stretched contentedly and then lit a cigarette.

An hour after Singsaker had come back to the station, he was sitting in his office when Jensen pounded on the door. It was a sound he always recognized and never turned away.

"Come in!"

Jensen looked worn-out.

"So, did you get him to talk?" said Singsaker as his colleague sank onto a chair in front of his desk.

"I'm starting to feel like he doesn't have much more to say. His story may be unusual, but I actually think he's telling the truth."

"Which is what?"

"He's gay."

"What?"

"Jonny Olin is gay. He says that he's kept it a secret for a long time and tried to have female lovers but that it just frustrated him. That's his explanation for the violent episodes."

"So he does admit to them?"

"Partially, but he tried to downplay it. He says that with Silje Rolfsen, he tried to break off the relationship many times but that she refused to accept it. He claims that she kept seeking him out and pestering him for a long time afterward. That was what finally pushed him so over the edge that he threatened her with a knife."

"And you believe his story?" Singsaker asked.

"I'm not sure. But we may be able to confirm that after coming to Trondheim, he took a male lover for the first time, and that the two of them spent last night at his lover's apartment. Gran is on the phone trying to verify his story."

"In other words, he's not our man."

"Not unless he's able to be in two places at once," said Jensen. "And we still need to find out from his neighbors whether Silje Rolfsen was seen near his residence during the past three weeks.

"Maybe Olin could tell us something about Silje other than the fact that he didn't kill her. After all, he did live with her, so he ought to be able to tell us what sort of woman she was."

"I asked him, but he didn't have much to say. Just a bunch of meaningless things that you could say about any young woman her age. She liked clothes and books and had apparently always been a gentle sort. I got the impression that he'd really been very fond of her, which fits with his explanation. There was one small item of interest. He said that she liked to sing. Evidently she'd been in a choir during her childhood, and she was always singing—in the shower, when she cooked, and when she walked along the street. I got the feeling her singing annoyed him."

"But maybe not enough to remove her larynx?"

"Hardly."

"Still, this might be significant. Where does Olin live?" Singsaker asked.

"He lives in Skyåsvegen, at the top, on Kuhaugen."

"So if someone heads over that way on foot from town, let's

say from the train station, wouldn't the crime scene be out of the way?"

"Well, it's not totally out in the sticks. Olin also confirmed that Silje Rolfsen had phoned him a couple of times after he moved to Trondheim and he came out. She had mentioned that she might come to see him. She may have decided to surprise him, maybe in an attempt to salvage a hopeless relationship that she refused to let go. Young Mr. Olin says he got a call from her that he didn't pick up, around the time she arrived in Trondheim, but he can't remember the exact date. He has voluntarily given us access to his phone records, so eventually we'll be able to confirm the precise time and date. But let's assume that she tried to call him from the station and couldn't get hold of him. So she started walking, maybe singing a song, attracting attention like that, and on the way something happened to her. The question is, What? And nothing explains the real mystery, if we believe her ex-boyfriend's claim that she wasn't staying with him."

Jensen let this thought hover in the air for a moment, and then Singsaker asked the next question.

"So, where was she those three weeks before the murder?" The minute he voiced the question, he realized there would be no pleasant answer.

A fly was living inside his skull, a diligent little insect that ambled around inside on those light, tickling insect limbs, but now it had stopped moving altogether. Could it be dead?

He'd taken good care of the vocal cords, placing them in an alcohol-filled jar, which now stood on the table in front of him. He rested his eyes on the pink membranes in the bottom of the jar. They looked like an as-yet-undiscovered sea creature, a deep-sea coral. Now and then he imagined that they stirred, as if preparing to sing. When he looked at them, he couldn't understand why her song had not been the one he'd hoped for. He sat there thinking about his wife. She'd been sleeping so soundly lately. He envied her. Would he ever be able to sleep like that?

When he finished his cigarette, he lit another one and read what it said on the pack: SMOKING KILLS.

PART II

6

Trondheim, 1767

Flies. There were far too many of them this summer. They crawled and buzzed over everything, on his hands and face and in his ears. They had even infiltrated his dreams. In one dream he'd eaten an entire meal that consisted only of flies. At this much too early hour of the morning, it took for Chief Inspector Nils Bayer a long time to realize that he was not dreaming. He grabbed at the fly that landed on his nose, catching it in his hand.

The festivities at the Hoppa last night had nearly done him in. As usual, he'd thrown up everything he'd eaten and drunk during the evening. He didn't feel nearly clearheaded enough to be wakened before the cockcrow. His back and all of his joints ached as if he'd crawled home on all fours from the inn, with someone beating him with a cane the whole way. He lit the oil lamp on the nightstand. Through the fog of sleep, the pale face leaning over his bed looked like a phantom.

Bayer wiped his forehead, sat up, and placed both hands on his enormous paunch. The hound of hell that lived inside his stomach woke up and issued a threatening growl. He belched and fixed a fierce gaze on the night watchman who had just stormed into his bedchamber to wake him so rudely.

"Pull yourself together, man," Bayer said. "You'd think you'd seen the Devil himself."

The watchman, a slight young boy with a reedy voice, was too easily frightened for the job he held, but even then, Chief Inspector Bayer had seldom seen him look as pale as he did now.

"I may not have seen the Devil himself," stammered the boy, "but I've seen his handiwork."

"The Devil's handiwork," muttered the inspector pensively. "Why can't the Devil do his work at more Christian hours of the day?"

Nils Bayer got out of bed, but he knew better than to try to stretch. He could see traces of vomit on his nightshirt.

"Wait downstairs. I'm coming," he said. "Get out, go, this minute! Who ever heard of a watchman afraid to wait alone on the street at night?"

When the watchman had reluctantly left the room, Bayer pulled the chamber pot from under the bed and threw up again. Then he took off his nightshirt and got dressed. He left his cloak behind and went out clad only in shirt, waistcoat, and trousers. He gripped his cane, which was new. The top was adorned with the Trondheim police chief's own emblem, the hand holding the city's coat of arms. It had been cast and wrought only a few weeks ago.

It was June, when the sun awoke before the rooster. A thick morning mist filled the streets, reaching over the walls of the buildings, making the prison on Kalvskinnet look like a hazy memory. The tentative bluish light from the morning sun settled over the marketplace rooftops down toward Skansen, the town fortress. Outside his front door, in the dawning light and fog, stood the young watchman, still looking only half-alive.

"Lead the way, boy," grumbled Bayer, scratching his belly under the tight waistcoat.

"But wouldn't the chief inspector wish to—" stammered the watchman.

"Wish to what?" Bayer brusquely interrupted him.

"Doesn't the chief inspector wish to hear my report before we go? I mean, wouldn't it be best to be prepared for—"

"Tell me, young man. Can I see this diabolical sight from where I'm standing right now?"

"No. You can't. We have to go beyond Skansen."

"Then let's not waste time with words. You ought to know the chief inspector well enough by now to realize that he believes only things he sees with his own eyes. Lead the way."

They walked in silence toward the city gate, which the watchman unlocked with one of the keys attached to a ring on his belt.

Morning was without a doubt the calmest time of day or night at Ila. By then peace had finally settled over this teetering, putrid row of buildings outside the city gate. The last tankards had been emptied, and the whores could at last take a rest. The only people in sight were a few incurable drunks lying in the gutter, a rattling sound issuing from their throats but not disturbing anyone. Chief Inspector Bayer might well have ended up in a similar position countless times if it hadn't been for her. He glanced up at the window of her room as he passed, knowing she was asleep. She always slept heavily after a long night.

After they'd gone past the stinking buildings of Ila, they followed the road that people used to transport drinking water from Ila Creek to the city. A bridge took them over the creek to below the sawmills. Then they continued along a narrow path to the edge of the sea. Heading westward, they came to the body that was lying on the beach.

Nils Bayer stopped in his tracks and looked at it.

These are new times we are living in, he thought. Dead bodies don't look the way they used to. Though he'd been chief inspector in Trondheim for only three years, he'd seen numerous corpses—people who had suffered unnatural death long before disease, accident, or old age would have robbed them of life. In Trondheim, not many weeks passed between murders or suicides. The homicides usually resulted from brawls involving knives and clubs. Occasionally a vicious devil would beat his woman one time too many. And then there were the gangs of boys that fought outside the city walls. Sometimes these fights would escalate into outright battles between the gangs from Ila and Bakklandet. Early one morning in Småbergan, Bayer and a watchman had found two bodies, their faces beaten to a pulp with clubs. But the chief inspector rarely encountered a case of cold-blooded murder.

Still, this corpse was different. Bayer couldn't yet identify a motive. But he was quite sure that strong emotions lay behind it, and that this case was without a doubt something entirely new. The man's lifeless body had been stripped naked. He lay on his back with his arms at his sides. His long red hair seemed well groomed. Bayer studied the man's face and thought that he might have seen it before, but if so, it had been after far too many glasses of spirits. A big red gash stretched from the groin all the way up to the sternum. The lower half of his belly was smeared with blood. Through the wound the man's intestines were visible. Flies crawled around the edges of the gash.

"What a fate," said the watchman, standing behind him.

Bayer turned around and saw that the young man was gazing out across the fjord, affected by its deep silence.

"Imagine dying so brutally. And in this place," continued the watchman, lost in reverie.

"Death is brutal. But that fact does not concern us," said the inspector with annoyance. "The only question we need to ask is, How did this happen? And you are mistaken regarding one crucial point. The victim did not die in this place."

"How do you know?"

"Look at all the blood on his belly."

"What does that say about where he died?"

"Look at the stones, young man."

"The stones? What about them?"

"Do you see any blood on the stones?"

The young watchman studied the ground close to the body.

"There is no blood on the stones, Chief Inspector," he remarked at last.

"Good observation. So what does that tell us?"

"That he didn't bleed on the stones."

"Quite right. And since we can ascertain that he did indeed bleed, what conclusion can we draw?"

"That he bled somewhere else?"

"Precisely. And if we add this fact to the way he's lying, with his arms neatly placed at his sides and his hair draped over his shoulders, we can conclude that someone must have carefully placed him in this position after he was dead and no longer bleeding."

They stood there for a moment, considering this possibility.

Then the young watchman said, "It must have taken a great deal of strength to drag a dead man all the way to the shore."

"Now you're using your head. But you haven't completed your thought," said the inspector.

"What do you mean?"

"You've examined the stones around the corpse, right?"

"Yes, I have."

"And besides the absence of blood, did you notice anything else?"

"No, not really. The stones are just lying here as if nothing happened."

"You've hit the nail on the head!" The poor watchman now looked even more bewildered. "And what is it that has not happened?"

"I'm afraid I don't quite understand what you're getting at."

"Think about what you just said, my young friend."

"You mean the part about how it must have taken strength to drag him here?"

"Exactly. Take another look at the stones from the end of the path and over to where he's lying."

The watchman stared intently at the ground. He looked at the undulating rows of rotting seaweed and the cobbles that covered the beach all the way up to the embankment along the shore.

"No traces on the ground," the watchman said at last. "He wasn't dragged here."

"Excellent!" said Bayer. "He wasn't dragged, nor has a heavy cart rolled across the sand in the last few hours. And besides, the path here from Ila cannot be traversed by cart."

"But how do we know that he has only been here a few hours? The fisherman who found the body had been at sea for two days. Few other people use this section of the beach. He could have been here for a long time without being seen. The drag marks and the blood could have been washed away by high tide. The body could even have come ashore from somewhere else."

"This body has not been in the water," the chief inspector said firmly. "I've seen bodies that have come out of the fjord. Neptune always leaves his mark. But there's one thing that tells us for certain that this body was put here only *after* the last high tide. If I'm not mistaken, that was two or three hours ago."

"How can you tell?"

"For God's sake, man! Here I was just thinking I could make a policeman out of you! There's fresh seaweed above the body, which tells us that the water from the previous tide would have submerged him where he's lying. Can't you see that his hair is dry?"

The watchman shamefully lowered his eyes.

"Of course," he murmured. "But if he didn't wash ashore here, and he wasn't dragged to this spot or brought by cart, how did he end up here?"

"Well, he could have been brought on a horse, which wouldn't have left as deep a track on the beach as a cart. But it undoubtedly would have left prints in the damp soil where the path passes along the creek farther up."

"Did you really notice that the path we were walking along had no trace of hoofprints?" asked the watchman with admiration in his voice.

"The job of the police is to reconstruct, to tell a story. And all stories leave a mark. An officer who doesn't use his eyes is useless indeed."

Again the watchman looked ashamed .

"We're left with what must be the most plausible explanation," he said, looking at the watchman, who paused to consider what that might be.

"He could have been carried here from the road," he concluded.

"Precisely! He could have been carried here. And that tells us something very important. Unless the killer possessed superhuman strength, there must have been more than one man who carried . out this crime."

"And you can tell all of this simply by using your eyes?" asked the watchman.

"We. We have understood all of this," said Bayer, aware that such modesty didn't really suit him. Then he said, "But I think there's more to learn. I am going to stay here for a while. Go and fetch re-inforcements. The body must be conveyed to the priest. But first I want Fredrici, the town physician, to take a look at it. Bring him back here at once."

"A physician? I'm afraid there is little a doctor can do for this fellow now."

"Do as I say. No one knows more about death than those who save lives," he grumbled crossly. Without further ado, the watchman took his leave and hurried up the path toward Ila. The chief inspector watched until he was out of sight. Then he began retching. He bent over three times but nothing came out.

About time for a dram, he thought, taking a small flask from the inner pocket of his waistcoat.

7

"You have a beautiful voice."

She looked up with alarm. She was often lost in her own world when she walked the dog, and she almost always sang, but she thought she did it quietly enough that no one would hear. But tonight she wasn't just singing out of habit. She was practicing a Bellman song for the concert that weekend. She loved the lyrics to Bellman's ballads and all the hidden references. Allegories. That was what they were called.

The man who had spoken was standing right in front of her outside the brown wooden house at the intersection of Ludvig Daaes Gate and Bernhard Getz' Gate. The glow from the streetlight settled on him from above, as did the huge drifting snowflakes. They were landing on his hair. In his left hand he carried two shopping bags. His right arm was in a sling. She couldn't tell how old he was, but he was definitely much older than she was.

"Thanks," she said. "What happened to your arm?"

"Could you possibly do me a favor?" he said without answering her question.

"What sort of favor?"

"I need help opening my door. It's not easy carrying everything with my arm like this."

"Of course," she said. "I didn't know you lived here."

"I live here off and on," he said.

She tied the dog's leash to the gate. Then she walked behind him along the recently shoveled driveway that led to the garage and the front door. She had looked at this house so many times before, since it was on her way to school. It was a grand old house. She imagined the creaking floorboards and empty rooms filled with the scent of nicotine and loneliness. The yard had long ago gone to seed. No one had tended it for years. Tonight its bushes, weeds, and general state of neglect were covered with snow, just like the rest of the world.

He paused at the door and turned to face her. She thought his cheeks looked flushed, as if he were embarrassed about something.

"If you wouldn't mind taking the shopping bags, I'll unlock the door."

Hesitantly she did as he asked. Using his good hand he turned the key in the lock and then allowed her to step into the entryway first. It didn't look the way she'd imagined. A big modern wardrobe with sliding doors stood against one wall. A new rug had been put down recently, and there was a new coat of paint on the walls.

"Would you please take the bags into the hall? There's a chair where you can put them."

The hall had not been spruced up. Here the ceiling was a dull yellow and the wallpaper was faded. A beautiful but dusty chandelier hung from the ceiling, and a worn Persian rug covered the stained wooden floor. She put the bags on the chair that stood against one wall.

"I was hoping you might like to stay awhile."

He had followed her into the hallway. She suddenly had an uneasy feeling as a question formed in her mind: Who had shoveled the path outside?

"I'd like you to sing for me," he said.

". . . his thoughts roamed where they liked, and no one could have guessed what thoughts he had—and that was a good thing!"

Music flooded over Felicia Stone the moment she entered Siri Holm's apartment. She opened the door without ringing the bell, even though she'd learned that in this country even good friends rang the bell. But the young librarian was not like other Norwegians. Besides, she'd become her best friend after Felicia had quit her job on the police force in Richmond, Virginia, and moved to ice-cold Norway.

The song she heard was by Cornelis Vreeswijk, and Felicia knew that Siri had become totally infatuated with him ever since she saw a film about the troubadour at the movie theater. In fact, Siri was so enthusiastic that she'd put her favorite instrument, the trumpet, aside as she taught herself to play guitar.

Felicia had expected to find the usual mess, so she was surprised by what she saw. Siri, who had confident green eyes, blond hair that curled somewhat messily, and a light dusting of freckles across her nose, was lying on a now-bare sofa in a room that had been completely cleaned and tidied.

"What happened here?" she shouted in an attempt to be heard over the music.

The great thing about Siri was that she refused to answer unless Felicia spoke Norwegian. This was something she had insisted on ever since Felicia started taking language classes. She'd even convinced Singsaker to do the same, and Felicia was grateful for it. It meant that she now spoke better Norwegian than most other Americans who lived in the country.

"Happened?" said Siri, using the remote to turn down the volume as she looked up with a nonchalant expression from the book she was reading.

"What happened to the mess?" asked Felicia.

"Oh, that. I cleaned," she replied, and then went back to her book as if it was the most natural thing in the world.

"You? Cleaned?"

"I needed things to be more organized."

Felicia paused to consider what her friend had just said. She knew she wouldn't get any further explanation. But she thought this might be the closest Siri would ever get to talking about her feelings. Felicia had a sneaking suspicion that the housecleaning was a reaction to the events of the previous fall, when a colleague, who had perhaps been more than that to Siri, had been viciously murdered.

"Plus, I have a visitor coming in a few days," Siri added.

"Oh, really? A man?" asked Felicia, though she knew Siri wouldn't clean her apartment just because a man was coming over.

"Yes, a man," said Siri. "My chief patron is spending a couple of nights."

"And by that, I hope you mean your father."

"Yes," said Siri, looking up at the ceiling. "So I'd advise you to stay away this weekend."

"Why's that? Isn't your father good company?"

"He's just a bit eccentric. That's all."

Felicia laughed.

"What are you reading?"

"It's called *Skin Deep*."

"Never heard of it. Is it any good?" Felicia looked at the book, which had a yellow cover with a skull and crossbones on it.

"I'm on page one fifty and I've already guessed who the killer is."

Siri had a notebook in which she kept a list of all the crime novels she'd read, and on what page she had identified the murderer.

According to Siri, she'd been wrong only seven times since she'd started keeping track hundreds of books ago. Nine times she'd pegged the killer in the first chapter. Felicia rarely read crime novels, but when she did, she preferred when the suspense was focused on whether the police would catch the guy. It reminded her of her former job as a homicide detective.

Siri put down her book on the abnormally empty coffee table and went into the kitchen. Felicia thought there was something strange going on, not just with the room but with Siri. But she couldn't quite put her finger on what it was. She seemed plumper, and a little more fatigued than usual. Siri was not a classic beauty, but she always looked fresh-faced and healthy, and men seemed to fall all over her. But today she didn't seem quite right.

"So, what brings you over here on a Monday afternoon?" Siri asked as she set the teapot on the kitchen counter. Felicia stood in the doorway, watching.

"Oh, there's not much going on at home. Odd is busy with that music box murderer, as they're calling him in the paper. It's been several days, but the police aren't making much headway. But that's not why I'm here. I've got my first case," Felicia said proudly.

Siri gave her an exaggerated stare and said, "See. What did I tell you? And it happened fast too."

"Fast? The Web site's been up for four weeks. I was starting to think there was nobody out there."

The Web site was called norwegianroots.org. Siri had helped Felicia set it up.

Felicia's first month in Norway had been carefree. She'd spent most of her time being in love with the thoughtful, absentminded, and much too old police detective she'd fallen for. She could have continued on like that for a while if it weren't for the Norwegian immigration laws. Eventually they had to decide what to do when Felicia's visa-free stay in Norway ran out. It meant that they'd been forced to put their feelings into words before either of them was really ready to do so. A few weeks had passed, until finally Odd had thrown all caution to the wind and proposed.

They were lying in bed one evening after making love. It was dark in the room, and they had no idea what time it was.

"I suppose we'll have to get married," he said.

She didn't say anything.

"So you can stay here, I mean. It's too soon for a proper marriage. I'm just talking about taking care of the formalities. Then if we still want to, we could have a real wedding in a year or two. But if things don't work out, well, no marriage is written in stone these days."

"Are you proposing to me, Odd Singsaker?" she asked, amused by her lover's clumsy approach.

"No, I'm just asking whether you'd like to be my imported wife," he teased. She thought that maybe this was what she loved most about him. Ninety percent of the time he fumbled with his words, but then he'd fire off some funny remark. She was beginning to suspect that she brought out this side of his personality. That this droll humor of his surfaced only when he was with her.

They both laughed and said nothing more.

The following week they were married. Suddenly Felicia was a newlywed in a foreign country. All because she had inexplicably fallen in love. It was an attraction she couldn't deny. Of course, then she'd realized she had to find some sort of work. Odd had assured her that he could afford to support both of them financially, but she had no intention of being *that* kind of "imported wife." For a while she considered getting her police credentials accepted. It would have been possible, but something made her hesitate. That was when she came up with the idea for the Web site.

The plan was for her to assist Americans who wanted to find out more about their ancestors in Norway. She would act as a professional genealogist for Norwegian-Americans. Siri was the one to persuade Felicia that money could be made by providing such a service, and she could have access to all the necessary resources through the Gunnerus Library, where Siri worked.

This library, a division of the University Library in Trondheim, was actually Norway's oldest research library. Originally founded as the library of the Royal Norwegian Scientific Society, it dated back to 1760. Today, the Gunnerus Library housed, among other things, a special collection of extremely rare historical reference materials. Because she worked there, Siri had access to a number of databases and external archives, so she could easily order any required materials. Yet Siri herself was the greatest resource. There was no doubt that her enterprising nature and vast expertise far exceeded the norm. Occasionally her resourcefulness could go a bit too far, as it had during the investigation of the flayed corpses a year ago. But there was little danger of that happening in connection with genealogical research.

Felicia knew that Siri would be a big help. Yet only a few weeks after she'd set up the Web site and posted the first ads on the Internet, Felicia started losing faith in the whole project. The e-mail in-box for norwegianroots.org had remained sadly empty. Until yesterday. Felicia Stone finally had her first customer. And that wasn't all. Detective that she was, she could tell that this was going to be a good case. Challenging, but not impossible.

Siri had finished making tea. They went back to the living room and sat down on the sofa. It was unusual not to have a pile of rare objects between them when they both sat there.

"A man from Lake Superior contacted me," Felicia explained. "He has a broadsheet from the 1700s, and he thinks it belonged to an ancestor from Norway. It's a ballad. The text and music were printed here in Trondheim."

Felicia went on enthusiastically, speaking a mixture of Norwegian and English. She pulled a folded sheet of paper out of her pocket.

"Look at this. He scanned it and sent it to me," she said, handing the paper to Siri.

She took a quick glance and then began humming the melody of the notes. Felicia, who had no training in sight-reading, listened carefully, memorizing the tune as best she could. She liked it. It sounded sad.

"The Winding Print Shop," murmured Siri. "This client of yours . . . does he know anything more about the ballad?"

"Not that he told me."

"The title page is missing. So we don't know the name of the song, or the composer, or even whether there were two composers—one for the lyrics and one for the music."

"I e-mailed the customer to ask him, but he hasn't replied yet."

"It's possible that the composer's name is on the full version of the broadsheet. If we're lucky, there are other existing prints from Winding. And in that case, there's a good chance that we have one in the Gunnerus Library. We have a big collection of old broadsheets."

"So you'll help me?"

"Of course. I'll get started tomorrow."

Then Siri turned up the volume of the music again. "*She has no demands, suffers not from diva indolence. Climb into her bed, men and boys, peasants and soldiers.*" Cornelis's playful, precise voice filled the room. The two women finished their tea and talked about other things—such as what they should buy for Odd's sixtieth birthday, which was coming up. They both agreed that they'd have to think of something better than a bottle of Red Aalborg aquavit, even though that was probably the only thing he wanted.

8

Elise Edvardsen had hurled a few more caustic remarks at her daughter before going to bed for the night. She didn't know why she was always so sarcastic. She didn't think of herself as malicious, and yet she couldn't hold back. She nagged her sixteen-year-old daughter about all sorts of trivial things. It might be about a test that didn't go well at school, or clothing she had bought that her daughter refused to wear. "So H&M isn't good enough for you anymore? I don't know how a daughter of mine could turn out to be such a snob."

The way the teenager smacked her chewing gum really pissed her off. "Do you really need to sound like a walrus drowning in its own spit?" Why did she say such absurd things? They hardly ever had a normal conversation anymore. And yet, they'd once been so close. Even Julie's singing annoyed Elise lately. It always woke her up. But not this morning.

All night she'd drifted in and out of dreams that were weighted with so many different thoughts. She had been arguing with Ivar, Julie, and herself about the strangest things, like Internet fees and the need for sunscreen during Easter vacation. It was odd to wake up to a silent house. Ivar breathed quietly beside her, almost as if he were making an effort not to disturb. She looked at his pale nose sticking out at the edge of the duvet. His nostrils flared and constricted with a calculated calm. She found it terribly irritating.

The bedroom door stood open, just as it always did. They had gotten into the habit of leaving the door ajar when Julie was little because she used to climb into their bed at night. And they'd never given up the habit. Right across from their bedroom was the bathroom, and that was where the sound should be coming from. Elise should have heard Julie singing behind the closed door, like she always did in the morning. She remembered when waking up to that song had been the best thing in the world.

She got up and thought back on last night. Julie had shown her an expensive pair of pants that she'd bought, and even though Elise knew her daughter had spent her own allowance on them, she'd still called her a stupid teenage diva. She could have said it like she was joking, but she hadn't. She had meant the words to hurt. They'd slipped out, and Julie hadn't replied. She'd just turned on her heel, put Bismarck on his leash, and left for their evening walk.

That had opened Elise's eyes. I can't keep on this way, she thought. So she had crept into bed alongside Ivar, who was already asleep. I'm a terrible mother, she had whispered to him as he dreamed. He had merely grunted and kept on sleeping. So Elise had lain in bed, listening for the door, the humming in the hallway, the dog shaking the snow off his coat. But she had fallen asleep before Julie came back.

But I was awake for a long time, wasn't I? she thought now.

She went into the hall and opened the bathroom door. Everything was just as she'd left it last night. No towels or dirty clothes tossed on the floor. And the top was on the toothpaste tube.

Without thinking, she went to the front door and pulled it open, staring out at the yard. It was not yet daylight. The frosty vapor issuing from her mouth made the world seem hazy, and she stood there, peering vacantly into the white space between the big trees.

Then out of old habit she looked down and found the newspaper lying on the doorstep. She read the front-page headline, which was about that awful thing that had happened on Ludvig Daaes Gate. It had shocked the whole neighborhood. For two days afterward she had forbidden Julie to go out alone after dark. But her daughter had refused to obey, which led to more arguments. So Elise had finally relented, though with a bad feeling in her stomach.

With a rising sense of alarm she went into the kitchen. The counter was clean, without a single crumb on it. In the living room, Bismarck wasn't sprawled on his pillow. For a moment she stood there, motionless, as if it were a great effort to draw a breath. Slowly, taking off-tempo steps, she went over to her daughter's bedroom. It was at the other end of the living room. An idiotic question suddenly occurred to her: Why did they sleep so far apart? For a moment she wondered if she were going crazy. Then she thought, This is just a dream. A horrible nightmare.

She stood outside her daughter's bedroom door for what seemed like a long time. Then she gathered her courage and opened the door.

9

In his mind, Grälmakar Löfberg relived the murder again and again, which was no more than a few days old. Sometimes he dwelled only on a single blow, a drop of blood, or a flash in her eyes. Other times, like now, he recalled the entire course of events and the atmosphere that had settled over everything. The blows, the sounds, the smell of blood and sweat, the dim light in the basement store-room. He thought about everything. It was the only thing that gave him any sense of calm.

He heard his own voice from that night with Silje Rolfsen.

"Sing!"

Then came the images.

The knife blade made a little hollow in the skin of her neck but did not cut all the way through. It wouldn't, since he held it very still, and she didn't move.

"Sing!" he repeated, taking the knife away so she could breathe. He turned it and set the point against her larynx.

Then she sang. He got up, taking the knife with him, and left the storeroom, locking the door behind him. He lay down on the mattress in the hall and listened to her singing. She had memorized every note and every verse. He heard her voice through the thin door, muted, like sound drifting in from someone else's apartment. For a while he thought he was getting drowsy, that he was drifting off to sleep. But his eyes refused to close. Then he heard the fly buzzing inside his head.

It wasn't working like it was supposed to.

Finally he got up slowly, leaned down, and put on a CD. It was Bellman. He turned up the volume. Then he went back into the storeroom. She had stopped singing. She stood there, her feet apart and her head bowed toward the floor.

He grabbed her by the hair and threw her against the wall. Her scream made him feel calmer. He slapped her cheek.

"Please don't. Please, please don't," she pleaded. "I don't want to be here anymore."

"You're not going anywhere, dear," he said.

And finally she understood.

She huddled on the floor. He threw himself at her, yanked her up, and kicked her in the stomach. She flew backward, rammed against the far wall, and then pitched forward. Slowly, she got back on her feet, motioned to him with one hand, muttering something, and then dropped to her knees. He lifted her up and pressed her back against the wall as he struck her. It was like hitting a mattress. Then everything inside her seemed to surrender all at once, and she sank to the floor. Her knees buckled; her head drooped. But then, a fraction of an inch at a time, she pulled herself up again.

She couldn't speak; she couldn't hear; she couldn't see. It was beyond his comprehension how she was able to breathe or stay upright. But she raised her head, made a few gurgling noises, and stretched her arms out to the sides. She stood like that for a moment; then she stumbled toward him. A clear tone issued from her throat, as if she were trying to sing one last time. Or maybe it was a plea.

He punched her on the chin. She fell to the floor like a sack of cement, and this time she didn't get up.

". . . *where time and death unite beauty and foulness in the same dust* . . ."

Behind him he could hear Åkerström's fervent bass voice.

The music filled the entire basement, coming from the little CD player next to the mattress outside the storeroom. The music made his thoughts float. He felt exhausted, as if all the blows had struck him instead of her, and he collapsed onto the mattress with the images of her motionless body imprinted on his retinas.

Now, several days later, he could still conjure up those images. They brought him peace.

Singsaker could feel the pressure against his chest, and the blood being pumped into the spongelike network of capillaries just under the surface of his skin. He had opened his eyes and could see the darkness below him, blurry through the salt water, like a question with no answer, a case with no resolution.

He hovered like that, staring through the waters with both arms stretched out to the sides. This numbness in his skin bordered on paralysis. It was no longer possible to determine whether he was freezing or warm. His body had somehow been set free, as well as his thoughts. It felt like an eternity, though it lasted only a few seconds. He couldn't hold his head under the ice-cold water any longer than that. Then he kicked his legs. It was a reflex and not a controlled action, but it happened every time he did this, and he shot upward. He still had his eyes open, and he could see the sun flailing like a golden octopus on the surface where a thin membrane of slushy ice had settled. He broke through, gasping for air at just about the same spot he'd jumped in. The surrounding water was still full of bubbles. Then he bellowed like a kid:

"What the fuck! It's just as bad every time!"

"And just as good," replied Thorvald Jensen, who was already sitting on the dock with a towel wrapped around him.

Singsaker swam quickly over to the ladder and climbed up to join his colleague.

"Good?" he said, grabbing the other towel from the dock. "It's times like this that make me think it might actually snow in hell."

Jensen smiled.

"Even Dante knew that. Wasn't it the traitors who ended up in Cocytus, the ice sea in the ninth inner circle of hell?"

"So if I betray you and give up this insane ice-bathing thing, is that where I'll end up too?" asked Singsaker, smiling wryly.

"Ironic, isn't it?' said Jensen.

They had issued a challenge to each other after the crazy homicide case in the fall. It was Jensen's idea. They would go swimming once a week all winter long. People said it was good for the health. Singsaker couldn't say whether that was why he'd accepted the challenge, or if it was because his life had been turned upside down in so many ways during the past year and that one more silly whim didn't really make any difference. Jensen had told him that he'd always been an avid open-air bather but that for a long time he'd dreamed of also being an ice bather, so he might as well get started before it was too late. Jensen was two years younger than Singsaker, so he too was approaching sixty. Singsaker had never had enough imagination to swim in the winter. He alternated between reproaching and admiring his friend—all depending on whether it was before or after their weekly swim—for this ice-cold lunacy.

He rubbed his body with the towel, the feeling starting to return to his skin. After a while he wrapped the towel around his waist, and together the two middle-aged policemen went back to the locker room. Singsaker was tall and rail-thin, even though he never worked out and only went hiking on the rare occasions when Jensen persuaded him to join him for a hunting expedition. Jensen, who was a real outdoorsman, had a solid paunch he'd never been able to shed, no matter how many heath-covered slopes he hiked in the fall.

Their old, naked bodies reminded Singsaker of two Roman citizens on their way out of the frigidarium, the cold section of the Roman baths. But the locker room of the swim club in Trondheim was about as different as you could get from Thermae Agrippae. While they got dressed, he thought about how nice a steam bath would have felt. But Jensen was in the conservative group of the swim club, those who probably would have chained themselves to the locker room to prevent the construction of anything like that. It was only because Jensen was a member of the club's hard-core group that they were allowed to borrow the key in the wintertime. The club was actually only open in the summer. Ice bathing was viewed with a certain skepticism by anyone other than the most dedicated open-air bathers in Trondheim.

Afterwards Singsaker locked the door to the swim facilities. Jensen was a clever one. He had let Odd keep the only key to the building, but several weeks passed before Singsaker understood why. If he had the key, he would have to show up. He couldn't use some pretext to get out of swimming, because if he didn't come, Jensen couldn't swim either. His colleague was a master at combining cynicism with friendship.

Together they walked from the pier to the police station. Jensen was on duty, but Singsaker had the day off. He couldn't say that he envied his colleague, since a pall had hovered over the department for the past few days.

Grongstad's prediction that they'd find very little evidence at the crime scene was correct. There was no organic material that might have given them DNA of anyone besides the victim. The heavy snowfall had effectively erased all footprints, and because of the cold weather, the killer had probably been bundled up and wearing gloves. Not even a partial fingerprint had been found on the music box. The truth was that they had almost nothing to go on.

In his final autopsy report, Dr. Kittelsen had confirmed that the victim had been severely beaten. She died when her throat was cut.

Singsaker, alone now, trudged along and crossed the bridge over to Bakklandet. He enjoyed walking through his city. It made him feel like a civilian, one of the people whose safety he had dedicated his life to protecting.

One time, a colleague from Bergen who had spent a few years working Homicide, had told Singsaker that the citizens of Bergen were patriotic but that those who lived in Trøndelag had a reason for their patriotism. He may have just been trying to ingratiate himself, but he did have a point. The people of Trøndelag were always the best, whether it was soccer, skiing, music, research, or merely being Norwegian. They were people who made their dreams come true. But Singsaker was a homicide detective. He knew that people's nightmares were just as awful here as any other place, and at times those nightmares came true. But he loved his city, both the good and the bad, and on clear winter mornings like this, it seemed to him the only place in the world to live.

Eventually he arrived at Baklandet Skydsstation.

The ramshackle tavern looked like it might topple into the street at any moment. Singsaker sat down at his usual table near the entrance. He hadn't gone out much during the last years of first his marriage, but ever since Felicia had come into his life, he'd decided that he should take her out for dinner once in a while. When he discovered that Baklandet Skydsstation served an excellent herring platter with homemade Danish rye bread, he'd started coming here on his days off to have lunch, often without Felicia. He'd become such a steady customer that the waiters had started to greet him by name.

He ordered his usual and then began leafing through the newspaper that lay on the table. The crime reporter Vlado Taneski, who wrote for *Adresseavisen*, was not Singsaker's favorite, but in the coverage of this particular case, he'd balanced the gravity of the situation with his obvious satisfaction at writing about something that was not confined to the city of Trondheim. If Singsaker felt any respect at all for Taneski, he might have been impressed.

But now he stared gloomily at the headlines.

WHERE WAS SHE? it asked in big letters above a photo of Silje Rolfsen. The article launched right in. It also had a quote from Singsaker.

"We're working with several different theories," he said. "That she was kidnapped by the killer is only one of the ideas we're looking at." For a change, Taneski had accurately cited what Singsaker had said. But that wasn't the whole truth. In fact, so far they didn't have a single plausible theory as to where Silje Rolfsen had been the weeks before she was killed. The idea that she might have been kidnapped by the unidentified perpetrator was the only angle that seemed credible. Over the past few days, their investigative efforts had almost definitely ruled out the likelihood that Silje had met Jonny Olin in Trondheim. But it had been verified that she'd bought a train ticket online from Oslo to Trondheim on the morning of January 3. Cell phone records had shown that she had used her cell twice at the train station that same evening. The police had traced these calls to her roommate in Oslo and to Olin, although the latter had not gone through, since Olin had been out of town with his boyfriend at the time. This had been confirmed by the boyfriend, as well as by records from the E-ZPass checkpoints to and from the coastal town. The police had also ascertained that Silje had not returned to her apartment in Oslo or visited any friends or family members. But most disturbing of all was the fact that after making those two calls from the train station in Trondheim, she had not used her phone again. The last purchase on her Visa card was for twenty-one Norwegian kroner on the Trondheim train on the same day she was reported missing. Neither her cell phone nor her wallet had been found on her body, or anywhere in the vicinity of the crime scene.

In Singsaker's opinion, there was only one scenario that seemed reasonable.

When she couldn't get in touch with Jonny Olin, whom she was planning to surprise with a visit, she must have started walking toward where he lived. Somewhere along the way she had met the unidentified perpetrator. Maybe she had mentioned that she was a stranger in town, which might have made her an easy mark. He must have enticed her to go home with him, maybe by offering to let her wait there until she could get in touch with her ex-boyfriend. Then he had held her hostage until he killed her three weeks later. That seemed like a plausible course of events, based on the facts of the case. But the question was, Why? What was the motive? The only thing this scenario told them about the killer—and this was something they could actually make use of in their investigation—was that he most likely lived somewhere close by. And that was actually very useful. It was always a relief to rule out what was every homicide detective's worst nightmare: a murderer who was an outsider, a random killer who just happened to be in the area. The section between the center of town and Skyåsvegen contained the highest density of apartment buildings and rental houses in all of Trondheim, other than Moholt, which was populated by university students. Plenty of students, welfare recipients, single-parent families, and divorced individuals lived in the blocks of apartment buildings in the Møllenberg district. They were constantly moving in or out, and not all of the residents were actually registered at the address where they lived. The well-established, highly educated people with an equally high mortgage lived in the area above Stadsingeniør Dahls Gate, toward Kuhaugen. But this part of town also contained a lot of lofts and basement apartments. This area was known for its many rental units, few of them with approved building permits, and all of them with a great deal of turnover. So even though the police had a vague idea of where the killer might live, it didn't help much in narrowing down the suspect pool.

Singsaker's lunch arrived, so he put down the newspaper and tried to think of something else. And he almost succeeded, once he'd downed his first glass of Red Aalborg aquavit. He realized it did him good to go ice bathing one day a week. He felt a tingling in his skin, which was now warm, and he felt a deep sense of relaxation. He was just about to take his first bite of herring in mustard sauce on a piece of rye bread when his cell rang. It was Jensen.

They hadn't said anything else when they parted company half an hour ago, so a phone call could mean only one thing: Something had happened. Something that was going to ruin Singsaker's day off.

"Having a nice lunch?" asked Jensen, sounding ominously cheerful.

"Until now," replied Singsaker, swallowing a small bite of herring.

"I'm afraid we could use a little help from you after all."

"I see. Does this have anything to do with the case?"

"No," said Jensen, pausing. "At least I hope not. A girl is missing."

"Missing?"

"Yes. Sixteen years old, in the tenth grade at the Rosenborg School. She disappeared quite suddenly from her home last night. Her parents went to bed early, and they haven't seen her since she took the dog out for his evening walk."

"I don't know, Thorvald. It sounds pretty routine. Teenage rebellion. You know how it is."

"Yeah. Normally I'd agree with you, but there are a few things that don't add up. Plus, we have to take into consideration where she lives."

"And where's that?"

"On Markvegen."

"Oh shit," said Singsaker. "That's awfully close to Bernhard Getz' Gate."

"That's why Brattberg wants to make it a priority. She wants you to go over there with Gran and have a talk with the girl's parents. You haven't got other plans, have you?"

"Of course I do," replied Singsaker with a sigh. "I'll be there as soon as I finish eating." And he ended the call.

Then he took his notebook out of his pocket. He placed it on the table next to his plate and wrote optimistically, "Routine case with Gran. Teenage girl on the roam." Then he crossed his fingers.

One thing bothered Grälmakar Löfberg:

Silje Rolfsen had sung for him. But only after it was all over had sleep finally come to him, and with it that strange, inexplicable dream with the giants in the sky. As if the blows and kicks had given him what he was hoping for, and not the song.

But no, not even the blows and kicks had given him what he longed for: to sleep each night, to dream, a slumber that would never end.

As he feared, he hadn't slept since the night he'd carried her motionless body out to the woods, cut her throat, and dug out her larynx. It had been liberating. But the effect had been so temporary, and all he'd won was a brief dream that he didn't understand. He hadn't found his way back to the world where his innermost madness and yearning were freed, where his hopes, passions, and forbidden thoughts could unfold each night, the world of dreams.

He couldn't say when something inside him had rebelled, when the raw emotions that belong to sleep had begun to force their way into the eternal waking hours. It had happened surreptitiously, slowly, like in his worst nightmare. Now he could barely make it through the nights anymore, with the warm duvet that tried to suffocate him. The dark in the room that had no substance but was filled with shadows that mocked him, and the gray nuances that disturbed his sleep as much as sunlight did. He could no longer stand the nights. The days were even worse.

But at last there was another opportunity for him to achieve some peace. This time he'd chosen the right girl. The lullaby was going to work. It had to work.

IO

You know, old man, you ought to be ashamed! Cecilia Lind is only a child. Pure as a blossom, shy as a doe. I'll be seventeen soon, said Cecilia Lind."

With a sigh, Siri Holm turned off the song by the lusty Swedish singer, took out her earbuds, and put her phone back in the pocket of her green pants.

She'd had her first sexual experience just after she'd turned nineteen. Maybe that was why she'd become so enthusiastic about the art of love. Over the past four years she'd had about fifty sexual partners. She hadn't been especially particular about who she went to bed with. For her, they were all good—old or young, ugly or handsome. She'd always been an explorer, and she saw no reason to change that. As with everything she did, the objective was to gain as much insight as possible. It had never occurred to her to look for a suitable husband. A quick calculation told her that she'd had an average of one partner per menstrual period, But she'd never been regular enough, either in terms of her period or her sexual adventures, for the arithmetic to add up perfectly. The important thing was that she'd had only one partner after her last period, which was about four months ago. So she knew who the father was of the child now growing inside of her.

But even though Siri had never been very particular about her sexual partners, there were actually a few men she could never imagine going to bed with. One of them was Gunnar Berg. He was a historian who worked as a librarian at the Gunnerus Library, and he was seated behind the office door that she knocked on now. He had no sense of humor whatsoever, but he did know a lot about broadsheets.

"Come in!"

His voice sounded like an out-of-tune fiddle in the hands of a child.

She opened the door with reluctance. It was depressing, being in the same room with someone who never laughed.

"Hi, Gunnar. Could you do me a favor?"

"That depends what it is." Berg looked up from the title page of a book. Apparently he'd been immersed in a difficult classification problem.

"I'm looking for a specific broadsheet," she said.

That caught his attention. His expression actually showed some measure of interest.

"A broadsheet?"

"Yes, I could try to find it myself, but I thought it'd be faster if I asked for your help. Especially since, as I understand it, you're the one who did all the cataloging, scanning, and digitizing of the library's broadsheets."

"That's right. It was quite a job. And now it looks as if we're going to have to do the whole thing over again."

"Oh, really?" said Siri, feigning ignorance about the impending conversion project.

"Yes, we've put all the broadsheets up on the Internet, but it's a Flash-based system called eRez. And it can't be read on any Apple devices. It is also unreliable. It's going to be a hell of a job to convert everything into open-source code, but it'll be worth it."

She looked at his somber expression, well aware of how much he was looking forward to doing the job itself and also being able to bitch about it. Then she handed him the broadsheet that Felicia had given her. He studied it for a long time before responding.

"Where did you get this?" he asked.

"Let's just say that somebody sent it from the States."

He continued to study the printout.

"Precisely. That makes sense. But I don't think it's the same as the one we had."

"What are you talking about? And what do you mean by 'had'?"

"This broadsheet, or another version of it, was stolen from the library a year ago. Before we had a chance to scan it."

"Really?"

She wondered if this might be significant for Felicia, but she decided it mostly just meant that the assignment was going to be harder to solve.

"So we don't have it here? Either on paper or in the computer?" she asked.

"That's right."

"Do you at least remember anything in particular about this broadsheet?"

"I most certainly do," he said in a pompous tone. "This is a lullaby. If I remember correctly, this is the fourth verse. The song is called 'The Golden Peace,' and the subtitle is 'Dreams Re-create the World Each Night.' The funny thing about this ballad is that it partially refers to itself. The title page boasts that the ballad can make anyone fall asleep. You only have to hear it once, and you'll sleep soundly and have sweet dreams every single night forever after. Not bad, huh? The verse you're holding is about how the song can even make a criminal fall asleep after committing a crime. But the last verse is my favorite. It's about how the troubadour himself falls asleep while he's singing, and thus forgets all his sorrows. This was without a doubt one of the best broadsheets we had in our collection.

"And if you ask me, we have the best collection in Norway. Trondheim was the printing capital of Norway in the seventeenth and eighteenth centuries. And Winding's was the foremost print shop in town."

"Do you recall who wrote this?" she asked.

"It was written under a pseudonym, which was customary at the time. Many of the composers were anonymous; very few songs can actually be attributed to known historical figures. We think that many of the anonymous ballads were written by well-known cultural figures who didn't wish to have their names associated with what was considered a low form of expression, even though they did benefit from the lucrative income that often came in from these."

"So the real author might be a well-known historical figure?"

"Theoretically, yes. But there isn't reason to believe that here, considering the pseudonym that was used. I think it was used only once, for this particular ballad."

"And what's the name?"

"Jon Blund."

"Jon Blund? The lead character in those movies from the 1960s? Those bedtime stories for kids?"

"Maybe. But Jon Blund has roots in Norwegian folklore, especially with short bedtime stories meant to lull children to sleep. In Danish, he's called 'Ole Lukøje,' which means 'Ole Shut-eye,' while in English he's known as 'the Sandman.' The name Jon Blund appeared around 1710 in a text by the Swedish poet Johan Runius. One of the most exciting things about the lullaby you've got here is that it's the first time that the name Jon Blund was used in a Norwegian text. It also shows up, of all places, in a police report from the same period. And as it happens, the report is from Trondheim. Later, Jon Blund is mentioned in the fairy tale 'An Old-Fashioned Christmas Eve' by Asbjørnsen and Moe. In that story the phrase 'At any moment Jon Blund would arrive' was synonymous with 'They would soon fall asleep.' In the old days *sleep* was often used in an allegorical sense to mean death, and so Jon Blund was sometimes associated with more sinister figures, like the Grim Reaper."

Siri Holm liked Gunnar Berg much better when he was talking about ballads and folklore than when he was droning on about classifications. He showed an involvement in the subject that might actually be taken for good spirits. It almost made him a little sexy. For a brief moment she stood there, considering the idea of seducing him. But then she told herself, Those days of being a woman footloose and fancy free are over for you, Siri, my girl.

"So you're saying that the author wrote only one ballad?"

"Not necessarily. If he didn't use another pseudonym, then it seems that he had only this one ballad printed in Trondheim. But both the pseudonym and the title point to Sweden as their place of origin. In Stockholm, there was an inn called the Golden Peace. It was just one of a number of inns where people would get drunk, which they did with great frequency. The water quality in Stockholm was terrible then, and so they drank liquor, which didn't spread infection as much. The Golden Peace actually still exists today. In fact, it's something of an institution in the city. I've been there myself."

Siri gave Gunnar Berg a look. She had heard of the Golden Peace. Vreeswijk sang about the place: *"Here we're all equal, you know, red ones and blue ones—skinny and fat."* But no matter how hard she tried, she just couldn't picture her colleague sitting in a pub, getting even slightly tipsy.

Berg went on: "There's something special about sitting in that place, imagining all the troubadours who drank there, having a grand old time and presenting their ballads for almost three hundred years. But in our case, the title doesn't refer directly to that inn, even though it may have inspired the song. I think it's describing sleep, the most golden of all peace. If our Jon Blund lived in Stockholm, he was most likely a contemporary of the famous troubadour Carl Michael Bellman, the true genius of the ballad tradition. But Blund undoubtedly lived in his shadow. It's even possible that he belonged to Bellman's circle of friends and drinking companions."

"One of Bellman's shadows," she said, mulling over the possibility. "Here in Trondheim. This is interesting stuff. Has anyone done any research on the subject?"

"No, oddly enough. Many of our broadsheets are real cultural treasures, but since they're also part of the folk culture, they're not taken as seriously as more canonized music and poetry."

She thought about what he'd just told her.

"But it's unusual for valuable items like this to disappear from the library, isn't it?" Holm then asked. She'd worked less than six months at the Gunnerus Library, and she'd thought that the case of the legendary Johannes Book, which had been the target of an attempted theft, was an exception. "I mean head librarian Hornemann seems very strict when it comes to security."

"Yes, but unfortunately it does happen. You wouldn't believe how many people have tried to walk off with valuables from the library. And the theft of the Jon Blund ballad got a lot of attention before you started working here. A police report was filed and everything. But the only result from the investigation was that it revealed how lax our security was. Hornemann's strict attitude on security is a consequence of the theft of that broadsheet. I think it was a real wake-up call for him. A library patron signed in under a false name and then was given access to the broadsheets. The ballads are stored in boxes, with several in each box. That was the only one the thief took. Presumably he just stuck it in his pocket and disappeared."

"Do you know what name the borrower used?"

"I remember it all too well. Anyone who listens to Bellman's work would recognize it."

"What is it?" asked Siri. Until just then, she'd thought that his interest in ballads extended only to the printed versions.

"Grälmakar Löfberg," he told her.

"And who was that?" she asked.

"Grälmakar Löfberg is one of the many figures who show up in Bellman's songs. Bellman created a whole universe that he populated with both fictional and real people who lived in Stockholm at the same time he did. Most of them were outsiders and drunkards. Often they were people who had fallen from grace and ended up in the gutter. There were lots of people like that in Stockholm during Bellman's day. Löfberg was not a central figure in the songs, so the only thing we know about the real person was that he was a quarrelsome sort. And Bellman wrote a lovely funeral hymn about his wife."

Siri had a strange feeling that this was somehow significant.

She thanked Gunnar Berg for his help, realizing that she now liked him better than before. As she closed the office door, she felt something in her stomach. Was it a kick? No, of course not. It was too early for that. She was less than four months along. Her stomach was just growling, that was all. But these days even the slightest stirring in her stomach reminded her of the tiny person inside.

"The little bell rings to the big bell's toll," she sang softly as she stroked her stomach and smiled.

The new singer was someone he knew from before.

He assured himself that everything was in order this time.

Then he lit a cigarette. The fly was not buzzing inside his head. Slowly he exhaled. Then he looked at the pink vocal cords in the jar of alcohol. They had begun to fade; the pink was slowly disappearing, as if their real demise hadn't yet occurred. But they still looked as though they might be able to sing from the bottom of the jar. What had been wrong with them? Why hadn't they worked the way they were supposed to?

Then he heard the dog barking. Why did I bring that mutt inside? he asked himself. He couldn't stand dogs that barked.

Down in the basement he walked over to the stall where he'd put the dog. The animal stopped barking and retreated to a corner with his tail between his legs the minute he opened the door. Then he began kicking it. Eventually he went out and knelt down on the mattress that he'd left outside the storeroom. She was inside, but she didn't make a sound. He could hear that his new songbird was breathing hard even though she was gagged. He wondered if she'd heard what he'd done to her dog.

With trembling hands he picked up the music box from the floor. Slowly, he turned the key until the spring was tightly wound. He set it back down and listened. A sad, metallic tune filled the basement. There it was: his lullaby, and it was just as beautiful as always. Tears ran down his cheeks. He sat and stared at the twirling singer wearing the white jacket until he felt calmer. Then he picked up the music box again. *That's enough for now,* he thought as he got to his feet. *We can play it again later.* Then he cleared his throat. He decided that he ought to say something to her, so he cleared his throat again.

"Good morning," he said finally. Just those two words. Then he turned on his heel and went back up the basement stairs.

I I

The fact that she was standing upright was the only indication that she was even alive. But then she said: "Thank you for taking the time to come here."

Elise Edvardsen sounded as if she were speaking to two workers she had hired. She stared blankly at Chief Inspector Singsaker, swaying. For a moment he was afraid that she was going to faint and pitch forward into his arms, and he wasn't at all sure that he'd be able to hold her up, even though she was awfully thin. At that point, all Singsaker knew was that she was an aerobics instructor married to an optician, and that they lived in a house at the end of Markvegen with a big yard and old trees that blocked the view from the neighboring houses.

Instead of collapsing, Elise pulled herself together and stepped to one side to allow the officers to come in. Singsaker entered first, followed by Mona Gran.

The husband, Ivar Edvardsen, sat on a chair in the living room. He was a short, plump man who looked worn-out. Even though Singsaker realized that his haggard appearance must be due to the situation, he had the feeling that Mr. Edvardsen always looked that way.

The two police detectives sat down on the sofa after shaking hands with him. He didn't say a word, merely nodded a greeting.

"Would you like something to drink?" asked Elise, who still hadn't sat down. "Coffee?"

Singsaker and Gran both declined the offer. Ivar was holding a cup in his hand, but Singsaker guessed that the man hadn't even taken a sip, and that by now the coffee had grown cold.

Elise sat down on the only unoccupied chair.

"Maybe we'd better start at the beginning," said Singsaker, getting out his notebook. Both parents looked at him as if they were having trouble comprehending his words.

"When did you last see your daughter?"

"Julie?" said Elise, sounding distracted.

"Yes, Julie," said Singsaker patiently.

"But we already told the police everything," said Ivar, speaking for the first time. His voice was surprisingly high-pitched for such a stout man.

"We apologize," said Gran, "but at the start of an investigation we often go over things more than once. It's important for us to hear what happened in your own words, since we'll be handling this case from now on."

Singsaker nodded agreement. It was Gran's direct but sensitive manner that made him sure that she would become an outstanding detective.

Mr. and Mrs. Edvardsen glanced at each other. Maybe they were able to communicate without words, as some couples did after many years together. Singsaker used to do the same with Anniken. His ex-wife had left him for a plumber. When she later regretted what she'd done, Singsaker had forgiven her. He forgave her and then moved on with his life. He didn't miss her, but he did miss the feeling of knowing someone so well. He wondered how long it would take before he and Felicia reached that point. Would they ever get there?

"I said good night to Julie a little before ten-thirty and then went to bed," said Ivar Edvardsen. "My wife talked to her until she took the dog for a walk, and she went to bed before Julie came back home."

Singsaker glanced at Elise, then began looking around while he listened to the others talking, their voices becoming a humming sound in the background. He only vaguely registered that Gran had begun asking them the usual, routine questions.

Hanging on the wall behind Ivar was a wedding photograph of the couple. They were young; she was dressed in white and he was in black. They looked contented, convinced of their future happiness. Singsaker thought about the red dress that Felicia had worn when they got married. The only other people present at the ceremony were Siri Holm and Thorvald Jensen. He recalled the numbing haste with which they'd fallen in love. He pictured the wedding scene, the second one in his life, as if an old 8mm film played in his mind, just slightly too fast. Had it happened too quickly? No, they couldn't have done it any other way, not if it was going to amount to anything, not if they were going to be together. And they were right for each other. The doubts he had were not about the two of them. He and Felicia had all the time in the world. Things couldn't have been better. It was the haste of the wedding. Had that been the right thing to do?

"I think we have enough preliminary information, don't you, Singsaker?" he heard Gran say as if from far away, bringing him abruptly back to reality.

Problems with his ability to concentrate. That was what his doctor had told him, adding that he was just going to have to learn to deal with it.

In Singsaker's profession, he had to hide this weakness as best he could. An inability to concentrate was not something a policeman could live with. But in a surprisingly short time he'd become expert at covering up these sorts of gaps.

"Yes, although we may need to come back to a few things later on," he said, even though he had no idea what they'd been talking about. Then he took a chance and selected a topic, speaking directly to Elise Edvardsen.

"How would you describe your daughter?" he asked her.

She didn't reply immediately. She looked from Singsaker to her husband. For a moment, Singsaker was afraid that he'd blundered and asked about something they'd already discussed. But then she opened her mouth and said, "Well, what can we say about her?" She was staring at a spot just above her husband's head.

"She's a very talented young lady," said Mr. Edvardsen.

"Oh, shut up, Ivar!" The rebuke didn't seem to surprise him as much as might have been expected. "For God's sake! Julie has disappeared. These officers aren't here to listen to us talk about how beautifully she sings or how many goals she's stopped in handball games."

"I realize that, Elise," said her husband with restrained indignation.

Gran stepped in and got the conversation back on track. "So, if you're being perfectly honest, how would you describe her?"

"To be perfectly honest, she's a teenager with a capital *T*. And I'm not handling it very well."

"I understand. A lot of door slamming?" said Gran.

"What I can't handle is how irrational she is. I know I should be more patient with her." She glanced at her husband, who smiled wanly.

"Does she have a boyfriend?" asked Gran.

"No," said Ivar firmly. But his wife was quick to correct him.

"We can't be sure that it's not still going on."

Singsaker took over. "So she did have a boyfriend?"

"His name is Fredrik. They've broken up and gotten back together about ten times. We never know whether they're on or off."

"And was it Julie or Fredrik who broke it off each time?" asked Singsaker.

"Who do you think? Don't misunderstand me. I love my daughter very much. And if anything has happened to her, I don't know—" Here Elise broke off and took a few deep breaths before going on. "But Julie isn't easy to deal with. She's moody. Sometimes I feel sorry for Fredrik, the poor boy, even though I can't say I like him much. He's too timid for a girl like Julie."

"Have you told Julie what you think of her boyfriend?"

"No, we don't talk much. In the past few weeks we've done nothing but argue about stupid things."

"Like what?"

"Just nonsense. Clothes, mostly. Julie put on some weight, so she went out and bought a lot of new clothes with the money she had been saving to buy a moped."

"Did you argue last night?" asked Singsaker.

"I guess I was a little harsh. And she was in a bad mood when she left the house. But you don't think that's why, do you? Did she run away from home to punish us? That wouldn't be like her. She's impulsive, but she doesn't stay mad for long."

"Is she usually the one who takes the dog out for a walk?" Gran interjected.

"Yes. She loves that dog. Every day she sits and sings to the dog as she pets him. He's her dog, and she's the one who walks him."

Singsaker got up to stretch his legs. The invigorated feeling he'd had after the morning swim was now gone.

"We'll need the full name, address, and phone number of this Fredrik," he said.

"Alm. Fredrik Alm," said Ivar as he too stood up. "I don't think we have his phone number, and they're not in the same class at school, but he lives on Veimester Krohgs Gate. You can probably look up his exact address."

"Thanks. What about girlfriends? Does she have any good friends?" asked Gran as she glanced at Singsaker, who had started walking around the room.

"Yes, there are a group of girls she hangs out with. But Julie's not the type to have one best friend. She's friends with all of them," explained Elise.

"We'll need a list." Singsaker sat down again, while Ivar went out to the kitchen. He came back after a minute with a sheet of paper.

"Here's a list of her classmates. I've underlined the names of the girls she spends the most time with," he said, handing the paper to Singsaker.

Then both officers stood up.

"We'll be talking to some of your neighbors, as well as checking with her friends. At the moment we're assuming that she's staying with someone she knows. It would be a big help if you could make a list of everyone you can think of whose house she might have gone to. Relatives, friends who aren't classmates, and the like. Let's hope that we find her very soon."

"So you don't think that she's . . ." Elise began hesitantly. "You don't think this has anything to do with that case?"

"If you're thinking about the murder near Ludvig Daaes Gate, it's too early to say anything about that," replied Singsaker. "There's nothing to indicate that there's a connection. The victim in that case was a stranger in town, and a good deal older than Julie. You should know that with most cases like this, the missing person shows up relatively quickly."

"I heard that a music box was found near the victim. How horrible. I hope you'll do everything to rule out the possibility that . . . that such a monster has taken our Julie."

"Of course," said Singsaker, hiding his annoyance that the detail of the music box had already been leaked to the public. "Don't worry. There's very little chance of any sort of connection," he added.

Something prevented Singsaker from feeling as optimistic as he tried to sound. He had no idea whether he had reassured the parents or not.

"We need a photograph of her. With a neutral expression, where she's not smiling," he told them now.

Ivar Edvardsen found one in a kitchen drawer.

The photo was of Julie standing in the yard outside. There was no snow on the ground, and yellow leaves covered the trees behind her. At her feet sat a Saint Bernard. Her expression was serious but self-confident, and she looked older than sixteen. She had shoulder-length dark blond hair and brown eyes. Her skin was tan after a nice summer. Singsaker put the picture in his coat pocket.

Then he and Gran thanked the Edvardsens for their time and stepped out into the swirling snow.

"And this was supposed to be my day off," said Singsaker as they walked along Markvegen.

"Yep," said Gran. "And I had a doctor's appointment."

"Doctor? Nothing serious, I hope," said Singsaker, immediately regretting saying that. He usually didn't broach personal topics with the younger officers. But somehow it was little different with Mona Gran.

"Nothing serious, healthwise," she told him. "But my partner and I are trying to have a baby. And it seems like nature may need a little help."

Singsaker felt himself blushing. He wondered if this was what separated young people from those of his generation—this willingness to talk about intimate matters.

"It was no problem changing my appointment. And I know why they called us in today. Don't you?"

Singsaker nodded.

"There's something going on here. I can see a sixteen-year-old running away from a mother like that. But what I can't figure out is the dog. Why take the dog along if you're going to run away?"

Gran stopped and looked at him. They had almost reached the

intersection of Ludvig Daaes Gate, and they could see the crime scene from where they were standing.

"I think we should talk to the boyfriend and the girls she hangs out with ASAP. Do you think we could get them out of class?" she asked.

"If we're discreet about it," said Singsaker, glancing in the direction of Rosenborg School. "No need to make a big deal. But we do have to have a little chat with all of them. What if I go over to the school and quietly make inquiries while you start knocking on doors in the neighborhood?"

Mona Gran nodded.

"I'll call Brattberg too. I think we should send out a more detailed description. The bus companies and the train service should be notified, with special attention paid to Oslo. That's usually where they end up, if they don't go stay with people they know," she said.

Singsaker gave her an approving look. He liked her decisiveness. He wouldn't be surprised if she was promoted to chief inspector before he retired from the force.

"She may have left Trondheim, but we're not going to find that girl hanging out with the junkies in Oslo," he said. He almost thought that it was too bad. If they found Julie Edvardsen with nothing more than a few tracks in her arm, they'd be lucky.

"What do you think about the father?" asked Gran. "Didn't he seem strangely unemotional?"

"He wasn't unaffected," replied Singsaker. "I've seen this so many times. Repressing emotion. It's not an uncommon reaction to dramatic events. It's his way of coming to grips with what's happened. He's probably convinced that she's going to come home at any moment, as long as no concrete evidence turns up to tell him otherwise."

"So there's no reason to suspect him?"

"Suspect him of what? But you know how it is. As long as we don't have a suspect, everyone is a suspect," said Singsaker.

Then they headed off in different directions. Singsaker felt the opposite of Gran; he felt ancient.

Julie Edvardsen was young. She'd never thought about dying. Not until now.

She lay on the floor in a locked basement storeroom, breathing hard in the raw air. Her forehead ached, and she could tell that she had a bruise there, even though her hands weren't free to touch it. He'd finally left the light on, so she could study the room. The floor was covered with patches of brown and dark red. The splotches on one wall were the same color, all the way up to the window, which was covered with newspaper. The sight made her feel sick to her stomach. She felt like giving up. At the same time, she knew that was the last thing she should do.

Slowly, as if over a bad Internet connection, the events that had brought her here lurched through her mind.

She had known something bad was going to happen the moment she set the shopping bag on the chair in the hall and turned around to look at him. Suddenly she didn't recognize him. Or maybe she saw him for what he truly was. The apologetic, even helpless expression that she'd seen in his eyes was gone. What she saw was madness. A look that seemed to come from another world.

"I want you to sing for me," he'd told her.

Then he slowly removed the sling from his right arm as she stood there in shock, and watched. His arm was not injured. She couldn't believe she'd fallen for such a ploy. How naïve could she be?

Under the sling he was holding something that looked like a black handle. She recognized the weapon from movies she'd seen. It was a stun gun, and she knew that one jolt could knock her out. Suddenly he pulled off his ring finger and little finger, and he stood there, holding the gun with three fingers.

Prostheses, she thought.

He casually tossed them to the floor and shifted the stun gun to his left hand.

"They just get in the way when there's work to do," he said. "But you have to admit they look quite real. Anyone who doesn't know me would never notice them. And there aren't many people who know me well." He laughed. "I'm like a magician," he went on. "The trick is to keep the left hand moving, so as to divert attention from the right."

Then he fixed his eyes on her, took a few steps forward, and swung the gun toward her. But he'd underestimated her reflexes. Julie Edvardsen had been a goalie for the Rapp handball club since she was seven, so she was used to reacting quickly. A small step back and a lightning-fast bending of her knees were enough for him to miss, and his arm passed over her shoulder. She grabbed hold and, panic-stricken, bit his upper arm, puncturing both his shirtsleeve and skin. She tasted blood. He howled as she rammed her knee into his diaphragm. He dropped to his knees, and at that instant she ran past him, heading for the door.

But she wasn't fast enough. His hand with the three fingers grabbed her ankle, and she fell against the door. Her head banged against the threshold and everything went black. Somewhere in the darkness she sensed a strong odor of sweat, and she thought she heard a voice humming a tune.

When she regained consciousness, she was lying here, on the ice-cold basement floor, bound and gagged. Julie swore at herself. How could she have been so stupid? He wasn't a stranger. He was somebody she knew. But she still should have known. Shouldn't she?

12

I *am quite convinced* that he has been impaled. *Horribile dictu.*"

"In other words, the venerable chief physician of the city agrees with my assessment. The young gentleman in front of us was killed in a highly irregular fashion."

Chief of Police Nils Bayer looked at the gaunt, pale doctor who had helped him turn the body onto its side so they could see the back. He saw the beads of sweat on the doctor's brow, underneath the new gray wig, which he'd had sent from the royal capital in Denmark only a few weeks ago. A wig like that must be hot in the summer, thought Bayer. He himself only used flour to powder his own hair, which he then tied at the nape of his neck. The Creator had been generous, giving him this much hair. It was at least as voluminous and robust as his enormous belly and his powers of perception.

Bayer thought it said a good deal about Dr. Fredrici that he chose to don his wig when they were the only two present. He shifted his gaze to the corpse. Visible between the shoulder blades was a small circular exit wound.

"I also find it highly implausible that he could have carried out this ungodly act on himself," said the doctor. "Some object struck him with deadly force in the midsection and then forced its way out, at least partially, through his back. The blow must have been delivered from below, possibly by someone who was either shorter or stood in a lower position."

"Not necessarily. The weapon could also have been thrust into him using an underhand blow by someone of the same height. Don't you agree?" said Bayer. "What sort of object do you think we're dealing with here, Dr. Fredrici?"

"That is precisely what troubles me. An ordinary lance or spear is out of the question. The injuries to the abdomen are too extensive for that. Perhaps we're talking about a large sword and only the very tip penetrated through the back, at the same time as it caused major wounds in front."

The two men again turned the corpse on its back. Crooking both his index fingers, the doctor pulled open the stomach wound and studied the entrails.

"Both the colon and ventriculus have been damaged. The weapon then continued upward, missing the *vertebrae thoracicae*, and then making a small hole in the cutis of the back. All this indicates a one-armed thrust from below. But in that case, I fear that a murderer is walking around the city with hugely powerful arms."

"What about all the blood in the stomach? And yet the back is clean. How can you explain that?"

"It tells us that the deceased most likely bled to death while lying on his stomach."

"Ergo, he was lying in a different position from the one than when we found him," said Bayer, pleased to have confirmed the observation that he'd already made.

"Yes, that ought to be our conclusion."

"What about his fingers? Can they tell us anything about this *cadavre silencieux*?"

"Nothing more than that they are still in the process of stiffening. Rigor mortis has set in but has not yet reached its peak, which usually occurs after twelve hours."

"So the corpse is relatively fresh, as I thought. But take a closer look at the fingers," said Bayer, lifting the fingertips of first one hand, then the other of the corpse. "Can you see that the fingernails are longer on the right hand, while they're cut short on the left? And on his left hand, the skin of the fingertips seems abnormally rough. Yet his hands have no scars or injuries. This man did not engage in manual labor. What do you think calluses on only one hand might signify?"

"In truth, I have no idea. But something tells me that you have a theory."

"In all modesty, I have to admit that a tiny suspicion has been aroused in my otherwise-simple brain," replied Bayer.

At this point the gaunt physician straightened up and glanced down at the police officer, who was still holding up the hands of the corpse.

"My distinguished chief of police, protector of the city and enforcer of the law, we both know that such modesty is ill-suited to a man of your background, nor is it genuine. Kindly tell me what is on your mind," said the doctor.

Nils Bayer was a bit offended to be so directly castigated. "As I see it, our cadaver was a musician. He played some sort of stringed instrument, using the fingertips of his left hand to press down the strings as he strummed them with the longer fingernails on his right hand."

The police chief glanced up to bask for a moment in the admiring gaze of the doctor, then looked down at the corpse again. He let go of the hands and did as the doctor had just done. He pulled apart the edges of the wound to peer inside the abdomen. Just inside the flesh, something caught his attention: a tiny, soft, foreign object. He plucked it out, holding it between his thumb and index finger. Then he straightened up and looked at the chief physician.

The doctor was no longer impressed. He looked disgusted. It's a strange thing about professional folk, thought Bayer. They couldn't stand to see untrained individuals doing their job. The doctor could carry out the most unpleasant operations on a human body without causing himself the slightest distress, but if he saw somebody merely touching a corpse like this, he turned pale, as if witnessing the most abominable witchcraft. Nils Bayer ignored the look of reproach.

"What do you think this could be?" he said, holding up the thin, soft, bloodstained object just a couple of inches from Fredrici's face.

"It looks like a tiny scrap of fabric," said the doctor, visibly shaken.

"And how do you think something like this ended up inside a naked body?"

"It's difficult to say. The most likely scenario would be if the victim had been wearing a shirt when he was killed, and the murder weapon tore off a piece of fabric as it entered his body."

"Are you suggesting that the victim was clothed when he was killed?" asked Bayer.

"Isn't that what you wish to suggest, chief inspector?"

"That is my conclusion, yes. The victim was killed while clothed. Afterward, his body was stripped and transported here. I wonder why."

"Something tells me that you have already answered that question," murmured the chief physician.

"Actually, I haven't. It's a mystery to me!"

Bayer gazed out over the dark fjord. He took a hip flask from his waistcoat pocket, took a long swig, and then offered the doctor a drink with an expression that said *bibamus, moriendum est* ("Let us drink, for death is certain"). Using both hands, Fredrici held the flask in a cruel grip, as if he pictured himself throttling Bayer. Then he emptied the flask in two big gulps.

"It seems as if my presence here has been unnecessary," said the doctor.

"By no means, my dear Dr. Fredrici. On the contrary, it has been most instructive. What I'm perhaps hoping might be superfluous, at least until times improve, is your fee. You know how limited my funds are as the city's chief of police. Three hundred *riksdaler* a year is hardly enough to pay my two officers and finance both an office and a decent home. And when you consider all the crimes that come with the ever-increasing numbers of tradesmen and fortune-seekers . . . I'm certain that you understand my position, and since I know you to be a noble man who gladly purchases medicines to be given free of charge to the city's needy when disease threatens, I am hoping it will be possible for you, in this instance, to extend your services to the city for the benefit of your own honor."

"There has never been anything wrong with your gift of speech," said the doctor curtly.

Then he handed the flask back to Bayer and took his leave without making any mention of a fee. Bayer knew that this time he had gone too far. He knew that the doctor also had trouble making ends meet, that he rarely demanded payment for many of the services he rendered, especially when it came to the truly needy people in the city. And he was planning to sell his country estate and move permanently to a place in the oppressive city air. Bayer was well aware of where the boundaries of common decency lay, and he knew that he'd overstepped them. He also knew that the doctor would quickly forgive him, and that he'd never again hear mention of a fee. But that was not the reason why his stomach was churning so ominously. Above all, he was hungry and thirsty, perhaps mostly the latter. He grabbed his cane and headed back into town. By now the Hoppa might have begun to serve breakfast.

He preferred the Hoppa to any of the other taverns in Trondheim because it happened to have one thing that no other place had. Her name was Ingrid Smeddatter. Her father, a blacksmith, and her mother had both died long ago in a fire, along with all their offspring except for Ingrid, who had been visiting a neighbor when the fire broke out. But Ingrid's cousin ran the Hoppa tavern, and he'd taken in the orphaned girl. She turned out to be the best thing that ever happened to his business. When she started serving beer, sales increased significantly. Ingrid attracted the menfolk, but she also knew how to spurn the most boorish of the lot. And she was skilled at telling stories, both true and untrue. Right now Bayer was interested in a story based on fact, and he was hoping that she was at work at this early hour.

The Hoppa had only five tables, but they were big, with room for many chairs around each of them. For that reason it was a favorite place for dice games, until the police chief started frequenting the pub. Right now no one was sitting at the tables. Feeling disappointed, Bayer sat down at the table in the back and surveyed the deserted premises. Then he took out a short pipe and a tobacco pouch from the waistcoat pocket not occupied by the flask. He filled his pipe and went over to the fireplace to light it from the embers. Then he went back to the table, slowly sucking on his pipe. In many ways he was not a patient man, but the Hoppa was one of the few places where he chose to hide any sign of irritation. Ingrid deserved as much.

After half an hour he heard someone moving about on the floor above. Then the hatch in the ceiling opened and a ladder was lowered to the floor, not far from where he was sitting. A few moments later, the hem of Ingrid's skirt came into view as she descended.

He sat at the table, calmly blowing smoke rings into the room. Ingrid was moving more slowly than usual. She fumbled her way down the ladder, as if reluctant to emerge from the night's dreams, longing to return to her bed. He knew that she detested change. Perhaps that was a feeling shared by everyone who had survived a fire, that the torment of waking up was as great for her as the distress of falling asleep. And that was why she would never marry him.

He watched as she went into the next room, and shortly he could hear the clatter of dishes. Then she carried a big basket of table linens out to the well behind the building. He refilled his pipe, and she didn't return until he'd finished smoking it. When she came back with a basket filled with dishes, she finally cast a glance in his direction and jumped so hard that she almost dropped the plates and tankards on the floor.

"Sweet heaven, Nils, you nearly scared me out of my wits!" she exclaimed, rolling her eyes.

He cleared his throat. It was something he had to do often if he hadn't spoken or had anything to drink for a while. His throat felt like it was plugged up with congealed gravy from a bad meal. A terrible cough rattled his chest.

"That cough doesn't sound good," she said, coming over to him. "You should get Fredrici to listen to your chest. He'll know what to do. Maybe you ought to smoke your pipe more often and switch to a stronger tobacco."

"That's possible. Or maybe I just need someone to take care of me."

"Don't start that again," she said, setting her basket on the table in front of him.

"One day you'll finally to have to relent," he teased her as he stuffed his extinguished pipe back in his pocket.

"Why are you here so early? Usually the whole neighborhood is still shaking with your snoring at this hour. I've heard that you even keep the prisoners in the jail awake at night. Is it really any wonder that I never let you spend the night here?"

"Your tongue is already wide-awake, I see," he parried drily. Then he added, "I've come to hear a story. And I'm hoping that you might tell it to me."

"I know plenty of stories," she said. "Are you thinking of one in particular?"

"Yes, this is a true story. It's about a troubadour with long red hair. It wouldn't surprise me if he'd been staying at one of the taverns around here. He can't have been in the city long, because otherwise I would have recognized him."

"I think I know the man you're talking about. He's been here a few times in the past months. Carrying a big old-fashioned lute. We never heard him play it. He was more interested in the dice games, and as the police chief knows, there's not much of that here lately."

"This man . . . does he have a name?"

"Yes, but I doubt that it's the one his mother gave him."

"What did he call himself?"

"Jon Blund."

"Jon Blund? That's a peculiar name to choose."

"Yes, a peculiar name indeed. But why are you so interested in him? He was just a vagrant."

"Because this Jon Blund has turned up down on the shore."

"What do you mean?"

"He's dead. Do you have any idea where he came from, before he ended up in our city?"

"He claimed to have come from here originally. Said he grew up here as a boy and attended grammar school in town. But his accent and vocabulary seemed to indicate that he'd lived for a long time over to the east. . . ."

"And he never mentioned why he'd come back here?"

"No, but I had the impression that he didn't give much thought to why he wandered. He seemed to be searching for happiness, in one way or another."

"I understand. When did you last see him here?"

"It must have been more than a week ago."

"And do you have any idea where he was staying?"

"I think he'd taken lodgings at the inn over in Brattøra, where the sailors often stay, and where ship's mate Per Jonsen has started serving beer."

Nils Bayer got to his feet, moving too fast for his stomach and noticing the twinge along his spine. Then he bowed in farewell.

"You're leaving without even trying to woo me? This troubadour must have made quite an impression on you, my dear Nils," she said with a laugh.

The sight of her dimples was imprinted in his brain.

"My lovely maiden," he said, bowing again as he struck the floor with his policeman's cane. "I can promise you that the wooing will be as copious as your refusals the next time we meet."

She laughed—a sound that tore at his heartstrings. Then he left before the laughter faded.

He'd forgotten to refill his flask. He'd also forgotten to ask for a drink while he was sitting there. Now he had to walk all the way out to Brattøra with this growing nausea. He hoped the beer served by this ship's mate was as good as the rumors claimed.

"A red-haired troubadour named Jon Blund? Yes. He's staying here. But I haven't seen him since yesterday morning," said Per Jonsen, the sailor who had come ashore and opened a pub, although he still clung to his former life, both in style of clothing and personal hygiene. It was said that he never noticed if he wet himself when he was busy behind the bar. Also, he never used perfume. He stank accordingly.

"The reason you haven't seen him is that he has kicked the bucket." Bayer glared at the old sea dog. On his way over he'd worked up a sweat and was now out of breath. He'd trod in a big horse apple and soiled one of his newly polished boots. He was not happy.

"How about a glass of beer? I had some full barrels delivered this morning," said the ship's mate.

The offer instantly put Bayer in a friendlier mood. He gave a slight bow to indicate his acceptance. A glass overflowing with foam was set in front of him, and he downed it in one long gulp, feeling the warmth spread through the depths of his stomach.

"How about a little smoked sausage? On the house, of course."

Bayer picked up the sausage, chewing as the former ship's mate refilled his glass.

"So what you're saying is that my lodger has departed this life? How terrible! Where did you find him?" asked Jonsen.

"On the beach, out past Ilsvika."

"What was he doing out there?"

"That's what I'm trying to find out. What do you know about him?"

"Not much. He arrived from Stockholm a few months ago with only an old lute, a few *daler* he'd apparently won gambling somewhere, and the clothes on his back. His money pouch was close to empty, especially since his gaming luck had been so bad the past few days. For a while he apparently earned a few coins by singing for the gentry out at Ringve."

Bayer nodded.

"Can I see his room?"

"Well, he's dead, isn't he? I hardly think he'd mind," said Jonsen with salt spray in his voice.

Jonsen led the way upstairs and unlocked the door. It was a small, drafty room that bore witness to a simple and restless life. It contained only a bed and a chair on which the lodger could place his clothes. At first glance Nils Bayer noticed two things: The troubadour's clothing was gone, but his lute leaned against the wall. Then he caught sight of a book lying on the pillow. It was a book in folio format, with soft covers. A notebook. He went over to pick up the book and turn the pages. It contained mostly fragments of texts, little rhymes and clever phrases. In some places musical notes accompanied the texts.

Bayer was not a musical man, and he liked music only in the company of strong drink. He couldn't say much about the musical notation on these pages. But he could tell that some of the completed texts had a certain distinction and finesse, and that the dead man must have had a talent for the art of words, and at least some amount of education.

One ballad in particular drew his attention. An introduction had been written to the song, explaining that this was not just any ordinary lullaby. It promised that anyone who heard it would fall asleep. In an aside, the author had added that this song would bring him the fame that he deserved, if only he could find the money to have it printed. Bayer read the words to the whole lullaby and had to admit that it was both beautifully poetic and gently humorous.

But the notebook revealed nothing that brought him any closer to why the man had died, this mystery that had begun to fill him with a thirst that was almost as strong as his thirst for beer. He tucked the notebook under his arm, thanked the innkeeper, and left the room. Down by the wharf he found a coach for hire that could take him to the office. He decided he'd walked enough for one day.

The police station was located on the floor below his bedchamber, with an excellent view of the jail across the street. Nils Bayer sat in his office thinking about Jon Blund.

I don't know what it is about that name, he thought, *but it has a sinister ring to it.* In truth, a gloomy gray light had settled over this day, while the ungodly forces that had brought the horrors of the day into view remained hidden under a pitch-black veil. He'd opened the police log to write his report, but he realized that these sorts of musings were material for a poet, not a public official. His thoughts were not yet clear enough to be recorded in the log. This seemed to have clouded his mind and made him sluggish. And there was no one with whom he could discuss the matter.

Police prosecutor Sivert Bekk was out at Brattøra to inspect a Dutch ship that had docked the night before. The two officers whom

Bayer employed, to whom he paid much too high a wage, were the illiterate and quarrelsome Torsten Reutz and the good-natured Jacob Torp. Both had been sent out to investigate. Reutz was to inquire at all of the city's taverns to find out whether any brawls had taken place the previous night and, if so, whether weapons had been drawn. Once the occurrence of such an event had been established, the officer was charged with finding out whether anyone had been injured or killed during one of these fights. This had to be done, even though Bayer was convinced that Jon Blund was not killed in a common pub brawl.

The other police officer, Torp, had been told to ask the city's coachmen whether they'd seen anything unusual during the night, such as passengers behaving oddly or wearing tattered and bloody clothing. Coachmen were often good witnesses. Unfortunately, the police chief had recently beaten a recalcitrant coachman with his police cane so hard that it broke, and the man had borne the imprint of the police emblem on his back for weeks afterward. Not that the coachman hadn't deserved it. He had behaved shockingly toward Torsten Reutz, who had done nothing more than attempt to mediate in an argument between two coachmen waiting for their masters outside the cathedral one Sunday morning. The mediation failed, and the coachmen wound up in a scuffle. Reutz had found himself with no recourse but to summon Bayer himself, and when the more hot-tempered of the two coachmen hadn't shown the chief the respect that his office deserved, Bayer had had no choice but to reprimand him. Regrettably, the coachman's master was a powerful man in town, and he had filed suit against the police chief. The case had not resulted in any fine, but Bayer had lost the cooperation of the city's coachmen. He was still hoping that Officer Torp, his most loyal assistant, would be able to get some information out of them.

Bayer was thinking about money—a never-ending topic for him. Four years ago, he'd paid the monstrous sum of 2,400 *riksdaler* to secure the position as Trondheim's police chief. It was sheer madness, of course. But it was those sorts of whims that governed his life. The loan he'd been forced to take at the time made it completely impossible for him to live on the three hundred *riksdaler*, the salary that came with the job. For that reason, he'd been fighting a long battle to be paid one *skilling* for every barrel of salt and grain that came into the city, such as the police chief in Kristiansand was allowed. He had also traveled all the way to Copenhagen to appeal to the king to increase his income by other means. But the chief administrative officer had refused to give him more. Bayer's last accounting showed that after he'd paid the interest on his debt and the wages of his officers and prosecutor, as well as the other expenses of the police station, he would be left with an annual income of thirty *riksdaler*. Trondheim's police chief was living in poverty, and he could only dream of ever starting a family of his own.

The police station consisted of one room with two desks, four chairs, a bookcase that held the police logs, and two windows that faced the street. The walls were bare timbers. The room also had one door, which had just opened. Torp's round face and worn clothing came into view. Torp was a pious man with a large family. Bayer liked the man simply because, in spite of much digging, he'd never been able to find anything negative on Torp.

"The coachmen refuse to cooperate," said Torp.

"Our good Lord and Savior! Do you mean to tell me that they're still brooding about that incident?"

"I'm afraid so."

"And here I thought that the city's coachmen had memories shorter than a fly's. By God, I'll change their minds. Where's my cane?"

Bayer got up from his desk and took a quick swig from the flask that he'd filled with poor quality aquavit at the pub in Brattøra.

"Bunch of damned riffraff!" he grumbled. "Where are they now?"

"A lot of the coachmen are over on Munkegata, where a dinner has apparently been arranged for the city's gentlemen. Not that I have any particular grasp of what's right or wrong in such cases, and no one can say that I don't have full confidence in the police chief's judgment in every matter, but wasn't it your cane that got us into this rather unfortunate situation to start with?" Torp ventured timidly.

"That may be, but let me tell you, I was not nearly generous enough with the blows I delivered. Those damned coachmen have no respect! This case won't be solved until they've got the seal of the city pounded into their skin, one and all. Ah, here it is."

Bayer strode across the room and grabbed his police cane, which was leaning against the wall next to the door. Then he threw on his coat, stuck the flask in his pocket, and left before Torp managed to voice any other objections.

On the doorstep, Bayer tripped and fell. He landed on the cobblestones on his stomach, knocking the air out of him. Furious, he tried to get up, but then he realized how exhausted he was. He fumbled in his coat until he found the flask. Then he slowly rolled onto his back and shook out the last drop. As he drank, something broke loose inside him. He felt tears welling up and was unable to hold them back. Those fucking coachmen, he thought. Fucking troubadours, fucking womenfolk, fucking life. Weeping, he got to his feet. There was now a hole in the right knee of his trousers. Then he picked up his cane and began slamming it against the ground. He kept on until it was completely shattered. The police emblem, the handle with the city's coat of arms, flew across the street and landed in the gutter. Then he opened his mouth and the contents of his stomach gushed out of him.

He went back inside, not to the office, but up to his room. There he washed the vomit from his mouth with water that had been left in a pitcher from the day before. He filled the chamber pot to the brim, then went over to the window to empty it before he sank his heavy body onto the bed. Only sleep could bring him peace.

"Chief!"

No more than an hour could have passed, and no dreams had managed to enter Bayer's hazy slumber before he was awakened by Torsten Reutz.

Bayer mumbled words that even he didn't understand and sat up. Instinctively he reached for his flask, but then remembered it was empty.

"I hope you have a very good reason for disturbing my deep ruminations," he said.

"Some would say that peace and order are more important than contemplation, for a police chief," said Reutz, that shameless lout. Bayer always wondered if he ought to fire this swine who drank more than he did and was insolent and coarse in every way. And he would have if Reutz hadn't proven so useful when it came to collecting fines and dealing with dishonest shop owners, or loose women who sold their wares from illegal stalls.

"What do you want?" Bayer growled, noticing that the gravy in his throat had once again congealed. He stretched and then took out his pipe and tobacco pouch from his waistcoat pocket.

"A brief report and an additional piece of information that I think will interest you," said Reutz, spitting on the floor.

"For God's sake, can't you see the spittoon over there?" Bayer pointed to the corner near the window.

Reutz ignored the remark.

"It was quiet in the city last night. Not a single brawl to speak of. But in a pub on Bakklandet, I made an interesting discovery."

"And what was that?" Bayer noticed that his curiosity was stronger than his annoyance.

"A Swedish gentleman took lodgings at the inn. He was apparently exceedingly well-dressed, in the latest fashion, as if he'd come straight from Paris. This gentleman inquired of the innkeeper whether he knew of a red-haired troubadour."

"Heavens! That *is* interesting. And where might he be now?"

"He wasn't in."

"Good. I suspect that a distinguished gentleman such as himself probably would not speak to anyone other than the city's police chief." Nils Bayer got up from the bed. He was just one small dram away from being in a very good mood.

PART III

PART III

13

"When did you last see her?"

The newly built Rosenborg School was bright and open. Fredrik Alm was closed and dark. He was such a teenager. A bewildering time of life, Chief Inspector Singsaker thought. He'd been given the use of a conference room that faced the cafeteria. The buzzing voices of kids standing in line outside reminded him of the sound inside his own head. He tried to tune out the swarming voices, but it took a lot of energy to do so.

Fredrik Alm nervously rocked his chair back and forth. He sat against the far wall. Singsaker was on the other side of the table, blocking the view to the door. It was probably best that he was alone with the boy. Two police officers in such a small space would have scared him more than was necessary.

"Yesterday," said Fredrik in a deep voice that sounded as uncertain as he looked. "She stopped by yesterday. We looked at pictures from the party."

"The party?"

"The party at Dina Svensen's house."

"A big party?"

"No, only a few kids were invited."

"I understand that you and Julie aren't together anymore. Is that right?" asked Singsaker, trying to catch the boy's eye. Fredrik kept his gaze focused on the table.

"Uh-huh," he muttered.

"Yet you both go to the same parties, and she drops by your place to look at pictures afterward. Isn't that a bit unusual?"

"I don't know."

Singsaker didn't either. He'd been young so long ago.

"Where do you think she is, Fredrik?" he asked, realizing that he was diverging from the script.

"I don't know."

"Does she often disappear like this?"

Fredrik looked up from the table, then lowered his eyes.

"I don't know," he said again.

Singsaker stared at him. *He's scared*, he thought. *Probably because he likes the girl*.

"I've never been able to figure out what she's thinking," said Fredrik.

"Do you think she went away of her own free will?"

He didn't reply, just stared at the table. Someone had written on the surface with a ballpoint pen: *Nadia Torp is a whore*.

"Was it you or Julie who wanted to break up this time?" asked Singsaker.

For the first time, Fredrik looked the inspector in the eye.

"What do you mean?"

"The two of you broke up. One of you must have decided to call it quits."

"Oh, right. It was her."

"Yesterday when she came over, was there anything else she wanted to talk about besides the pictures from the party? I mean, couldn't you have just posted them on Facebook?"

Fredrik was again staring down at the table. He held his hand in front of his mouth as he said, "No, there was nothing special."

"Did she want to get back together?"

"We didn't talk about that."

Singsaker could tell that he wasn't getting anywhere, so he switched to more concrete questions.

"Are you aware that Julie often takes her dog out for a walk in the evening?"

"Yes, she does every night."

"And did she ever mention anything unpleasant that happened when she was out with the dog?"

"No."

"Nobody who talked to her or bothered her? Nothing like that?"

"No, except . . ."

"Except what?"

"I went on the walk with her one night last week. There was a man shoveling his driveway. He asked her about something."

"Do you remember what it was?"

"He asked her why she wasn't singing. Julie always sang when she was out alone. But then he noticed me walking a few steps behind, and he didn't say anything else. Julie seemed to know who he was."

"Did she say how she happened to know him?"

"No, and I didn't ask."

Singsaker asked Fredrik to describe the man and the house where he lived while he took notes, thinking that they needed to check this out. He also jotted down the following frightening thought: *"There's a similarity between Julie Edvardsen and the murder victim: Both of them sang when they went out walking. Coincidence?"*

The first two girls on the list of friends couldn't tell Singsaker even as much as Fredrik had. Neither of them had seen Julie since the party on Saturday night. She'd been acting perfectly normal. Now Singsaker waited for the next girl. Feeling a bit embarrassed, he stared at the graffiti on the tabletop with the unflattering statement and realized it was referring to someone with the same name as the next witness. He spat on his thumb and tried to rub off the words before she arrived, but they were impossible to remove. So he decided to cover it with his notebook. That meant that he had to stretch out his hand in a rather uncomfortable position in order to write anything down, but he'd manage.

Nadia Torp had been more liberal with her makeup than the other two girls Singsaker had spoken to, but it was still discreetly applied. Had something changed with the way girls wore makeup? Something he wasn't aware of? He assumed that she also had what her girlfriends would call "her own style." She was wearing an oversize old T-shirt with a picture of the equally old Norwegian punk band Kjøtt on the front. She must have gotten it from her father or a cool uncle. Over it she wore a reddish brown ribbed-knit cardigan with ruched sleeves. It looked expensive. Singsaker didn't think she looked like a whore at all. He thought she looked cool.

She fixed her eyes on him as they shook hands. Then she sat down without seeming the least bit nervous.

"What's happened to Julie?" she asked.

"That's what we're trying to find out. She didn't come home last night."

"Really?"

"I'm afraid so. That's why we need to talk to everyone she knows and ask a few questions."

"Sure."

Nadia Torp suddenly looked much too small for that cardigan she was wearing.

"When did you last see Julie?"

"At choir practice on Friday."

"You weren't at the party on Saturday night?"

"Wasn't invited."

"But you sing in the choir with Julie?"

"Yes. We're both in the Nidaros Cathedral girls choir."

Singsaker made a note in his book.

"You can move your notebook back to your side of the table," she told him. "I know what it says underneath it."

Singsaker gave her an embarrassed look and moved his notebook closer.

"That's not a very nice thing for someone to write," he said.

"Maybe it's true," she said.

He blushed, wondering if he should respond, or just ignore it. He chose the latter.

"So you have choir practice every Friday?"

"No, we actually practice on Tuesdays and Thursdays. But this was an extra practice session at Ringve for some of us who were selected to participate in the concert on the weekend."

Singsaker paused to think and then looked back through his notebook.

"The concert at Ringve," he said. "Bellman, right? Isn't it Professor Høybråten who's going to direct?"

Nadia nodded. And Singsaker thought he glimpsed something in her eyes that he wanted to know more about.

"So Julie was also selected for this concert?"

"Are you kidding? She's better than any of us. Nobody has a voice like hers. You should hear her sing. She was Høybråten's first choice, of course."

"Is Julie good at anything else, besides singing?"

"Julie is good at everything—school, handball. Everything."

"Is she well liked?"

"Yeah, strangely enough."

"Why is that strange?"

"Some people get jealous of people like Julie who are good at so many things. But she never brags or pretends she's better than anyone."

"What's her favorite thing to do?"

"Singing. She's good at everything else, but she loves to sing. She's always singing, even during handball games. She's really looking forward to the concert this weekend."

Singsaker paused for a moment. He couldn't put the other case entirely out of his mind. He thought about the music box and the vocal cords that the killer had removed. If there actually was a connection, then it had to do with singing.

"Jan Høybråten—is he a good choir director?"

"He's good at a lot of things," replied Nadia caustically.

"What do you mean by that?"

"Nothing," she said, perhaps realizing that he wouldn't believe her.

"Is he a good teacher?"

"That too. Or, well . . . I don't know."

"What is it you don't know?"

"A teacher doesn't do things like that."

"A teacher doesn't do what?" Singsaker was breathing calmly. The feeling he had at this moment was the same as when he went hunting with Jensen. This was how he felt when they finally had circled around the prey and were ready to shoot. It was really the only thing he liked about those hunting trips.

"Forget it," she said now.

"Forget what?"

"What I said. I don't like him. That's all. I think he's disgusting."

"Disgusting?"

"Yeah, you know. He's old. What do I know?"

"Has he done something to you, Nadia?" asked Singsaker, looking at her without blinking. At the same time he could sense that the prey was about to disappear into the underbrush.

"Aren't you here to ask me about Julie?" she said.

It was too late. If there'd been something important in this conversation, it was gone now, vanished somewhere behind Nadia Torp's expression. She was less confident and open than when they'd started talking. And she was right: He had diverged from the topic at hand.

"Do you know of anyone Julie might be staying with?" he asked.

"No," she said sullenly.

"No one she happened to mention, relatives she likes, or friends only a few of you might know about?"

"I don't really know her that well," said Nadia Torp.

Odd Singsaker felt bad about letting her go back to her class. She had been skirting around something. She had wanted to confide something to him. Should he have pressured her more? Or maybe she told me enough, he thought. He phoned Mona Gran.

"How's it going?" he asked when his colleague picked up.

"I started on the other side of Stadsingeniør Dahls Gate," she told him. "Haven't found out much. What about you? How'd it go at the school?"

"I couldn't get much out of Fredrik Alm. But that's probably because of his age. He seems harmless enough."

"The harmless ones are usually the most dangerous. You know that."

"True enough, but I seriously doubt that he had anything to do with this. He seemed just as bewildered as we are."

"What about her girlfriends?"

When he told Mona about Nadia Torp, he omitted certain details. Then he ended the call and stuffed his cell back in his pocket as he turned on his heel and left the school.

Outside, he paused to look across Festningsgata at the defensive tower of Kristiansten Fortress. The white cube stood there like a hard drive filled with secrets; the arrow slits were like data ports that had stopped functioning long ago. Inside the edifice was stored everything that had ever happened in Trondheim since it was built in the 1700s. He tore himself away from his reveries to turn his attention back to the case. Again he got out his cell phone and looked up the number for the music institute.

The secretary told Singsaker that Høybråten had the day off to do research. On those occasions he usually worked at home. She gave him the professor's cell number and his address, which was in the Singsaker area.

Singsaker put away his phone and plodded off in the direction of the part of town that happened to share his last name.

Jan Høybråten, professor of music theory at the Institute of Music at NTNU closed up the manuals, put them away in the desk of his home office, and sighed heavily. He was an old man, but he worked out every day, and he still felt youthful and strong. He devoted one day a week to his own research. Lately, he'd been working on a pet project, translating the poetry of Lars Wivallius from seventeenth-century Swedish into Norwegian. These poems, which had once been set to music, were considered some of the earliest examples of Swedish ballads. But in those days the musical score was rarely included in printed collections or on broadsheets, and so the melodies had been lost, while the lyrics had lived on as poems. No one would ever know how these tunes sounded in the pubs of the 1600s. But Høybråten felt that he got closer to the melodies by translating the texts.

When the doorbell rang, he was deeply immersed in a ballad called "Wivallju Dream." Annoyed, he called to his wife, asking her to answer the door.

Odd Singsaker was breathing hard. After Felicia had learned that the name of one of the sections of Trondheim was the same as his surname, she'd started calling his genitals Lower Singsaker, which she said in Norwegian with her thick American accent. But Upper Singsaker was the very steep part of town where Professor Høybråten happened to live.

Singsaker pressed the doorbell and heard a low buzzing through the oak door. He stood outside the large walled house and looked at the view. He could see the fortress and Rosenborg School and almost all the way to the crime scene. He thought to himself that Julie Edvardsen must be down there somewhere. And that thought made him impatient. Then he heard movement inside the house, and Høybråten's wife opened the door. She was wearing expensive-looking clothes, but they didn't make her look any younger. Nor did her obvious dye job.

Singsaker showed her his ID and explained that he wanted to speak to her husband, so she stepped aside to let him enter.

"He's in his office, working."

She didn't need to say anything more. Her tone of voice conveyed quite clearly that her husband did not like to be disturbed.

"Odd Singsaker. What a surprise," said Høybråten when the inspector opened the door and entered the room without knocking. But the professor's voice revealed more irritation than surprise. "What brings you here?"

"I wanted to find out if you'd learned anything more about that ballad," Singsaker told him. He sat down on a leather chair that looked comfortable but wasn't. But he stayed where he was, his back to the window.

"Didn't I say I'd contact you if I found out anything?"

"Yes, but I'm afraid that nagging people is part of my job," said Singsaker.

"I really have nothing to tell you."

"That's too bad. We seem to have reached a stalemate with this case." Singsaker searched his pants pockets, then the pockets of his coat, which he hadn't taken off, but he couldn't find his notebook. He must have left it at the school.

"Maybe he wrote it himself," Høybråten suggested impatiently, running his hand through his hair.

"That did occur to us. Are you sure there's nothing else you could tell me about the song?"

"No, I already said that."

"All right," said Singsaker, making a move to get up. "By the way, there's one more thing I wanted to ask you about, now that I'm here. This concert at Ringve that you mentioned last time . . . It's this weekend, right?"

"Yes. What about it?"

"Julie Edvardsen," said Singsaker. He let her name hover in the air for a few seconds while he studied Høybråten's expression. And he thought he saw something there. A trace of the same uncertainty that he'd noticed when they'd last met in the professor's office. "She's supposed to sing, isn't she?"

"That's right. But I don't see what this has to do with anything. Aren't you investigating a murder?"

"Yes, but I'm afraid that a police officer frequently has to handle more than one case at a time. There's always a lot going on in a town like Trondheim. And Julie Edvardsen has disappeared. She took her dog for a walk last night and hasn't been seen since."

Høybråten stared at him for a moment.

"What are you saying?" he finally asked.

"Julie Edvardsen has been reported missing. She's your best pupil, isn't she?"

It looked like Høybråten was again carefully choosing his words before he spoke.

"Yes," he said at last. "Julie sings because she loves singing. She's the sort of singer every choir director dreams of. Sensitive and receptive. But I don't know the girls well, not personally. When we get together, our focus is always on the music. Julie was made to sing Bellman, and Bellman's music was made for her. She has the same bittersweet humor about her that can be found in Bellman's lyrics. But I don't know if that's of any help to you. What do you think happened?"

Singsaker pretended not to hear the question.

"So you say that you don't know them personally? Is that true of all the girls?"

"Of course. What are you getting at?" said Høybråten, glancing out the window at the bare branches of the maples and the wintry weather.

"I just had a talk with a few of the girls," said Singsaker.

"What did they say?"

"What do you think they said?"

"I have no idea. This conversation is over. If you're going to accuse me of anything, I want to know what the charges are first. And the next time we talk, I'll have a lawyer at my side."

Well, well, Professor Høybråten, thought Singsaker. *That doesn't sound like something an innocent man would say.*

All of a sudden he felt terribly tired. The truth was that there was no basis for charging the professor with anything, and Singsaker suspected that Høybråten was well aware of this fact.

There was nothing more he could do except thank the professor for his time and leave.

He phoned Mona Gran on his way back. She was almost done with her canvassing, so they agreed to meet on Bernhard Getz' Gate. Singsaker caught sight of Gran through the snow as he arrived at the designated meeting place.

"Some weather, huh?" she said cheerfully.

Singsaker fixed his eyes on her uniform jacket.

"What have got so far?"

She had very little to report. She hadn't found anyone who had seen Julie and her dog the previous evening, nor did anyone have any clue where she might have gone. Those who knew her at all described her as a sensible girl who would never do anything stupid. Gran had also talked to Brattberg on the phone. Their boss said that all attempts to track down the girl at the homes of relatives and friends had been fruitless. Gran had then recited a list of all the addresses where no one was home, and they both decided that it would be necessary to knock on more doors later in the evening.

Then Singsaker told Gran about his conversation with Nadia Torp and his visit with Høybråten.

"You know what this could mean, don't you?" she said eagerly.

"It could mean that Høybråten knows more about the tune on the music box than he's willing to admit," he replied carefully. "But most likely it just means that he's a dirty old man."

"No matter what, we now have a possible suspect in the case," said Gran. "He might not be involved at all, but at least he's a lead we can follow up on. We can bring him in for questioning, check his alibi, and interview the other girls in the choir. All those things that we're good at. This means there's some movement in the case, Singsaker."

"Yes, I suppose so," he replied, sounding distracted.

"But it doesn't add up. For one thing, there's the matter of his age," Gran went on. "Could a man of seventy beat up a woman the way the perp did to Silje Rolfsen?"

"I wouldn't rule it out," said Singsaker. "There's nothing wrong with Høybråten's physical condition. And in general we tend to underestimate elderly people. Silje Rolfsen was a petite young woman, and Høybråten is definitely much stronger than she was."

"Another thing is that the killer most likely knows a lot about music and broadsheets," she added.

"You're right, Gran. We've got some work to do here," he replied. But it was almost dinnertime. She was headed up to Tyholt, where she lived with her partner and two cats, while Singsaker was on his way to Møllenberg. He stood there for a moment, watching his colleague as she disappeared around the corner.

When he turned to go, he suddenly tripped and found himself lying on the sidewalk. He had landed so that he was looking at the grove of trees across the street. Only a few days ago they'd found a body there, and now he was lying on his stomach, staring at the crime scene. And what had they accomplished in the meantime? Nothing. They were nowhere near catching the person who had killed Silje Rolfsen.

Singsaker got up and brushed the snow off his coat. As he did that, he remembered that he'd left his notebook at the school. He started walking, hoping he'd be able to get inside to look for it. But the building had already been locked up for the night when he got there.

14

Winter *was seeping* into the house somewhere. Elise Edvardsen followed the draft to see where it was coming from. At first she thought the front door might be ajar. It had warped in the winter cold and didn't always close properly. In the front hall she felt the door and decided it was closed. Then she opened it and peered out into the dark. Evening had arrived.

It's been twenty-four hours since Julie disappeared, she thought.

But the time couldn't be measured normally. Before she awoke this morning, minutes, hours, days had passed. Now all that was gone, replaced by breaths, footsteps, creaking floorboards, glances at the door—an eternity of tense movements and anxious waiting.

She closed the door. On her way to the living room, she felt the draft again. The bathroom. It must be coming from in there. She opened the door and saw that the small window high on the wall was open, which it never was in the wintertime. Then she saw the flies. There had to be a couple dozen of them squeezed together on the sill behind the weather stripping. This spot, when the window was closed, formed a warm niche for the insects to spend the winter. At first the flies seemed lifeless. But all of a sudden one of them moved, vigorously beating its wings, almost convulsively. But it didn't take flight; instead it merely buzzed around its half-dead fellows. Elise shuddered, not sure if it was because of the cold or the disgusting sight. She climbed up on the toilet seat and was about to close the window when she heard the song. Faint individual notes, played slowly. The pure, thin sound made her think of a music box.

Then she glimpsed a figure outside in the dark. Did she really see someone? For a few seconds the person stood perfectly still. It's him, she thought, and she recalled the articles in the newspapers over the past few days; all of them had mentioned the music box that had been found with the woman's body over near Ludvig Daaes Gate. He's the one who took Julie, she thought.

Then the figure vanished among the trees, taking the music with him. She listened intently, but all that remained was a faint rustling of the wind in the trees.

I'm going crazy, she thought as she climbed down from the toilet. I'm not thinking clearly. I'm dreaming even though I'm wide-awake.

She found her husband in the hallway. He was holding a spray can.

"The window in the bathroom was open," she told him.

"I know," he replied. "I was cleaning the bathtub. When I opened the window, I saw that the ledge was covered with flies, so I went to get some bug spray."

"Cleaning? Our daughter is missing and you're washing the bathtub?" She felt the urge to slap him, but she didn't.

"It's better to be busy. I can't just sit around waiting. Besides, she's going to come back. That's what the police said too. They think she ran away to aggravate us."

"This is making me crazy," she said. Then she met his glance. "Come with me."

She took him out in the yard and led him through the deep snow until they were standing in front of the bathroom window. Near the big oak tree, they saw tracks in the snow.

"Someone has been here," she said. "I'm not crazy, after all."

"It was probably just some of the neighborhood kids," he said. "They're always coming into our yard."

In the crusty snow they couldn't see clear footprints, just a jumble of tracks. It was impossible to say who might have made them.

"I guess you're right," she said. "But what if it was him?"

"Who?"

"The man who took her. What if he's coming after us now?"

"Nobody took her, Elise." He said this with such conviction that she nearly believed him.

"He was playing a song," she said. "It sounded so peaceful. Almost like a lullaby."

"You're tired, sweetheart. You're just imagining things because you're scared and worn-out. It's cold. Let's go back inside."

All of Singsaker's thoughts were transferred to Felicia's shoulder, where he was resting his head. He definitely wasn't paying attention to the movie they were watching.

"We had a dozen cases like this in Richmond every year," said Felicia, shifting on the sofa. "I can count on one hand the times when we didn't find the kids alive, or when they didn't turn up on their own."

"That's exactly what makes it so difficult. Experience and common sense tell us to play it cool. But what if this is one of those exceptions? What if it has something to do with the homicide? And what if the old professor is involved in both cases? You should see the parents. Especially the mother. Fear and a guilty conscience combined with something else."

"Combined with what?"

"I'm not sure. But I think it's contagious. I feel it too."

"Feel what? You're being awfully vague." Felicia had switched to English, which she did whenever he annoyed her.

"It's just a bad feeling. Nothing specific. The thing is that I think this is one of those times when the kid isn't going to come back. And then all hell is going to break loose, whether the two cases are related or not."

"I know," she said, deciding to humor him and follow his train of thought. "But let's hope there's no connection between the cases, because if there is, we're dealing with a serial killer who has struck twice in an unusually short period of time. And we don't know when he might be planning to kill Julie and start the hunt for his next victim."

"Thanks for the encouragement."

She gave him a resigned smile.

The doorbell rang. Felicia turned off the movie. Michael Winterbottom's *The Killer Inside Me* vanished and the screen went blank.

"We weren't really watching anyway," she said, and went out to the hall to open the door. She came back, accompanied by Siri Holm.

Singsaker said hello and then went in the kitchen to make tea.

When he came back, the two women were having an intense conversation. Felicia looked up with a smile.

"Siri is helping me with my first job. That Norwegian emigrant that I'm looking for. It turns out he used a pseudonym."

"What was it?"

"Jon Blund."

"This is the same Jon Blund who wrote the broadsheet? How can you be sure he's the same person who emigrated to the United States?" he asked.

"We're not sure. In theory, anybody could have taken it over. For instance, maybe his son, or even someone else decided to take credit for a ballad that Jon Blund had written. The pseudonym is the only thing we have to go on. We still don't know his real name," Felicia said.

"I think the smart thing to do would be to follow the pseudonym," said Siri. "My colleague mentioned that a Jon Blund was entered in a police log from the 1700s here in Trondheim. That might lead us to more answers. I've checked around a bit, and the log is kept at the National Archives. I've requested an interlibrary loan so it can be sent over to the Gunnerus."

With that plan in place, they drank their tea. It was past eleven by the time Siri went home.

Odd and Felicia remained on the sofa. They looked at each other in silence.

How did I ever get her? thought Singsaker, looking at her creamy complexion beneath her dark hair. It was the sort of thing he asked himself when he was too tired to make love to her.

They talked for a while about Odd's son, Lars, who lived in Oslo with his wife and two children. Felicia had developed a real affection for him and his wife when she met them at the christening of their youngest child. Since then, she'd been back to visit them twice on her own. And that pleased Singsaker. He felt that Felicia had brought him closer to his son than he'd ever been while married to Lars's mother.

Felicia changed the subject.

"Did you notice anything different about Siri?"

"No, I don't think so. She drank just as much tea as usual, didn't she?"

"Don't you think her stomach had gotten rather plump? And her cheeks are a little rosier than before."

"What do you mean?"

"You know what I'm talking about. Are you a policeman, or aren't you?"

"Pregnant? Are you kidding?" he said after a brief pause. He sat up straight. A crazy thought occurred to him. An impossible thought. A terrible, ruinous thought.

"How far along do you think she is?" he asked.

"Since she's starting to show, I'd say she has to be at least three or four months pregnant. But it can vary a lot from one woman to another."

In his mind, he began calculating dates, back to a day in the midst of the chaotic investigation of last year's Palimpsest murders. Singsaker had made a mistake a police officer should never make and had a secret a married man should never have to keep. In a moment of weakness, he'd had sex with his wife's friend. Even though this occurred before Felicia became his wife, even before they'd met, way before the two women became friends. But it wasn't that long ago. Did it make any difference when it had happened? He'd never told Felicia. By Singsaker's count, it had happened five months ago. But was that really reassuring? They didn't know exactly how far along Siri was. Could it be five months?

It was going to be a sleepless night.

15

Fredrik *was the only one* who knew about the child she was carrying. If he hadn't told their parents about it by now, that is. He'd gotten her pregnant, and the night before she was taken, she'd gone to break the news to him. Julie was worried what her parents would say if they found out.

What a stupid thing to worry about. There was really no point in thinking about anything at all. The real world was somewhere else, somewhere beyond her. This became especially clear whenever she fell into an exhausted sleep. Those hazy seconds before waking or sleep, before reality set in, she wasn't fully aware of where she was; it might be anywhere. In those moments she wasn't bound and gagged. Or lying on a hard floor. For an instant, her dreams were like a mattress of warm air beneath her. How strange. So far she hadn't had a single dream about being tied up. His voice hadn't managed to reach into her sleep. She had dreamed about her dog, Bismarck, but not about how he was whimpering in a dark room far away. She dreamed that she was sleeping with her head resting on his stomach, just as she'd done in those confusing middle years when she was still afraid of the dark but too old to sleep in her parents' bed. She was surprised to find that her dreams had very little to do with the mistakes she'd made or the one wrong step that had taken her away from her world.

Some things now seemed closer, some things more distant. Her friends were far, far away, while the memory of other things was still so strong, like the bathroom at home with the Donald Duck comics next to the toilet, and the feeling of her bare toes on the warm tiled floor in the morning. Her anger had disappeared. Instead, she recalled the fine hairs on her mother's arms and the way her mother would hesitate in the midst of a quarrel, as if she was about to stop and have a good laugh at the whole thing. These things had all come closer. As Julie lay there, she spent a long time thinking about these things: the snow creaking under her feet as she shoveled, the streets in her neighborhood, the flickering light behind the letters in her father's eye tests, the notes that were difficult to reach. A sick thought haunted her: Was this a test? Could something good come out of this?

She stood up. It was hard to do without using her hands, but she'd developed a technique of shoving her body against the wall and slowly rising. She tugged down her sweatpants and then sat on the bucket. A little while ago he'd come in to bring her food. At first he'd threatened to kill her, but then he'd gone back upstairs. Finally he'd come back and taken off the gag. That time he hadn't said anything about killing her if she spoke. That was the first time he'd offered her food. The sandwiches reminded her of the ones she'd made when she was ten years old. She hadn't said anything. Not one word. Nor had she touched the food. It was important to show strength even if her stomach was practically numb with hunger. At the moment she thought this somehow gave her the upper hand.

Most worrisome was Bismarck. His whimpering had grown fainter. The fear and anger that she'd heard in his barking when they were first down here in the dark had now gone. It sounded like he had given up, like the only thing he hoped for was not to die alone.

As she sat on the bucket, she looked down at the sheets of paper he'd left with her. They were copies of an old printed booklet.

She'd read the text several times. It had to do with sleep, written in a mixture of Danish and Swedish, and it reminded her a bit of a lullaby that Bellman might have written. The man had talked to her about this tune.

"You need to learn this song," he'd told her. "I want you to sing it for me."

Then he'd played a tune for her on the music box. He'd played it over and over outside the door. It was a dreamlike melody, and in a strange way it seemed to belong down here. This ice-cold basement room was not the real world.

When she was done, she used the wall to get up and then slid down onto the floor again. As she waited to fall asleep, she rubbed her bound hands over the small of her back. That was as close as she could get to caressing the baby now living inside of her. She wept, wanting to sing to it. She could hear Bismarck whimpering in the distance. Death cries, she thought. Death cries, music box tunes, and a baby that she could neither hear nor feel. This was all a dream. Sooner or later she would wake up. That was the thought that prevented time from stopping altogether.

Then he came down the stairs.

Go ahead and play that damned tune of yours, she thought.

But this time the music box didn't start. She heard him go into the room where the dog was being held, and she knew this wasn't good. He'd gone in there several times, and she'd heard what he'd done to Bismarck. If only she could have plugged her ears. But she heard everything. This time the kicks striking the dog's body were louder than his whimpers.

Exhausted, she again got to her feet. She'd noticed something when she slid onto the floor. This time she made her way along the

wall. The rope tied around her wrists rubbed against the rough surface. If she kept moving like this, up and down, maybe the rope
would shred.

I have to get out of here, she thought. Not just for my own sake,
but for Bismarck and the baby.

16

Nothing could compare with the smell of an infant. There was a peace in that smell that perhaps stemmed from some far, distant memory. It made him think of Denmark and his own childhood, of newborn calves, heat from the stove's dying embers, and a newly washed linen sheet against his skin on warm summer nights. Every child had his own smell, yet all of them bore the faint scent of a woman's breasts. And for that reason, there was something vaguely arousing about the smell, although not enough to disturb the calm of the moment. Besides, babies smelled mostly of things belonging to the future—hazelnuts, sourdough, and young saplings—

If they weren't in need of a diaper change, of course.

The baby boy that Nils Bayer was holding did need to be changed, but he wasn't quite ready to call for the nurse. He wanted to hold him a little longer. It was these morning hours that gave him strength. He was glad that Mother Anne, who was in charge of the orphanage, allowed him to come here in secret to see to the children once in a while. She understood, even though they had never discussed the matter, that what he wanted most in the world was his own child.

Sometimes he imagined that this might be the solution to all his problems—the perpetual drunkenness, the upset stomach, and his hot temper. But he was too good a judge of character to really believe it.

He thought about yesterday afternoon and his fruitless efforts to find the Swedish gentleman who might be able to cast some light on the strange murder case he was now investigating. He'd waited in the pub until almost midnight, but the man had never showed up. Finally, he'd gone home to drink himself to sleep.

Today he'd woken up with a clear head. It had occurred to him that a gentleman such as the one he was looking for would most likely have introduced himself to others of equal standing and birth shortly after arriving in the city. And so Bayer decided to pay a visit to his friend Søren Engel. But since he'd awakened so early, even before the flies, he decided to stop by the orphanage first. Now he sat here, holding this warm, soft little body against his enormous stomach, thinking about how everyone starts off in life with a world of possibilities ahead of them. *It's strange what a mess we make of things,* he thought to himself. *Why does that happen? Is it language that leads us away from our original state of harmony? Is it because of words, the tongue? They bind us together and yet can make us so unhappy. Or is it because of the way we look at things, seeing only the exterior?*

Then he noticed the flies that had started to settle around the boy's eyes. Why had all these flies invaded Trondheim this summer? Was it the abnormally high temperatures that made them multiply? He figured it was time for him to give the child back. He summoned Mother Anne and thanked her for allowing him the joy of holding the little tyke. Then he gave her a few *skillings*, his usual contribution to the orphanage.

From the orphanage, he set off at a leisurely pace for town and then made his way to Engel's newly built mansion on the market square. Bayer stood at the front entrance, staring at the knocker. Like everything else, it was new. It was made of brass and may have been forged in town, using copper from Røros. Engel's coat of arms had been engraved on the knocker. The same shield hung over the door, carved into some kind of hardwood and painted in bright colors. Engel's coat of arms was of newer origin; it was not an old family crest. People called him a nouveau riche. That was the only kind of wealthy person that Bayer liked: one who had earned his own money. Engel was an educated man; he had studied in both Copenhagen and Leipzig. He had taken his father's modest fortune, made in the timber trade, and multiplied it many times over. He was a very wealthy man by the time he came to Trondheim, where he became even richer through his sawmills, the shipping business, commodities trading, and his interests in the mines of Røros. He married into a higher social class, commissioned a coat of arms, and built a mansion where he could live whenever he wasn't at his country home.

At the moment he was devoted to his books. It was said that his library housed close to seven thousand volumes. The police chief assumed that the actual number was about half that, but it was still an enormous number of books in a small town like this. People said that Søren Engel singlehandedly financed Winding's print shop, even thought most of his books were purchased from Danish, French, and German printers, booksellers, and collectors. Bayer had spent some of his best hours reading books that he'd borrowed from the erudite and wealthy man. The chief was especially fond of the latest French titles that spoke of the free nature of human beings and the enlightened mind.

After Bayer knocked on the door, it was opened by a servant, a pitch-black African, the only one of his kind in the city, a fellow with piercing eyes and an impeccable knowledge of many languages. Apparently assuming that the police chief had an appointment, the servant ushered him inside and then took his coat and cane.

"The police chief is not carrying his official cane today," the servant remarked.

"I've ordered a new one," mumbled Bayer as he looked up at the ceiling, which had not yet been painted. The floors, on the other hand, had recently been treated with linseed oil and still gave off a strong odor. This was the first time he'd come to see Engel in the new mansion. It hadn't yet been inaugurated with a grand celebration. From what he'd heard, Engel was waiting for a ship to arrive from France, bringing cases of a particularly fine champagne. The workmen labored with the last areas that required painting, and they still needed to attach the wine fountain to the wall in the ballroom.

On the evening before the body was discovered, Bayer had attended a drinking party of sorts at Engel's former villa. Engel was the only upper-class gentleman in the city who ever invited the police chief to any high-society gatherings. The merchant found it entertaining to listen to Bayer's shrewd observations and his amusing stories about Copenhagen. He especially enjoyed hearing about the lives of the petty thieves, street urchins, poor folk, and whores in the king's city. Bayer had hundreds of tales from the time he was a police officer in his homeland. He, in turn, couldn't get enough of Engel's stories about life at university. But above all, he came for the books and booze.

"Have a seat and I'll fetch the master," said the servant after showing Bayer into a large, bright library with big windows and a glass door that led to the garden in back. Outside he could see several gardeners hard at work, planting flowers that had come from distant lands and bore names Bayer had never heard. At the far end of the library, the most important volumes had been placed in a bookcase that covered the whole wall. Bayer couldn't help going over and running his index finger along the spine of a book bound in calfskin on which the author's name, Jean-Jacques Rousseau, had been stamped in gold leaf. He limited himself to touching it, resisting the urge to take the book from the shelf and start reading.

Then he took a seat, choosing one of the comfortable gold-embroidered chairs that faced the garden. He closed his eyes and felt a light prickling on his forehead. The numerous windows allowed the sun to fill the room with a scorching heat. Not thinking about anything in particular, his hand found its way to the small pewter flask in his waistcoat pocket. He took it out but realized at once that it was empty. Nevertheless, he raised it to his lips and, using his tongue, he managed to get a few drops from the flask.

Then the door opened, and a narrow, pale face appeared in the doorway. Bayer recognized Oda, the youngest of Engel's daughters. She was thirteen and thin as a flower stalk.

She looked at him with alarm, then took several steps into the room, curtsying and apologizing. As she came forward, her skirts seem to glide across the floor, as if moving on their own. She was like a baby bird.

"I didn't know anyone was here," Oda said. "I was on my way outside to look at the new flowers."

Bayer smiled and gestured toward the garden. "Don't let me detain you, young lady," he said.

She curtsied again, a bit timidly, and went over to the glass door. As she opened it, Bayer said, "Where is your sister?"

Eva Engel was three years older and far more spirited. Bayer wasn't particularly fond of young girls; he often found them to be anemic, with overly shrill voices. He preferred men with whom he could talk sensibly and tell a joke without making them blush—this applied equally to his tastes regarding women. But he'd liked Eva from the moment he met her. Not that they'd talked much since then. Like any self-respecting gentleman and father, Søren Engel protected his daughters like a jealous rooster, and they were always sent to bed before any strong liquor appeared on the table.

"Eva has gone away," said Oda, fixing her eyes on the floor.

"Gone away?" he said. "Your father didn't mention anything about that the other day."

"It was hastily arranged. I only learned of it myself yesterday."

Bayer thought the girl seemed offended for some reason. As if she disapproved of her sister's sudden departure.

"Do you know why she left?" he asked.

"She went to visit relatives in Denmark."

"And how long will she be away?"

"I was told that we won't see her again until next spring. But now you must excuse me. *Les fleurs.* Aren't they beautiful?" She laughed, turned toward the garden, and went out to look.

Bayer sat in the library, watching her go and looking at her blond tresses gleaming in the sunlight. Then Søren Engel came into the room, eclipsing the sun with his presence.

As always, he was smiling, as if he knew no other demeanor. Engel had a broad chin and dark brown eyes, hinting at ancestors from southern climes. Today he wore no wig, nor had he powdered his hair. Bayer viewed it as a sign of friendship that Engel was willing to receive him so informally. Yet he was well-dressed, as always. His long jacket of reddish brown velvet reached to his thighs and his coat of arms was embroidered on the breast pocket. He bowed and then sat down in a chair next to Bayer.

"So, what brings the police chief to my new abode at this early-morning hour?"

"I apologize for the inconvenient time, my dear friend and protector of the city."

"Kindly refrain from the flowery speech. It doesn't suit you, and we should be able to speak freely with each other. Have you had your morning dram?"

"I'm afraid I overestimated how much was left in my flask after I took my nightly libation." Bayer gave a wry smile, which was immediately returned. Engel rang a little bell that sat on the table between them. A different servant instantly appeared in the doorway.

"A bottle of our best aqua vitae and two glasses, please," said Engel without looking at the servant.

"So, you still haven't answered my question," he said to Bayer after the servant had closed the door. "What brings you here?"

"I need some help with a difficult case," replied Bayer. "Have you by chance heard about the body that we found outside of town?"

"Of course. The body on the shore. The attorney Martinus Nissen told me last night, when we were drinking beer together. We were celebrating the imminent publication of his investigative newspaper—the first and only of its kind in the city. He asked me whether I thought it was a good idea for him to write a small article about this mysterious corpse, but I advised against it. It would merely attract frivolous readers and contribute to unnecessary gossip. Not to mention the disparaging effect it would have on his publication in general. 'No, that's a police matter,' I told him. 'Leave it in Bayer's hands. Your publication ought to concentrate on the things that will bring honor to its advertisers.' The man is an astute jurist. My suggestion was to focus on topics of a more fundamental and legal nature."

"I couldn't agree with you more," said Bayer with satisfaction. "That will elevate his newspaper above the more trivial publications. We've seen so many of those lately. How will it end if all the papers in this country are filled with reports of every sordid crime?"

"Nissen is a sensible man. The city is lucky he's running this gazette."

"Very true. But back to the corpse. My investigations indicate that the deceased died in a most suspicious manner. I've also discovered that the man had arrived here only recently, and by all accounts he came from Sweden. For that reason, I am looking for another Swede who has recently taken lodgings in our city. We have witnesses who claim that the two Swedes knew each other. Since the one who is still alive happens to be of some social standing, I thought he might have made the acquaintance of the most prominent members of our local gentry."

At that moment, the door opened. The servant crossed the floor, hardly making a sound. He set a bottle and two glasses on the table between the two men, then left the room. Engel filled their glasses as he spoke.

"So you're wondering if I've encountered a high-ranking Swedish gentleman in the past few days?"

He frowned, as if considering the matter, and Bayer couldn't help thinking he was laying it on a bit thick.

"I'm afraid I have to disappoint you," said Engel at last. "But I wouldn't want your visit to have been completely in vain: *Skål!*" He raised his glass.

Bayer followed suit, downing his drink in one gulp.

"But what about the dead man? Did you ever meet him?" asked the police chief.

"I heard he was a simple vagrant who earned his keep by singing and gambling."

"Precisely. Our city lacks musicians of high quality. Don't people of your social class often hire troubadours from the inns or itinerant fiddlers to play at your festivities?"

"You certainly are thorough. You don't give up easily, do you? Those are qualities that I value in you, though I know that not everyone shares my view," said Engel with a sigh. "It's possible I heard something about a Swedish troubadour out at Ringve. That was at least two months ago, and I haven't seen him since. But now you really must excuse me. I have important matters to tend to. Business related to the society, you know."

Bayer nodded respectfully.

"I hear things are going well with that," he said.

"Yes, the boys have made remarkable progress. Our city now stands at the forefront for developing our own Norwegian scientific research."

The "boys" Engel was referring to were no less than Bishop Johan Ernst Gunnerus, university president Gerhard Schøning, and State Councilor Peter Frederik Suhm; together they had established the Trondheim Society seven years ago. The latter two pioneers had since moved away from the city, but thanks to the efforts of all three men, the society had attained an excellent reputation in scientific scholarship, not only in Norway but also in the rest of the world. This meant that the society could soon expect to receive the royal stamp of approval and call itself the Royal Norwegian Scientific Society. Bayer was proud of this achievement. This man, holding a schnapps glass and leaning back in a chair that had cost more than a police officer earned in a year, was a major contributor to the society's efforts to create an independent Norwegian scientific entity. He also possessed the financial resources necessary to keep such an enterprise going.

"By all means, help yourself to another drink. One of the servants will show you out when you ring the bell. Good-bye, Bayer," said Søren Engel.

The merchant rose and headed toward the door. Bayer couldn't remember the last time he'd seen the older gentleman without a smile on his face. Engel paused, his hand on the door handle.

"My dear Nils Bayer," he said somberly, "you know that I think a great deal of you, even though you're evidently a man who does not think much of himself. You seem to have planned your own ruin. You paid more than two thousand *riksdaler* to become police chief. That wasn't a good investment. Perhaps the prefect and I ought to have a talk about this skilling per barrel that you are so eager to obtain. The prefect is always amenable to listening to my advice."

"You would do that for me?" said Bayer in a measured tone.

"It's the sort of thing one does for a friend."

"And what would be expected in return from this friend?"

"Bayer, your suspiciousness offends me deeply. Of course, it's a useful quality in anyone in charge of police matters. But before I leave, I would ask you to consider which matters should concern a police chief and which ones do not come under his purview. When was the last time you inspected the goldsmith's scales or the baker's flour? What about the prostitutes? Of course a gentleman might feel the need for some entertainment now and then, but it should cost him a bit more effort than it does in our city these days. Spending your time running around after a murderer who must have long since disappeared—don't you think that's wasting the time you owe to our king?"

Bayer sat in silence for a moment. Then he said, "Petty sins have never interested me."

"But they ought to. Don't you, as the police chief, realize that petty sins lead to even greater sins? I wouldn't be surprised to learn that gambling or whoring were to blame for this poor Swede's death."

At this point Engel opened the door, bowed to a painting on the wall behind the police chief, and left.

Alone in the room, Bayer took the flask out of his pocket and filled it with Engel's liquor. Then he rang for the servant.

It looked like it was going to be a hot and sunny summer day, an excellent one to go out to the country, perhaps in the direction of Ringve Manor.

His horse, Bucephalus, was an old nag that he'd paid too much for, much too long ago. The horse had come with him from Copenhagen.

He led Bucephalus, who sadly enough was his oldest friend, out of the stable that he shared with a shoemaker and rode off toward the ferry landing in Brattøra. He was lucky enough to find the boat on the right side of the river.

Once he reached the other shore, he rode to the Bakke Inn and stopped there to have a glass of beer. While there, he argued with the owner, who said that the police chief must have better things to do than go searching for a killer. Take, for example, the trash that filled the city streets. When was the last time the chief had posted a placard threatening fines for such conditions? Bayer didn't leave

Bakke until close to midday, which meant he had to travel in the strongest sunlight of the day. When he eventually arrived at Ringve, he was sweating profusely and in a foul mood.

He rode over to the stable and left his horse with one of the lads before he headed for the main building, a long, narrow house built in the sturdy Trøndelag style.

A freestanding portal with carved, painted pillars made the entrance a sight to behold. On the little roof above the portal sat a worker who was attaching a beautiful weather vane made from cast iron.

"Are the master and mistress at home?" asked Bayer.

The young man climbed down the ladder at once and went inside the house without a word. A moment later Captain Preben Wessel appeared in the doorway. Although his stomach was no match for Bayer's, he was still a gentleman of ample girth. His wig was slightly askew, and his shirtfront a bit rumpled.

"Police Chief Bayer," he said with a smile. "To what do I owe this rare honor?"

Bayer cleared his throat.

"Oh, Dr. Fredrici advised me to spend a day in the country. It's this cough I have," he said as he took his pipe out of his pocket.

"The city air can be ghastly. I never use our house in town during the summer," said Wessel.

"Well, I just happened to be riding past, and so I wondered if you might offer a traveler a dram and bite to eat." He started filling his pipe.

"But of course, Police Chief. You must know that we have our own licensed tavern out here."

The captain pointed toward the inn called Nybryggen, a pleasant place where Bayer vaguely remembered getting drunk on some previous outing.

"So come with me, by all means. You are most welcome, as my private guest." There was genuine hospitality in Wessel's smile.

Bayer was invited upstairs to a large room with windows facing each other on either side. A place was set for him at the table while Bayer looked out at the courtyard. From here, he could peer down at the straw hat the laborer was wearing as he resumed his work on the weather vane above the entrance. Then Bayer crossed the room and looked out at the garden in back. A woman holding a spade was bent over an empty black flower bed. The gown she wore was much too nice for that sort of work.

"My wife loves to dig in the ground," said Captain Wessel as he came over to join Bayer. "I think it's because of her provincial background. She just can't stay away from a bed of newly turned earth. It's funny that a seaman such as myself should fall for a peasant type like her." He spoke with genuine love for the woman he'd married.

Bayer nodded and then sat down at the table, which now held dishes of soup, cheese curd, bread, and bacon. A big mug of beer and some good aquavit had also been set on the table.

"I see that you enjoy music," said Bayer, pointing to several types of stringed instruments hanging on one wall.

"It's my wife who is the musician," said the captain, looking a bit uncomfortable. "I can only manage to produce screeches from those things."

"Do you ever invite musicians out here, Captain?"

Wessel looked at him for a moment without speaking. Bayer helped himself to the soup and some beer.

"What I'm asking is this: On festive occasions, is it only the captain's wife who plays, or do you ever hire fiddlers?"

"Once in a while, yes, but I'm uncertain what you mean by this line of questioning."

"Oh, this is just a friendly conversation between two friends. I happened to stop by Bakke on my way here, and they told me about the big celebration you had out here in March. At Bakke, they seemed to think there might have been a Swedish fiddler present. Could that be right?"

"We had a fiddler, yes. But whether he was Swedish, I can't

remember. He played for us only one evening here in the house, but otherwise I think he played several evenings in the tavern."

"And he hasn't been back since then?"

"No. Why do you ask? I must say that you disappoint me, Police Chief Bayer. You say this is a peaceful visit, but in truth you've come here to dig into my private affairs. I demand to know what this is all about."

"Fine," said Bayer, taking a healthy swig of beer. "This Swedish fiddler was found dead yesterday morning on the outskirts of town. I presume you haven't heard of the case yet."

"No. News travels slowly out here in the country, as you well know. But why do you need to talk to me about this man?" Wessel's expression was still strained.

"You have every right to ask. The fact is that we know very little about him except that he was out here in March. Since then, he apparently spent most of his time playing dice in some of the pubs in town, and he made very few acquaintances. He's something of a mystery to us."

"I wish I could help you," said Wessel, now looking significantly more relaxed. "But the man who played for us was here and gone in a matter of a few days."

Neither man said anything more for a while as they ate their bread.

Then Bayer said, "Did he play well?"

Again Wessel's expression turned stony.

"You will have to ask my wife about that. I have no ear for music."

Having finished his meal, Bayer thanked his host and then had his horse saddled up. Wessel had come out to the courtyard to see him off.

Bayer began the slow process of mounting his horse. For a man of his size, it was an effort that he couldn't handle more than a few times a day, and after a day of traveling, his strength was almost gone.

"Are you sure you don't want one of my servants to ferry you across the water to town? I think there might be enough room for both you and your horse in my new boat, which is docked in Ringve Bay."

The captain watched the police chief with barely concealed glee. But Bucephalus knew his master well, and he was also a patient mount. Finally Bayer managed to haul himself into the saddle. He declined the offer, wondering whether the captain was more doubtful about space in the boat for him or for his horse. Then he asked one last question: "Have you met any other Swedes out here lately?"

The police chief silently counted as Wessel blinked four times before answering.

"No. Why would I? We're not at war, you know."

"I know. Tordenskiold's time is long past," said Bayer, referring to the captain's ancestor and previous occupant of Ringve Manor.

Then he recalled that Tordenskiold was said to have run away from home when he was very young. He also remembered hearing that the captain had lost a son at a young age. Their ship had gone down during a voyage to Copenhagen, and the boy did not survive.

And so it was with a feeling of compassion that he rode away from Ringve Manor. We all have our ghosts to bear, he thought.

It was evening by the time he returned to the city. He was worn-out, and after putting his horse in the stable, all he really wanted to do was fall into bed. But he decided to make a quick stop at his office. There he found Torp sitting in the dim light, waiting for him.

"What are you doing here at this hour?" asked Bayer with alarm.

"I've been waiting for you all day," replied Torp. "It's about the body, that Swedish singer we took over to the hospital chapel yesterday. The priest came over right after you left this morning to give us the news. The body has been stolen from the chapel."

17

A *glass struck* the kitchen cupboard and shattered. Most of the glass shards fell into the sink, while the rest slid across the counter, and a few landed on the floor. The next glass struck almost the same spot. This time, more of the shards ended up on the oak parquet floor.

Elise Edvardsen hadn't been able to accept that the music she'd heard from the yard was something she'd imagined. All attempts to sleep had failed, and finally she couldn't stay in bed any longer. Now she was standing in the kitchen, howling and kicking at the pieces of glass. She grabbed another glass from the counter and flung it without taking aim at anything specific. It struck the door to the living room, raining glass shards all over the threshold. She had an urge to take off her slippers and jump on the pieces, to feel them slicing into the soles of her feet. She imagined her warm blood seeping out, and there was something strangely comforting about that thought. Then she sank to the floor, sobbing.

I need to call the police and tell them about what I heard, she thought.

But she stayed where she was until Ivar came in from the yard. He hadn't been able to sleep either, so he'd gone to shovel the driveway. It had snowed again in the night. He'd said that this would save him from having to shovel in the morning. As if that was important for some reason.

"Elise, what happened?"

Not that fucking phony voice again, she thought, and then wailed, "What the hell do you care?"

He didn't reply, just began sweeping up the pieces of glass on the floor as she sobbed quietly. Finally he said, "You're not being fair. You know I'm worried. That I care just as much as you do. I'm trying to stay positive. I still think they're going to find her." He opened the cupboard under the sink and emptied the dustpan into the garbage. "Do you know what this is?" he asked. "Smashing glasses is the kind of thing we do when we've given up. And we haven't given up yet. She ran away. They'll find her."

"Shut up, you stupid bastard!"

He wiped off the counter and put away the glasses that were still intact. Then he went over to her and leaned down.

"You don't mean that."

Now she looked up at him. "I know. I'm sorry," she told him.

Then he took her hand and helped her up. She put her arms around him and pulled him close. For a few minutes they stood there like a couple of teenagers at a dance. Her tears slowly seeped into his shirt at the shoulder.

"Let's call the police," he said. "You're right. Maybe somebody was outside."

Then the tune started up again.

At first she didn't know what it was. It was so sad that it could have been part of her own thoughts. Then she realized that it was coming from outdoors.

"Did you close the door when you came in?" she said, suddenly noticing the icy draft.

"I heard you crying," he said. "I must have forgotten."

Together they went out to the front hall. Through the open door they saw the figure of a man in the dark amidst the swirling snow. This time they both saw him. There was no longer any doubt.

Elise watched as her husband opened the wardrobe in the hallway. That was where he kept his guns. The figure outside must have seen them, but he just stood there, motionless. The melody was just as unhurried as before, but much clearer this time, and closer. It was definitely coming from a music box. The notes sounded metallic and pure. Now Elise saw her husband open the gun cabinet and take out his shotgun. It's not locked, she thought. The shotgun's easily accessible. He must have believed me after all.

Now she saw him dash for the door, holding the gun in his hand. After that, everything was a blur. She fell to the floor; still conscious but too dizzy to get up, she lay there listening. Ivar bellowed. Then she heard the sound of running footsteps that vanished into the night.

Ivar Edvardsen had hunted small game ever since he was a teenager, but he'd never gone after larger animals. He couldn't stand the thought of all the blood, the big carcasses dropping to the ground. He'd never imagined he would ever aim his shotgun at a human being. As he ran out to the driveway, he told himself that the last thing he wanted to do was kill the man who was probably holding his daughter captive somewhere. He was struck by how swiftly he'd come to this conclusion. Half an hour ago, he'd still wanted to believe that his daughter had simply run away from home, and that her disappearance had nothing to do with the murder at Kuhaugen. But all it took was for him to hear that tune from the music box for any doubts to vanish. Elise had been right all along. This man had her. The monster had come to their door, and somewhere he was holding their daughter prisoner. Ivar felt like shooting him dead, but he couldn't.

By now he was out on Markvegen. There he stopped and looked around. The street was very quiet. He saw no one. He paused, noticing the vapor coming from his mouth, as he pondered what to do next. They had both seen him. They were not imagining things.

All of a sudden the man was standing right in front of him. He rose up from behind a parked car like a petrified shadow, only five yards away. Startled, Ivar took a step back, instinctively putting his finger on the trigger.

Aware that Ivar was scared, the shadow took a step closer, then another. At that moment Ivar stopped thinking. He wanted to turn on his heel and run back to the house. Call the police. But before he managed to go anywhere, he slipped and fell to his knees. The gun went off as he tried to scramble to his feet. He was hardly aware that he'd squeezed the trigger.

The man standing in front of him cried out, then turned and limped away quickly, snarling furiously.

What have I done? thought Ivar Edvardsen as he crouched on the ground, watching the man leave. Now I've wounded him. I've wounded the monster.

Then he caught sight of the music box in the snow.

For a few seconds Elise was completely out of it. When she opened her eyes again, she wasn't quite sure where she was. What happened? Was she dreaming?

Then he was standing over her.

Her husband held the shotgun in one hand. In the other he had a blue heart-shaped music box with a tiny figure on the lid. She stared at it in disbelief.

"Is that the one we heard?" she asked.

After setting the music box on the floor, he squatted down next to her and slipped his hand under her head to help her sit up.

"I had no idea it was loaded. I must have left a shell in the chamber."

"That's so unlike you," she said.

"Let's just hope I didn't kill him."

"Let's hope you didn't." She sat up straight, finally feeling clearheaded. For the first time since last night, they were in agreement.

"He took her, didn't he? It was him, wasn't it?" he asked.

"And that's why we have to hope that he survives," she said. "But that's the only reason."

He nodded and she saw tears trickling down her husband's cheeks. She had been more prepared for this turn of events than he was. And that was why she was the one who got up to make the call.

She was no longer in any doubt. Those were bloodstains on the floor and walls. The realization had completely paralyzed her at first, but then, oddly enough, it had made her more determined than ever.

She moved along the wall. She'd been doing this for several hours now. She hadn't heard any sounds in the house for a long time, so she thought he must have gone out. If she hurried, she might be able to get her hands free before he came back. She could feel the rope very slowly fraying and getting looser around her wrists. Finally it pulled apart with a faint ripping sound. At the same moment she felt as if a tight, invisible rope was also released from around her chest. She pulled her hands out of the rope and took several deep breaths, then sank to the floor. She could feel how tired her thighs and hips felt. She placed her hand on her abdomen for the first time since she'd been tied up.

"Are you there?" she whispered.

The rope had been wrapped three times around her wrists, so now that it was off, she had a piece of rope that was more than a foot and a half long. She dropped it to the floor. Then she began untying her feet.

When she was free, she stood up and stretched, running her hand over her belly one last time. She needed to act before he came home. She had already decided what to do. She knew the door was locked, and that it would take too long to kick it open, even if she had enough strength to manage it. That meant she would have to leave her dog behind. The window was her best chance. The police could come back to get Bismarck. If he was still alive.

She went over and loosened the hasps, but when she tried to open the window, it refused to budge. When she studied the frame, she saw the nail heads. She stripped off her sweater, wrapped it around her right hand, made a fist, and slammed it against the pane. The newspaper covering the window tore apart and the glass underneath shattered, but she didn't hear any shards fall outside, as she'd expected.

It took a few seconds before she realized why. Behind the torn newspaper and broken window she saw snow. A big, heavy layer of snow just outside the basement window. That explained why it had been so dark whenever he turned off the light, and why she'd never noticed any sunlight. The window was totally blocked by snow. She cursed herself for not thinking about that possibility. Now she stared at the snow, trying to figure out whether it was night or day. Her inner clock told her that it was late in the evening on the second night of her captivity. But the tightly packed snow gave little hint as to whether she was right or not.

Then she unwrapped the sweater from around her hand. She saw that it had protected her as she'd hoped. Cautiously she shook the shards of glass out of the sweater and put it back on. There were still sharp pieces sticking out from the window frame, so she began prying them loose. At the same time, she removed the scraps of newspaper and the glass that were embedded in the snow. She put everything in a pile on the floor.

I've got to get out of here, she thought. *If he comes back and sees this, who knows what he might do next.*

After clearing away all the glass, she started digging. But she soon realized she wasn't tall enough. Even if she stood on tiptoe, she could only manage to make a hole a couple of feet outside the window. To get through the last part she needed something to stand on. And there was only one choice.

With an intense feeling of disgust, she went over to the bucket and picked it up, trying not to look inside. Then she dumped out the contents as far away from the window as possible. Quickly she went back to the window and turned the bucket upside down on the floor. Standing on top of it, she was up high enough to dig properly.

Not long after, she reached her goal. Her hand broke through the snow into the air. She pulled it back, and through the hole she could see that she had guessed right: It was nighttime. A streetlight gave off enough light to see outside as she kept on digging, making the hole bigger. Finally the opening was big enough for her to get through.

"Will the snow mess everything up?"

It was a regular snowstorm, and chief inspector Odd Singsaker stared at the dog that Jens Fjellstad, one of the guys from the canine unit, was holding on a leash. Less than an hour had passed since Elise Edvardsen had called the police.

"Not if we hurry. An hour isn't very long. He can usually pick up a scent, and aside from the snow, there isn't much to distract him on a deserted street like this."

The dog found the traces of blood on Markvegen outside the Edvardsen home, traces that Grongstad had secured by covering with a tarp. The dog picked up the trail instantly. Singsaker and Fjellstad followed the dog across the street, along with two other officers, both of whom wore guns on their belts.

At the first intersection, a snowplow had recently driven through, headed in the direction of the crime scene and then down the slope of Åsbakken. Singsaker cursed when he saw the fresh plow marks.

"Is this a problem?" he asked, holding his breath. They couldn't lose him now. This was a golden opportunity, the perp's first big mistake. They really had a chance of catching him. Singsaker could feel it. They were so close that he practically felt he'd picked up the scent himself.

Fjellstad reassured him. "A plow isn't enough to throw him off the trail."

The dog stopped abruptly in the intersection, then continued down Åsbakken. But the highly trained German shepherd didn't get far very before he paused, looking confused.

Fjellstad allowed him to sniff for a while before signaling for him to go back to Markvegen.

"A typical T movement," he remarked as they trudged back up the hill. "That can be a bigger challenge than a snowplow. He walked partway down the street and then turned. He probably went past Markvegen when he got back up there. He wandered around. If he did that a lot, we may have a few problems."

Singsaker was breathing heavily. This could mean two things. Either the perp was smart and knew how to fool the dogs or he was confused after being shot and was roaming aimlessly.

"The subject could be psychotic. At any rate, he's wounded and probably furious as hell," he told Fjellstad.

Up on Markvegen the dog picked up the scent again, and they all jogged toward Bernhard Getz' Gate, continued to Ludvig Daaes Gate, and turned onto a path near Lille Kuhaugen, not far from where the body had been discovered.

It was pitch-dark among the trees. Singsaker turned on his flashlight and aimed it ahead of the dog, who was still on the trail. Any visible signs of the likely perpetrator had now been covered by snow. Singsaker tried to breathe calmly, straining to hear any sounds besides the footsteps of the three officers accompanying him. The man might be still hiding here in the woods.

The path led up the steep slope to the view overlooking the city. Out there on a rock outcrop stood a small transformer station, sprayed with graffiti. The dog tugged at his leash until they'd made one full circle of the dilapidated brick building.

Then the dog stopped.

"Shit," said Fjellstad. "He turned around and headed back the same way we came. So most likely he took another detour somewhere. The problem is that it could be anywhere between here and Åsbakken."

"Are you saying we've lost him?"

Singsaker sighed heavily as he stared down at Trondheim, seeing the lights gleaming in the dark. Then he aimed his flashlight back at the path they'd just taken. The dark forest wasn't giving up any answers.

Fjellstad didn't reply either, only shrugged as they headed back, walking in their own footsteps.

They went all the way back down to the street.

There Fjellstad pointed at the plow marks.

"Now this could be a problem. The plow may have disturbed the spoor in the snow. Enough so that the dog can't find where the subject turned off from the original trail. Especially if the man went into someone's yard—or, even worse, got into a car."

And Fjellstad's prediction turned out to be right. The dog led them right back to their starting point on Markvegen.

They stood there staring at Grongstad's tarp, which by now was almost completely covered with snow.

"We could start a new search from here, but I'm afraid that the snow is too deep and time has run out for us," said Fjellstad.

Singsaker sighed. They had been so close. They'd almost caught him. But then they'd been led on a wild-goose chase. He'd had enough of all the false leads in this case.

Even so, he asked Fjellstad to do another search while he went inside the Edvardsens' house.

Singsaker stared, mesmerized, at the tiny figure in the white tuxedo. He had clear blue eyes and long hair pulled back in a ponytail. It was certainly first-class craftsmanship. The figure had been made back when toys really meant something. The music box stood on the counter in the Edvardsens' kitchen. Singsaker had wound it up, wearing a pair of white gloves that he'd borrowed from Grongstad, who had just come inside the house. Even though Mr. and Mrs. Edvardsen had both touched the music box after Ivar found it, there still might be some important prints on it.

Singsaker listened to the tune. It was the same melody played by the music box they'd found in the woods. He knew all too well what that meant. And since the discovery of the music box at the murder scene near Kuhaugen had already been covered in the press, Ivar and Elise knew it too.

When the notes faded, Singsaker picked up the music box and handed it over to Grongstad.

"This is the top priority. Look for fingerprints and any biological traces," he said.

"Biological evidence won't be a problem," said Grongstad. "The blood on the road should be enough to obtain a satisfactory profile. Maybe we'll find a match in our database."

"He's toying with us," said Singsaker. "Do you think he wants to get caught?"

"I don't know," replied Grongstad. "But this sure is no ordinary killer we're dealing with."

"And yet I have the feeling that we're not going to find him in the system, no matter how good the fingerprints or DNA evidence are. This guy has been operating under the radar for a long time."

"You know what I like best about your gut feelings, Singsaker?" said Grongstad with a wry smile.

"No, what?"

"That they're not really feelings. That's just what you call them so you don't have to explain exactly what goes on inside that brain of yours. And you've gotten better at it since the surgery."

Singsaker didn't laugh. Then he left Grongstad to work while he rejoined the Edvardsens. They were sitting in the living room, where he and Gran had interviewed them the day before. But this time they both sat on the sofa, and Ivar had his arm around his wife's shoulders.

Singsaker asked them to describe the man, but without much success. It was so dark, and Edvardsen was terrified. Apparently the man had been wearing a hood, a cap underneath, and a scarf around his neck. His face had been partially hidden by the hood. Ivar described the man as unpredictable, but that was largely based on his behavior.

Then Singsaker told the couple that the police would have to take the shotgun into evidence. It was also his duty to investigate the shooting. He told them it was possible that they'd be charged with unlawful use of a firearm and even negligence. And this was regardless of whether or not the victim of the shooting had kidnapped their daughter. At the same time, the injured party in the case had undoubtedly represented a threat, and considering all of the emotions involved, there were obviously mitigating circumstances, since Ivar had reasonably assumed that he was facing a murderer on their property.

Finally, Singsaker sighed and then told them, "Due to time pressures and a shortage of resources, it may be necessary for the police to downgrade a number of criminal cases. I can assure you that Julie's disappearance isn't one of them, but separate matters that may arise—let's say slightly peripheral to the case—might easily land at the bottom of the list."

"So what you're saying is that you're going to take the shotgun but that you might not investigate the shooting any further?" asked Elise. Singsaker understood. They'd just discovered crucial evidence that their daughter hadn't run away from home but was most likely in the hands of an unpredictable and manipulative killer.

"If the injury to the suspect isn't serious, your husband hasn't really done anything but provide the police with good evidence in the case. The important thing right now is to make sure that both of you receive the proper protection. We're going to position officers here in the house with you."

The Edvardsens nodded.

"I know that you're hoping to get your daughter back soon," Singsaker said. "We thought it was more probable that she had simply run away. Unfortunately, that doesn't seem to be the case. But I want you to focus on one thing: This has led us closer to a resolution. The perpetrator has shown his face, and we now have concrete evidence. And perhaps most important of all . . ." Here he paused. He could feel a headache brewing, and for a moment he wondered whether what he had to say would provide any solace. "I think she's still alive. I think that's what this behavior pattern is telling us."

Singsaker instantly regretted his words. His profession had taught him never to promise more than he knew he could deliver.

Julie launched herself upward, noticing as she did so that the bucket fell over and slid away, but she had enough momentum to shove her body into the narrow snow tunnel to freedom. She lay there with her head sticking out into the faint glow from the streetlight as she struggled to free her hands.

That was when she heard him. The lonely sound of footsteps in the quiet night, solitary and distant, as if created by the dark backdrop beyond the streetlights. Only when he got closer did she hear how rapid and agitated his breathing sounded. Was he angry? No, it sounded more like he was in pain.

As he came through the front gate that was no more than twenty yards away, she could see the top of his head behind the banks of snow cleared from the driveway. He was wearing a hood. Instinctively she pulled back a bit.

Suddenly she started sliding backward on the slippery snow. Desperately she flailed her legs, trying to find a foothold. Then she fell back into the room and landed on the toppled plastic bucket. She heard it split in two beneath her.

She wanted to scream, but she was afraid he might hear. He was on his way into the house. Her one opportunity was gone.

She got up from the stinking, filthy basement floor and picked up the length of rope. Feeling stiff and bruised, she staggered over to the corner near the door, not remembering that was where she had emptied the bucket. Leaning against the wall, she waited motionless, listening. She heard him rummaging about upstairs with violent, abrupt movements. Finally he settled down. She heaved a sigh of relief, hoping he would stay in one place for a while or maybe even go out again. If he came down here, he would discover that she'd tried to escape the moment he came into the room. Her mind was working in high gear. Was there any other way for her to reach the window now that the bucket was broken? She had nothing but her clothes and her boots. What if she took off everything and piled them in a heap on the floor? No, it wouldn't be high enough. She went over to the window and jumped up. She managed to grip the ledge with her fingers, but when she tried to pull herself up and into the tunnel of snow outside, she lost her grip and fell back down. Without something to stand on, it was useless. But she kept on trying.

After the fifth attempt, she heard his footsteps cross the floor overhead and come down the stairs to the basement.

He's coming to kill me, she thought. When he sees the broken window, it's over. But maybe he'll just wind up the music box and leave.

Again she took up her position next to the door. If he came in, she had only one chance. She had to try to overpower him in some way.

He was right outside the door now, but he didn't wind up the music box. Instead, he started talking. This was the first time he'd spoken to her through the door.

"I went to visit your parents," he said. "I thought they should hear the tune. I wanted them to know that you're sacrificing yourself for something beautiful, something unique. But they didn't appreciate the music. Maybe it's not important. Maybe what I think of them is more important. What should be done with people who shoot somebody? Should I seek revenge? I have no idea. I just wanted you to know that I went over there. Something tells me that it might motivate you. And if you sing the song properly, I'll probably forget about any thought of revenge. I'm almost sure of that."

Her hands shook with fear and rage, but she forced herself not to say anything. He must not find out that she'd taken off the gag.

Then he said, as if he could smell her emotions, "Fear. I think it should be sung with fear in your voice. But it should be the fear of someone who is brave and is almost able to hide it completely. That's how it should be sung. Not the way Silje sang it."

Of course the thought had occurred to Julie long ago, but this confirmation of her worst suspicions almost made her legs give way beneath her. She felt herself starting to slide to the floor, but she forced her legs to hold her up. He was the one who had killed the woman in the woods. The story had been in all the newspapers.

She couldn't keep a small sigh from escaping her lips.

He fell silent on the other side of the door. Had he heard her?

But then she heard him get to his feet and come toward the door. He put the key in the lock, and a moment later the door opened. She was standing behind it, hidden from view. To him, the room looked empty. He must have seen the broken window and the tunnel through the snow. He hobbled over to the window and screamed.

This was her chance. She could slip out the door and hope he didn't turn around before she'd made her escape, but already he'd started looking around uncontrollably. Any second he'd catch sight of her. If she was going to slip around the door and run out, she would have to get so close to him that he'd be on her before she crossed the threshold. Her best chance was to knock him to the ground before she ran off.

Then she saw his leg.

He'd torn off his pants leg above the knee and wrapped a dressing around his calf. The bandage had been recently applied, but blood had already seeped through the white cloth.

Cautiously she stepped forward and took aim. Then she kicked him right in the middle of the wound. He howled and bent over to grab his leg.

Holding the rope between her hands, she threw herself at him from behind. At the same instant, he abruptly stood up so that she was hanging from his back with only the tips of her toes touching the floor. She felt his body tense as the rope tightened around his neck. She pulled as hard as she could and heard him gasping for air.

Then he took two steps back just as she regained her footing. She pulled on the rope one last time, and he sank down. The back of his head struck the brick floor with a thud.

She looked down at him and saw his eyes staring at her, his expression empty and lifeless.

Then she ran. She dashed out the door but paused in the hallway. Something held her back.

She found the storeroom door where she thought her dog must be imprisoned and went over to touch the handle. The door opened. Inside she found Bismarck huddled in a corner. When he saw her, he got up and limped toward her. He was hurt and it took effort for him to walk.

Then she heard the man moving in the room next door. How was that possible? How had he managed to get up so quickly?

She leaned down and kissed the dog on his snout.

"I'll come back for you," she whispered, and then turned to run.

He came out of the room just as she reached the bottom of the stairs. In four bounds she was at the top, yanking on the door handle.

That was when she realized that she had lost. She'd done everything she could, and there was nothing more to do. All hope had vanished.

And time stood still.

Her head was filled with the strangest images. Walking Bismarck along snow-covered roads. The woman with no throat from the newspaper stories. Fredrik naked in the dim light of his room. A fetus somewhere deep inside her. Her mother, with a rare smile on her face. A choir singing. Fragments of a life about to slip away.

The door refused to budge. He'd locked it.

She held her breath as she turned around.

He'd stopped halfway up the stairs, knowing he had all the time he needed. Then he slowly started moving upward. He paused on each step until he was three steps below her. She tried to meet his eyes but found them empty of all expression. It was like he was somewhere else entirely.

At one time she'd thought she knew who he was. But she had been terribly mistaken. He didn't even belong in the same reality as she did.

Then he came up the last steps. His hand with the missing two fingers grabbed her by the hair right above her ear.

He took two steps down, yanking her hair. She lost her balance. He let go and she tumbled down the stairs. She lay on the basement floor, gasping, as she looked around in confusion. Bismarck was standing in the doorway to the storeroom, staring at her. He looked exhausted and frightened, and he was too worn-out to come to her aid.

"Don't try to save me," she whispered to him. "No one can save me now."

Then the man was standing over her.

"What do you want from me, you sick bastard?" she screamed. Something in her was still fighting back, trying to fend off the inevitable. "What do you want from me?"

"But my dear Julie Edvardsen. You know what I want. I want you to sing."

He grabbed her hair again and dragged her into the room with Bismarck. There he dropped her on the floor.

Before she could get up, he took the dog and left. The sound of the key turning in the lock was like the cocking of a gun. Then the music started. This time it wasn't the music box. It was from a CD. Bellman. She recognized the song as the one she was supposed to have sung at the concert in Ringve, in another lifetime that was all over long ago.

"Drink up your glass, see death outside waiting, whetting his sword as he stands at your door."

He was trying to bring his breath under control. The Bellman tune was slowly having an effect and he calmed down. He stood still, one hand touching the bandage on his leg. The shot had grazed his knee. He'd used tweezers to remove four pieces of buckshot, and he hadn't been hit anywhere else. By now the bleeding had stopped.

The pain had been awful. It hurt so much that he'd almost blacked out after he'd stanched the bleeding with a strip of cloth he'd torn from his shirt at the foot of Åsbakken. He'd trudged through the streets for a while, unable to think clearly until he'd almost reached Kuhaugen. And that had frightened him. It was the first time that he'd felt completely gone. Not even the fly inside his head showed any sign of life. He'd been like a sleepwalker, but it was not sleep that he'd experienced; it was total darkness. Fortunately, it hadn't lasted long. His mind had cleared, and he'd turned around and come back to the house, only to discover that she'd tried to escape.

He'd arrived just in time.

He'd carefully chosen what he'd told her about her parents. It would make her think. He thought she was getting ready to sing for him now. It wouldn't be necessary to prepare her for as long as he'd done with Silje Rolfsen. Maybe he'd waited too long with Silje. But what he'd said about Julie's parents wasn't quite true. He wanted to give them a shock—because he didn't like them. He'd seen them before, outside, sometimes with Julie. Once he'd heard her mother yelling at her. He couldn't stand that woman. People like her didn't deserve Julie. The girl was too good for those two, and he'd been right to give them a shock. And their response had been to wound him. What should he do with people like that?

Then he took the dog and climbed the basement stairs. After what he'd done to the animal, the dog could barely walk.

18

Gro Brattberg was a good leader when things weren't going well. She was even better when they were. She considered it a lucky break that the suspected perpetrator had been shot. At least as long as he wasn't dead. Brattberg was a pragmatist, and she knew how significant this would be for the investigation.

Joining her in the conference room on this morning were Singsaker, Jensen, Gran, and Grongstad.

"So what you're saying is that he's most likely still alive?" Brattberg said to Grongstad.

The crime technician paused before he replied, furrowing his brow. Then he gave his boss a sidelong look.

"We didn't find a lot of blood. But before the snow really started coming down, we were able to gather enough to run the necessary tests. But there's nothing to indicate that he's going to bleed to death. The blood traces stop a few hundred yards from where he was shot. That means that he managed to get control of the bleeding, possibly by wrapping the wound with his own clothing. I'd guess it was a superficial injury and not a deep bullet wound."

"What about the music box?"

"We found a strand of hair inside. My guess is that it'll show the same DNA profile as the blood. Provided that it doesn't belong to anyone in the Edvardsen family, that is."

"Could it belong to the daughter?"

"Hardly. It's from a person with short hair. As far as I know, Julie Edvardsen has very long hair."

"What color is it?" asked Brattberg.

"I'd call it gray."

"So it's from an older person?" said Singsaker with interest.

"Not necessarily. Plenty of people start going gray in their early thirties. And sometimes the gray is so sparse that no one really notices. So in theory the hair could just as well have come from a younger or middle-aged man."

Singsaker nodded. Then he said, "The music box is interesting. I think it can tell us just as much about his state of mind as it can about his outward appearance."

"Yes, this is a turning point for us," said Brattberg. "By all accounts, we're dealing with a mentally unbalanced individual, and the motive for this new kidnapping seems more or less irrational."

"That's right," said Singsaker. "It's possible that our perp will be in the system. But the police don't have access to the records of psychiatric patients. Our hands are tied here because of doctor-patient confidentiality laws and privacy rights."

"We'll just have to use the resources that we have," said Brattberg with a sigh. "Gran, I want you to spend the morning on this. Take a fresh look through police reports, complaints filed, and the criminal records. Is there anything we've forgotten or overlooked? We're looking for individuals who may have behaved in a disturbing way, been reported for stalking or other types of irrational actions. Put on your psychiatrist's glasses."

"All right," said Gran. "Even though Mr. Edvardsen couldn't give us a good description of the man, except to say that he was wearing a coat with a hood, there's one thing we shouldn't forget. The person we're looking for has now been branded. We can identify him by the gunshot wound."

"Are you thinking of Høybråten?" asked Singsaker.

"We need to check him out."

"No matter what, we should bring him in for questioning sometime today. Even eliminating him from the list of suspects would be progress," said Brattberg.

"One more thing," said Singsaker. "We have to expect even more media attention. How can we keep Edvardsen and the gunfire out of the news?"

"We can't," said Brattberg. "He shot someone, after all. But for the time being, we'll call it an accident, and devote our energy to finding the girl."

Singsaker stopped just outside his apartment building. On his way inside he hummed the tune from the music box, which had lodged inside his brain against his will.

When he came in, he found Felicia sitting in front of her computer at the desk in the living room. He headed for the kitchen.

"Want anything to eat?" he called to Felicia and then went back to humming. She appeared in the kitchen doorway.

"Where'd you hear that tune?" she asked, sounding particularly interested.

"It has to do with the case I'm working on," he told her. "Why?"

"It has something to do with my case too," she said.

She went back to the living room and returned, carrying a piece of paper. It was the broadsheet her client had sent her. She handed it to Singsaker.

"Take a look at the score," she said.

"Felicia, this is me you're talking to. You know I can't read music," he replied with a helpless gesture. He handed back the broadsheet.

"I'm not very good at sight-reading either, but Siri hummed it for me. Listen," she said and began humming.

A cold shiver ran down his back.

"What the hell?" he said in shock.

She nodded.

"That bastard knows the tune to a ballad that is almost totally unknown," she said. "Music that has existed only as some sort of heirloom of a Norwegian-American family, and on an original broadsheet that was stolen from the Gunnerus Library. And he was so taken by the tune that he made a music box that would play it for him. But why?"

"That's something I'd really like to know. How's it going with your research?"

"I'm actually waiting for Siri to find out more about this Jon Blund," said Felicia.

"Oh, right. Jon Blund," he said, thinking out loud. "That's one name that should never get to the editorial desk at *Adresseavisen*. I don't even want to think about the headlines they'd come up with. Maybe we should go over to talk to Siri right now."

"We can, but she mentioned something about having time off this morning. I think she was going to work out."

Singsaker made himself a ham sandwich to take along.

"Come on," he said, heading for the front door. "I know where she works out."

His worries from the night returned. Was he about to become a father again? How was he going to tell Felicia? And was he prepared for such an enormous responsibility at his age?

"I've got an idea," said Felicia as they drove.

They were stopped at an intersection, and Singsaker swallowed the last bite of his ham sandwich before he glanced at her.

"What is it?" he asked

"I've only had contact with my client by e-mail."

"So?"

"He has a Gmail address, and I didn't really think much about it until now. But I think the English he writes is rather formal. He doesn't make any grammatical errors, but the way he formulates his thoughts seems a bit stiff. As if they were written by a foreigner who has a good command of the language, but it's not his mother tongue."

Singsaker thought about this as the light changed to green and he started driving again.

"So what you're saying is that your client might not be who he's pretending to be?"

"Well, don't you think it's too much of a coincidence that this particular ballad should show up in a case that I've taken on, while at the same time it's a crucial element in your investigation?"

"You're right," he said, noticing that he was clutching the steering wheel a little too hard as he braked to take the exit toward the Trondheim martial arts center. "But why would the killer do something like that?"

"I don't know. Maybe he wants to find out more about this Jon Blund without drawing attention to himself. A fake inquiry on the Internet could be just the cover he needs. We have to assume that Jon Blund and this ballad are somehow connected with the twisted reasons he has for killing."

19

The art of moving hands and feet. Siri Holm had long since stopped using her mind when she fought. The impulses behind every movement emanated from her fingertips and the soles of her feet. That didn't mean she was no longer thinking, that there was no consideration given to each blow. But these thoughts were different, automatic and carefully reasoned and yet endlessly creative. This might well have been what she liked best about *kyorugi,* which in tae kwon do was both sparring and fighting—the fact that her hands and feet understood things that her brain couldn't put into words. But her focus had started shifting inward, into her body. Her abdomen became a focal point around which all her movements circled. As if she were constantly engaged in a defensive battle for what lay inside her.

Today, the battle felt more real than ever. Usually she didn't feel anything when she struck a blow or connected with a kick. She was merely aware of how many she'd landed and how many she'd received. The same could be said about sex, in some instances. Or at least it could be said about the sex she'd had with her opponent, Rolf

Birger Gregersen, her only real competition in the Trondheim Tae Kwon Do Club. She'd slept with him almost without noticing it, just once, right after she moved to town and joined the club. Afterward she explained to him that she'd done it simply in order to get to know him better. And that she liked the way he fought better than the way he made love. He'd understood. Besides, he was married. They'd become regular sparring partners and now sweat together, but without any erotic contact.

They were an even match. She kicked and then retreated. Paused for a moment. Right now they were tied. They were approaching the part of the fight when she usually took the advantage. Slowly, they started up again. That graceful, deliberate dance. Eye contact. He looked at her and yet did not. This gaze of his was his best weapon, both in battle and in love. Both of them lunged but didn't strike. Then she felt a pinching in her belly. For an instant she lost focus, and that was all he needed. Quick as lightning he struck. For a moment she lost her balance, but she managed to stay on her feet. Then the time was up.

"It's been forever since I beat you," he said.

The truth was that he'd never beaten her since that first week she was in town. And then she'd let him win so she could come down in his *doboken*.

"I can't understand why you don't compete," he said, breathing hard as they headed for the bench against the wall.

He wasn't the only member of the club to say this. Siri knew she was the best one there, and that she could have gone far, possibly even to the Olympic Games, if she'd wanted to. But for her, tae kwon do was primarily a way of thinking. A totally different form of rationalizing than she couldn't find anywhere else. If she started competing, it would become just like everything else in her life. While she was fighting, it would distract her to know that a medal was waiting for her when she won. Just as the baby inside her was distracting her now.

"I've been thinking of taking a break," she said.

"What do you mean? Why?"

"Relax! It's no big deal. It'll just be a break of about nine months, minus the four that have already passed."

"You mean that you're . . ." His face turned pale.

"Take it easy. It's not yours," she said with a laugh. "Although I could have you locked up for a previous pregnancy attempt." They both laughed.

"Shit, Siri. Congrats!" He seemed relieved.

"Thanks," she said.

"Is this your last training session, then?"

"Yes. But don't say anything to the others until I've showered and left the premises."

"Why not?"

"I know things about you, Rolf Birger Gregersen," she replied.

"Fine. My lips are sealed. Fuck, I'm going to miss you."

"You're just going to miss aiming for my boobs," she said, smiling. Then she headed for the locker room.

After showering she went back into the hall to get a towel she'd left behind. That was when she saw two familiar people at the door, and she went over to them.

"Felicia and Odd? What are you doing here?"

Singsaker told her about the music box and the melody it played.

When he finished, Siri said, "I've requested the police log from the 1700s that we talked about, and I'm expecting it to be delivered to the library today. I could go over there, even though it's my day off."

"Good," said Singsaker. "That's what we were hoping. If the kidnapper was inspired by this lullaby, we might need to find out exactly who this Jon Blund was."

At that moment, Gregersen walked past, carrying a bag on a shoulder strap.

"I'm going to miss you, lady," he said jokingly as he went out the door.

"I'll miss you too," Siri called after him.

Singsaker and Felicia looked at her.

"I'm going to take a break for a while," Siri answered Singsaker's questioning look.

"A break? Why?"

"I don't know," she replied. She didn't feel ready to tell them yet. She wasn't sure how they'd react. "I'm not feeling very motivated. That's all."

Neither Singsaker nor Felicia said anything more about it.

Singsaker was having trouble concentrating on his driving. At the first stoplight Felicia pointed out that he was in the wrong lane, headed toward the harbor instead of the center of town. So there was no longer any doubt about Siri. And he could think of only one reason why she didn't want to tell them.

"Felicia," he said as he steered the car into the right lane when the light turned green and the traffic started moving. "She's really pregnant, isn't she?"

"Didn't I tell you?" she said, smiling.

"There's something . . ." he said.

"What's that?"

"The thing is," he said, mustering up his courage, even though he knew he ought to leave it alone. He plunged ahead anyway. "The thing is, I might be the father of her baby."

She didn't say a word.

"Don't misunderstand me. It happened before you came to Norway. I didn't know you yet. And I was feeling confused after going back to work, especially after that insane case was foisted on me."

"Confused?" she said, her voice ice-cold. "Were you confused when you met me too? It couldn't have been more than a few days later."

"No, I wasn't confused when I met you. Or maybe I was, but our meeting each other has nothing to do with that feeling of confusion. I've never been more certain of anything in my life than when we . . . when we . . ."

"Stop the car!"

"What?"

"Stop the car!"

"But why? Didn't you hear what I just said? It didn't mean anything."

"The two of you are friends, Odd. She's my best friend. And neither of you ever said a word about this to me."

"Why would we want to tell you about something that was going to hurt you, when it's of no importance whatsoever?"

"Stop the car," she repeated.

This time he did as she said. He pulled into a bus stop near a café and stopped. She opened the door and got out.

"Go to work and don't come home for a while," she said. Her voice was about to break.

"Wouldn't it be better if we went home together and talked this through?"

"I don't want to talk," she told him. "Christ, I hate talking!"

She'd switched to English. Then she slammed the car door.

He sat in the driver's seat, watching her in the rearview mirror as she headed for the crosswalk near the park.

"Fuck!" he said out loud. "Fuck, fuck, fuck!"

A headache began deep inside his brain, the kind of headache that sounded like traffic blasting by at high speed, and it quickly spread.

20

H*is cell phone rang* just as he was pulling away.

It was Brattberg. "Professor Høybråten is on his way into the station," she said. "We'd like you to be here when he arrives."

Singsaker cleared his throat and said he'd get there as soon as he could.

"Jon Blund," said Singsaker, giving Jan Høybråten his most penetrating stare.

Next to the professor sat Terje Bjugn, an older defense attorney. Singsaker knew him. Bjugn had once joined him and Jensen on a hunt. But he didn't like to shoot, so he'd hadn't gone again. He seemed cautious, always relaxed, and there was a sleepy glaze to his eyes, as if he spent too much time staring off into space. Yet Singsaker knew that the man had a sharp tongue, which he saved for appropriate occasions.

"Jon Blund?" Høybråten looked genuinely surprised by the way this interview was starting. He was sitting on a chair that was clearly not as comfortable as the one he was accustomed to. The interview room had sterile white walls and plain furniture. The table, with Singsaker on one side and the professor and his lawyer on the other, was from IKEA. Singsaker was startled to see a green potted plant standing in the corner behind Høybråten. It was new. Who had put it there? He had his suspicions, but then he started wondering how long it would last without any natural sunlight. The next instant the door next to the plant opened and Mona Gran came into the room.

"Yes, Jon Blund," Singsaker repeated as his colleague sat down beside him. He was annoyed to see that she leaned forward to make sure that the tape recorder on the table was switched on. Which of course it was. He'd gotten more forgetful, but he wasn't completely senile yet. He continued with his line of questioning.

"The ballad the music box plays was written by a composer who called himself Jon Blund."

Høybråten stared at him. Singsaker stared back. He'd already noted that there was no sign of a bullet wound in the skin that was visible on Høybråten's body. But the professor might still have a bandage somewhere under his clothing.

"Oh, of course. That's why it sounded familiar. The ballad collection in the Gunnerus Library, right? Now I remember. How silly of me. Forgive me, but it's been years since I last looked at the ballads, so I've forgotten the tune. Of course. Jon Blund. Sure. And I was correct about it being a lullaby, wasn't I?"

"So it seems."

"'The Golden Peace.' Isn't that what it's called? I remember it now. It's a lovely ballad."

"And apparently lethal," said Singsaker.

Høybråten looked at him, and it was clear that he now recalled the poorly disguised accusations that Singsaker had voiced the last time they'd met.

Singsaker went on. "Isn't it a little odd that you remember the tune only now?"

"Not really. I've never worked with the ballads in the Gunnerus Library. That's mainly because very few of them have ever been set to music. The one you mention is an exception. I did see it several decades ago. But the tune didn't stay with me. Not even a professor can remember everything."

Singsaker studied him carefully and realized that he might be telling the truth.

"Don't think that we're just going to forget about your relationship with the girls in the choir, Professor Høybråten," said Singsaker. "But we're aware that you've come here voluntarily, and at this stage we are treating you as a witness. And I assume that your attorney has no objection to that. Am I right?"

Attorney Bjugn nodded a bit warily.

"Now that you evidently do remember certain things about the ballad, let's follow that for a while. Can you tell us anything we don't already know about Jon Blund?"

"Jon Blund is a pseudonym," replied Høybråten.

"That much we do know," said Gran. And Singsaker was relieved that she had chimed in. "What we want to know is whether you know anything about the man behind the name."

"Not much, I'm afraid. But according to an old police log, someone with that name was murdered in Trondheim sometime in the 1760s. That's why we believe that 'The Golden Peace' was written close to that time."

"Is that the only source of information we have about Jon Blund?" asked Gran.

"Yes and no," replied Høybråten.

"What do you mean by that?"

"A few years ago a letter was found in the wall of Ringve Manor when the section from the eighteenth century was being renovated. This letter was stolen almost immediately after it was discovered, and so no one has been able to study it properly. But it was said to be about Jon Blund."

"And no one knows who stole the letter?"

"Not to my knowledge. But you police officers would know more than I do," said Høybråten spitefully.

Singsaker stood up, having decided they'd followed the Jon Blund lead as far as they could go. There were other, more pressing reasons why they wished to speak to Høybråten.

"I don't know whether you realize it, but as of last night we're investigating the murder at Kuhaugen and the disappearance of Julie Edvardsen as one and the same case."

"I see," said Høybråten, displaying no sign of emotion.

"May I ask why?" asked Attorney Bjugn, clearing his throat.

"For the time being, we can't divulge much information. What I *can* tell you is that last night there was a confrontation between the perpetrator and Julie's parents, during which a wound of unknown severity was inflicted on the suspect. As a result, we now have an opportunity to check witnesses who are associated in some way with the case. We have DNA evidence from the perp, and we also know that he has a wound somewhere on his body. What we are hoping, professor, is that you will agree to see a doctor, who will examine you for wounds. It would be in your best interest, and it would greatly help us with the investigation," Singsaker concluded, amused with his own diplomatic formulation of the request.

Høybråten cast an uncertain glance at Bjugn, who nodded almost imperceptibly.

"All right," the professor said with a sigh. "If that's all you need."

Gran stood up and escorted Jan Høybråten to the doctor while Singsaker went back to his office.

21

Hi, *this is Siri Holm* at the Gunnerus Library. I talked to you earlier about borrowing a police log from the 1700s. It's rather urgent that I see it, but I understand if you feel uneasy about sending such an old document over here by messenger. If it suits you better, would it be possible for me to stop by the Dora to have a look at it there?"

Siri was sitting in her office on her day off. She yawned, partly because she was bored by her own formal tone of voice, and partly because it was now afternoon and she'd had only two cups of tea and nothing to eat all day.

"Ah, Miss Holm. I was actually just about to call you," said a polite and gentle-sounding male voice on the phone. An archivist named Erik Nilsen was on the line.

The man she was talking to was sitting somewhere in the Dora. The building itself was a monstrous submarine bunker that the Germans had constructed during the war. With a roof and walls made of armored concrete more than ten feet thick, the structure was so massive that when the war ended, it proved impossible to demolish.

It was said that blasting it apart would require so much dynamite that the whole town would be put at risk. And besides, it would be too costly. Instead, the building had been sold for one single krone. By now this investment had paid off, to put it mildly. The Dora was a protected landmark in the harbor area, and it was fully occupied. The enormous building housed, among other things, the National Archives of Trondheim and the University Library. Every time Siri talked to the people at Dora on the phone, it was like hearing a voice from the deep.

"I just talked to the police about it," Nilsen replied.

"The police?" she repeated. "Don't tell me. Has it been stolen?"

"It has. It was usually kept in a box in the archives. When I went to get it yesterday, I discovered that someone had taken it."

"I thought this might happen," she said. "Who has access to the archives?"

"Generally we allow access to anyone who wishes to use them. Mostly researchers, historians, and an author or two. Innocent people. But they all have to sign the register before they can gain access to our materials."

"And of course you've already looked at this list of names to see who visited the archives lately, right?"

"Yes, I have."

"Was there any particular name that struck you as—how should I say it?—a bit odd?"

"Yes, when you put it like that, there actually was one that I noticed."

"Let me guess. Could it be Grälmakar Löfberg?"

"How did you know? Yes—he entered his name in the register several months ago. He may have been the one who took the logbook. There haven't been many visitors since then, and none of them was interested in the police logs. I wasn't working here when this guy arrived. But I think he might have been someone that the archivist on duty at the time knew, at least by sight, someone she trusted, and so she didn't look at what name he wrote down. Nor did she check whether the contents were still in the box when he turned it in. So how do you know about the name?"

"We've had a visit from him over here too," explained Siri Holm.

After finishing her conversation with Nilsen at the National Archives, she sat at her desk and pondered what she'd learned. I wonder if there's a facsimile, she thought, or a secondary source. Now she wanted more than ever to find out what that police log said.

Gunnar Berg looked up with a start from his book when Siri opened his office door without knocking.

"Siri? What can I help you with?" he asked after collecting himself.

"I wanted to ask you about something, Gunnar."

"Will it take long?"

"That depends. It has to do with a ballad and old police logbooks."

Berg thought for a moment.

"This is definitely going to take a while," he concluded. "I'm just about to pack up for the day. If you like, you could come along and we can talk on the way."

She accepted the offer. This way she wouldn't have to walk up the hills to get home from town.

Half an hour after Gran left the interview room with Professor Høybråten, she informed the investigative team that they no longer had a primary suspect in the case. Jan Høybråten had no gunshot wounds or any other injuries on his body that had punctured the skin.

"So that rules him out, right?" she asked her colleagues.

"We agree with Ivar Edvardsen that it's almost certain that he confronted the man with the music box last night. And it's just as certain that the man with the music box is our perpetrator. That's the only thing that makes sense," said Jensen.

After a brief meeting, Singsaker and Mona Gran were the only ones left, standing together in the corridor.

"Back to the drawing board," he said with a sigh.

"I'm afraid so," she replied.

"Did you put that potted plant in the interview room? You do know that there's no natural light in there, and it's going to die faster than you can say *greenhouse,* right?" he asked.

"Then it's a good thing I bought it at the dollar store. It's plastic."

"Are you kidding?"

"No. Take a closer look next time, Chief Inspector."

Gran headed for her office, while Singsaker decided to go outside. As he made his way downstairs, he realized that he was feeling pretty good. He was glad they had Gran on the team. They needed someone like her who could keep their spirits up. But when he stepped out into the sunlight, his good mood evaporated as he headed toward the canal bridge in Brattøra. Even though he'd tried not to get his hopes up, he had to admit that he'd been convinced there was a link between Høybråten and the killer. But now that theory had fallen apart, and they really had no leads whatsoever.

When he reached the canal on the other side of the street, he sat down on a bench. He started thinking about Felicia again. *Is it irrevocable, what happened between us? It can't be. Can it?* He was immersed in these thoughts when his cell rang.

"You said I could call you if there was anything," said a voice, which despite its deep timbre lacked any hint of authority.

"Who is this?" Singsaker asked.

"It's Fredrik."

"Fredrik?"

Singsaker dug through his memory. It felt as if the rest of his life was stored on some computer server in a distant country.

"Fredrik Alm?" he ventured after a moment. "What is it?"

"You said I could call you if there was anything."

"I did. And is there something?"

"I want to talk to you."

"If I'm not mistaken," said Singsaker, "that's precisely what you're doing right now."

"Not on the phone."

"I see." Singsaker sighed heavily and did his best to pull himself together. He'd already been dealt a few good blows today, but there was no reason he should take his frustration out on the boy. "Where are you right now?"

"I stayed home from school today. I'm not feeling well."

"Okay, give me your address and I'll be there in five minutes."

"The Swedes have an incredibly strong and ancient ballad tradition. Lots of people think that it began with Bellman, but there were many great troubadours before him. My favorite is Lasse Lucidor," said Gunnar Berg as he turned onto Prinsens Gate near the Trøndelag Theater.

"I don't think I've ever asked you where you live," said Siri.

"I actually live in Tiller," he replied. "But I need to stop by a place that I'm renting. Lasse Lucidor wrote a number of beautiful ballads in the 1600s. He's best known for a number of so-called occasional ballads." Gunnar was unstoppable once he got started talking about these kinds of songs. Siri hadn't yet had a chance to ask him about the police log, which was why she'd wanted to talk to him in the first place.

"Wedding songs and funeral ballads were his specialty. He was once arrested for writing a wedding poem titled 'The Suitor's Anguish.' It was intended for Konrad Gyllenstjärna's wedding. The song was so offensive that it was banned by King Karl X Gustav himself. Lucidor defended his work, saying that he had simply listened to his muse. He managed to win the case against him by acting as his own defense counsel, and so the case is considered an important victory for free speech in Sweden."

They had now reached the premises of the Student Association. He switched lanes to take the exit toward Singsaker and Rosenborg.

"What's interesting about Lasse Lucidor is that after being found not guilty of slander, he ended up dying in a duel at a tavern in Stockholm in 1676. It happened after a heated exchange of words with the officer Arvid Christian Storm. After killing Lucidor, Storm fled to Norway and soon afterward became the commandant in Fredrikstad. His descendants became very prosperous and eventually married into the well-known Wedel Jarlsberg family. That's how things were, back in those days."

They had reached the Fortress Park and were approaching the Rosenborg School.

"It's not far now," he said.

The Alm family lived in a big apartment building that had a sweeping view.

Fredrik opened the door when Singsaker rang the bell.

"Home alone?" he asked as the boy led the way into the living room. Fredrik nodded mutely. They sat down near the big picture window that looked out over the fjord. Fredrik looked ill at ease. Singsaker suspected that he was the type of person that didn't really feel at home anywhere.

"What is it you want to tell me?" he asked, having taken a seat on the sofa.

The magnificent view of the fjord made him think about Siri Holm's apartment. What he remembered most from that hour of dalliance with her was that he'd felt dizzy the whole time. Now he wondered if it had been because of the view. Or maybe it was the nagging suspicion he'd had even then that he was doing something that would have far-reaching consequences. But at the time he didn't know what those consequences would be. If he'd known, would he have done it anyway? No, he thought. No, no, no. Or maybe he would have.

Would he be able to get out of this without being honest with himself? He'd never had an experience like that. He and Siri had put everything, and yet nothing, into it. It was that impossible combination of joy and vertigo, of feeling completely free and yet knowing there could be unanticipated consequences that had made their encounter something he would never forget. What he couldn't explain to himself, much less to Felicia, was that it took nothing away from his feelings for her.

"She's pregnant," said Fredrik Alm, his voice sounding as it came from far away.

Singsaker was just about to say, I know, damn it all. But then he realized who Fredrik meant.

"Julie? Julie's pregnant?"

"Yes."

"Are you the father?"

"Yes."

"So the last time she came over, it wasn't to look at pictures, was it? She came here to tell you about the baby. Am I right?"

"Yes."

"Do your parents know about this?"

"No. Just Julie and I, and her doctor, of course. Now you know about it too."

"Did you talk about whether she should keep the child?"

"Yeah, we talked about it."

"And?"

"We couldn't decide. We couldn't make up our minds."

What a fucking mess, thought Singsaker, looking at Fredrik Alm.

He was too skinny. At the same time, there was a new self-confidence in his gaze. This wasn't the way to become a grown-up. Yet this was what had happened. A mentally disturbed man had kidnapped his girlfriend and his unborn baby. In that situation, no one could remain a child.

"You realize that I'm going to have to phone your parents, right?"

The boy nodded.

"And Julie's parents need to know about this too."

Again he nodded.

"You did the right thing, telling me," he said, and then took out his cell.

As Singsaker punched in Brattberg's number, Fredrik said, "It all seems so unreal. I know it's true, but her stomach was still so flat. I couldn't believe there was anything inside there."

After Singsaker filled Brattberg in, he got ready to leave.

"How much did you tell each other?" he then asked Fredrik as they stood in the hall and he was putting on his coat.

"What do you mean?"

"If somebody had treated her badly, would she have told you about it?"

"Maybe. What are you getting at?"

"Did Julie ever tell you about anything that happened at choir practice?"

"Like what?"

"Did she complain about any of the choir directors?"

"No, not really. But she said something about a man she thought was disgusting, someone at the practices for the Bellman concert."

"Did she tell you what he did?"

"No, just that he was staring at her in a creepy way."

"Do you remember his name?"

"No. We didn't really talk about it. It was just something she happened to mention. I think she likes saying that sort of thing, just to bug me."

Singsaker thanked Fredrik for his help and then left. By now it was late afternoon, and he headed home for dinner.

The man Julie had described as disgusting was probably Høybråten. He was clearly the sort of man that had more than one reason for working with a girls choir. But that didn't bring them any closer to the killer.

On his way home, Singsaker realized how much he was hoping that Felicia would be there, and that she'd calmed down by now. He tried to phone her, but she didn't pick up. As he passed the Rosenborg School, he happened to think of his notebook. He recalled that he'd jotted down quite a bit of information, and it might be important for him to follow up on some of it. But once again, the school was closed and deserted.

When they reached Rosenborg, they stopped in front of a huge old building.

"This is where I rent a place," said Gunnar Berg. They both got out of the car. "Do you want to come in, or do you need to get home?"

"Well," said Siri, feeling a cool breeze ruffle her curls, "I haven't even asked you about what I wanted to discuss."

"Can you stand it if things are a mess?" he asked.

"Can't live any other way," she replied with a smile.

"Then come on in."

She followed him to the entrance, where he unlocked an old, worn door and ushered her inside. From the front hall they proceeded downstairs to the basement.

"This is the room I'm renting," he said and paused outside the door. Then he insisted, a bit bashfully, that she cover her eyes as he opened the door and led her in.

Then he told her to take her hand away from her eyes, and what she saw did not match the image she'd had of him up until now. There were dirty dishes piled up all over the floor, pages of notes were spread out on a table, and behind that stood something that looked like a big mixing console, with the top removed so that wires stuck out in all directions. The whole place smelled moldy, and she noticed that she was standing on something sticky, but she didn't want to know what it was. She almost felt like she was back in her own apartment a week ago, before she'd decided to clean up.

She turned around and took a step back, slipping on something underfoot. She saw Gunnar Berg coming toward her a second before she regained her balance, and then she fell backward, with him on top of her. Something struck the back of her head. And then everything went black.

22

Elise *Edvardsen was lying* on top of her husband, pounding on the mattress with her fists. Her thighs trembled as she wailed.

"Hush," he said. "There's a police officer outside."

That only made her wail louder.

"I don't care!" she screamed. Then she continued shouting incoherently.

"Now, now, sweetheart," he said, trying to stroke her hair, but it was no use. She wouldn't lie still. Then he wrapped both arms around her waist and tried to rock her. They'd gone to bed at eleven, and both of them had actually fallen asleep. But she'd been awakened by some horrible dream and rolled on top of him. He couldn't remember this ever happening before. She was like an animal. But animals probably didn't experience this sort of boundless grief and terror. She no longer saw any reason to hold back.

She moaned, loud and strident, clawing at his back. Then she calmed down and finally lay still, clinging to him as she sobbed.

"I was going to be a grandmother," she gasped. "You were going to be a grandfather. Could it get any worse than this?"

It had only been a few hours since Chief Inspector Singsaker had phoned to tell them what Fredrik had said.

"Shhh," said Ivar. "This is just as terrible for me."

"I know," she said. "I know."

He felt her start to relax. Gradually, her breathing eased. The tension was seeping out of her limbs, but she didn't let go of him. Slowly, she began to caress him. She was wearing only panties and a T-shirt. He reacted to her movements, knowing that it wasn't appropriate. It wasn't possible, not now. There simply wasn't room for so many different emotions at once, was there? He tried to roll her off of him.

"No," was all she said. Nothing else. She stayed where she was. Then she took off her panties.

She awoke in the morning filled with guilt. How could they have done that last night, in the midst of this awful situation?

Her husband was still sleeping. She stroked his forehead.

"What's going to happen to us?" she asked quietly, not wanting to wake him. She thought, I feel closer to him now. Before this happened, I didn't know whether I still loved him. Now I know. And yet everything around us is black.

She got up, put on her robe and slippers. She went straight to Julie's room, not even glancing at the policeman sitting on a chair in the kitchen.

Of course the room was empty. Julie hadn't suddenly come home. She wasn't sitting on her bed, laughing and saying that she'd sure fooled them. The bed was empty and unmade, just as it had been since Julie had disappeared. Elise went over and sat down on it. Under the pillow was a comic book that Julie had been reading. She loved comics. This one was called *Sandman*. Julie had tried to get her mother to read it, saying that it was so good. But Elise hadn't understood why she should read something like that. Now she took it with her to the kitchen, deciding to leaf through it as she ate breakfast.

The police officer there told her he'd started his shift at two in the morning.

Good, she thought. That means he didn't hear anything from the bedroom.

"I'll get the newspaper for you," she said and put the comic book down on the table.

Snow struck her face as she opened the door. The whole stoop was covered with snow, piled up by the wind. She was about to turn to get a shovel in order to dig out the newspaper when she saw it. Two black eyes staring at her from the snow.

She fell to her knees and began digging. Soon the dog's fur came into view. She sat there holding Bismarck's head in her hands. The rest of his body was still under the snow. The dog's body was ice-cold and completely rigid. Elise let him go and ran into the house, screaming. Where was that damned policeman who was supposed to be keeping watch? Why hadn't he heard anything?

23

When Singsaker had gotten home the previous afternoon, Felicia was gone, and when he tried to call her, her cell was switched off.

He went to bed, hoping that she'd show up during the night and crawl under the covers next to him, but that didn't happen. It wasn't Felicia who woke him in the morning, softly humming some nineties hit song as she got dressed. It was his phone. As usual, he thought about how he still needed to change the shrill ringtone.

"Singsaker," he said in a gravelly voice.

"Brattberg here. Did I wake you?"

"What are *you* doing up?" he said, looking at his alarm clock, which wouldn't go off for hours. But he couldn't be really angry with his boss. It was a weakness that he'd learned to live with.

"I got a call, same as you," she told him.

"So there's a development? Tell me it's good news."

"If a new lead in a case is good news, then yes. But from any other perspective, no."

"Don't tell me something happened to the girl."

"No, it's her dog. The perp beat the dog to death and then left him on the doorstep of the Edvardsen home. It was basically just an icy lump of flesh and fur by the time they discovered it this morning."

"Shit. What kind of psychopath is this guy?"

"I know, Odd," said Brattberg, who always knew when to use his first name. "But you have to leave your personal feelings at home. Get over to Markvegen ASAP."

"Okay, boss."

Singsaker ended the call and went into the kitchen. This morning he needed three shots from the bottle of Red Aalborg to get his brain functioning. The pickled herring he ate tasted of sadness. Felicia had made it herself. She'd spent an entire morning studying recipes in Norwegian cookbooks as she prepared the herring filets and onions, with tears in her eyes, all for him. She couldn't stand herring. Right now, he couldn't wrap his mind around the whole situation. He could think only of her, and he tried to figure out a way to present himself as innocent, but couldn't. Her reaction was completely justified. She had every reason to feel hurt and upset. But even though she was in the right, it wouldn't necessarily stop her from doing something stupid. Several weeks ago, she had told him about being raped in her youth, and about her subsequent drinking problems.

"I don't know whether I'm really an alcoholic. I think it was more an attempt at suicide rather than a real abuse of alcohol," she'd told him. "But I've never really considered examining the issue."

And now is not the time, he thought as he went out the door.

"Damn it, Felicia," he muttered to himself. "Come home!"

24

Felicia Stone *was naked*. Someone had smeared Tiger Balm in her eyes and repeatedly hurled an anvil at her pale forehead. That, or she was horribly hungover.

She peered through the bottle that stood on the room service menu on the nightstand, catching a glimpse of the label on the other side. A few colors shone through the label, but she couldn't make out the brand.

She'd heard once that alcoholics have one type of booze that they prefer over others, and that they get drunk on other kinds only if they can't find their favorite. When she thought about it, she realized she must have read that in some sleazy detective novel. In reality, most alcoholics weren't that snobbish; they drank whatever was at hand. So what about her? What was her favorite poison? She turned the bottle around and saw that it was Smirnoff vodka that was flowing like barbed wire through her bloodstream. She propped herself in the double bed and saw, to her relief, that she was alone. She couldn't remember *how* she'd ended up here in this hotel room with only an empty liquor bottle for company, but she did remember *why*.

She'd fallen in love. Which had led her to make a whole bunch of irrational decisions and overlook some obvious pitfalls, such as the fact that the man was old enough to be her father. Or that for practical reasons she'd had to move in with him before they'd really gotten to know each other and share confidences, like how he'd slept with the best friend she'd made in Norway.

But inevitably things had fallen apart. Reality had caught up with her, and now here she was in a hotel room in a foreign country. She had believed that she had friends here; she had started feeling at home. That might be the worst part about what she'd lost. Right now, she just felt empty.

She went into the bathroom, where she found her clothes. Before she got dressed, she took a shower. The cold water helped her start to think more clearly. Fully dressed, she went and read the hotel information on the desk, which told her that she was in the Rica Hell Hotel.

She used to joke with Odd about Hell, a small, densely populated area near the Trondheim airport. She was always amused by the road signs on the way here. In the lobby of the local hotel, where they'd stopped for brunch one Sunday when they were taking a drive, they'd seen a poster that said in English WELCOME TO HELL. They'd had a good laugh about that one.

So now Felicia found herself in the Hell Hotel. And true to its name, it was no place to linger. But fortunately there was also one thing that set the hotel apart from the purgatorial Hell. It had its own airport with a departure hall.

She hadn't brought any luggage, but she wouldn't need any where she was going. She did have her wallet and her passport. So she checked out of the hotel and walked the short distance over to the airport at Værnes.

A little while later she had a plane ticket in hand. She wondered if she'd be able to buy herself a beer after going through security.

This is the test, she thought. This is when I find out. She thought about a time, long ago, in the basement of her parents' home in Richmond. There was a table covered with empty liquor and pill bottles, a ratty-looking sofa, the smell of mold, and childish pictures on the walls. She had almost killed herself with booze and drugs in that secret club room of her childhood. But nobody got addicted in such a short time, did they? She'd wanted to die back then, not just numb herself. This time was different. She didn't want to escape life permanently. Just drink so she could stop thinking, so she wouldn't have to answer all those damned questions that kept scraping at her brain. What was she doing here? Did she really love him? Was she ever going to figure him out?

A strange thought kept nagging at her; it was probably what bothered her most. What if he had simply forgotten that he'd slept with Siri? Was that why he hadn't said anything? Maybe he'd only recalled the incident when he found out that Siri was pregnant. Someone who had been through such an extensive brain operation as Odd had endured, who had lost parts of his memory, must have also lost some of himself. And if he didn't know who he was, how could he be sure that she was the one he wanted?

25

Singsaker trudged through the snowstorm. He was on his way to the station, his head filled with gloomy thoughts. He tried to send Felicia a text message. It was the same one he'd already sent several times that morning: "Where are you? Do you want to talk?" She had every right to react the way she had, but why did she have to disappear the very moment that a homicidal maniac was roaming the streets? Again and again he reminded himself that Felicia was a tough cookie, with police training to boot. She knew how to take care of herself. Plus, the killer had no reason to go after her in particular. Still, that didn't make him feel any better. The perp had been on her Web site, after all.

He'd gone over to the Edvardsen home and watched Grongstad pack up the frozen body of the Saint Bernard in plastic. Grongstad acted as though the dead dog was good news, because it would undoubtedly provide a treasure trove of evidence. Singsaker, on the other hand, regarded the discovery as yet another failure, and he thought that the next good lead in the case might be finding Julie's dead body. This time, he had no idea what to say to her parents, so he left the task to Jensen. His colleague had made just as bad a job of it as Singsaker would have. All in all, it was a miserable way to start the day. For the very first time since he'd started ice bathing, he'd actually looked forward to the freezing dip. An icy swim would suit him just fine.

Singsaker couldn't stop himself from brooding. No matter how hard he tried not to think about Felicia, he couldn't push it aside. He had only himself to blame for what had happened between them.

Maybe it was the black belt that Siri had worn around her waist as they engaged in that easy, sweaty fuck in the midst of that frenzied investigation late last summer. Ever since he had fallen asleep in her messy bedcovers after making love, he had feared the consequences. He had pictured getting in trouble at his job, since Siri had been a key witness in the case. If it had ever come to Brattberg's attention that he'd had sex with a witness, he wouldn't have been able to defend himself. But strangely enough, the prospect of being suspended from the force hadn't worried him much. After the brain surgery, his job hadn't seemed as important as before. No matter what happened, his wounded head always came along with him. And sometimes working felt like more drudgery than it was worth. That was definitely the way it felt today. But his error in judgment with Siri Holm hadn't had any effect on his job. Bad decisions weren't really bad if they didn't have repercussions that truly stung. After he met Felicia, he quickly realized that there were worse things than losing his job. What had happened now was a disaster that had been waiting to happen. He just hadn't seen the signs in time.

When Singsaker reached the station, Gran had some surprising news for him.

"Høybråten is back," she said.

"Did you find anything on him?" asked Singsaker, wondering

whether this would give him any sense of satisfaction, but he wasn't sure.

"Not regarding the music box case, I'm afraid. But Nadia Torp mustered her courage and decided to report him. She says that he touched a lot of the girls in the choir inappropriately, and that one night after practice he asked her to stay, and then forced her onto a table. She managed to get away before he could rape her. We have more than enough to charge him. This morning, after we brought him in, he confessed to Brattberg. He totally fell apart. He's been sobbing like a little kid. Actually, he asked to speak to you personally."

Singsaker entered the interview room. The professor was seated next to his attorney.

Singsaker sat down across from them.

"I don't expect anything in return," said Høybråten. "And my attorney has already told me that the Norwegian police don't grant lighter sentences in return for information, the way they do in American movies."

"Is there something you want to tell me?" asked Singsaker, noticing that a sudden tension had replaced the listless feeling he'd had all morning.

"He had something on me, and I had something on him," said Høybråten. "That's why I didn't say anything about this before. I was afraid he'd talk—about the stuff with the girls."

"What are you trying to say?"

"I know who stole the letter that was found at the Ringve estate," replied Høybråten. "It has to do with Jon Blund, and was supposed to be turned over to the Gunnerus Library."

"Tell me more," said Singsaker.

And Høybråten began to talk.

26

He'd walked alone through the storm and had the city all to himself. The dog was inside a plastic bag. It was night. The streets were deserted. It was just him and the dog, whose body was still warm, and the snowflakes melting on his face. As he walked, he realized that from now on, there was only one path to take.

After unpacking the dog and placing him on their doorstep, he went home. Not to his childhood home that he was renting, not back to her, but home to his wife. There he had fallen asleep, and he had finally dreamed again.

The dream took him right back to the doorstep of the Edvardsen house. The dog lay at his feet. A police car was parked in the driveway, but no one had noticed him. He was looking up at the sky. There he saw the man with the hood again. This time he thought he caught a glimpse of the man's eyes, and in one of them shone a star brighter than any other in the sky. Then he realized who the man was and understood.

Then the man with the violin appeared.

And then the procession with the coffin, but this time he was absolutely sure that it was his father inside.

He stood there bewitched as the murky giants trudged across the sky. The world around him felt like it was falling apart, as if there was nothing more to hold on to or believe in. He was looking at himself from the outside as he watched the procession, and he saw things that he couldn't explain or describe. New figures were following the coffin. He didn't know who they were or whom they were mourning. But it didn't matter. One of them was a dog. All of them were up there in the sky. At the end of the line, behind all the others, were two girls he recognized. One of them was hesitating. She took a step and then paused, as if she'd forgotten what she was doing, and then she moved forward a bit. Blood was running out of her mouth. The other girl, the very last in the line, looked as if she wanted to sing. She opened her mouth. Then she stopped. She stopped under the moon and looked at him. Looked at him and opened her mouth.

Now he was in the bathroom at home, staring at the bottles of sleeping pills. Full bottles. Empty promises.

A thought occurred to him. He'd slept well for two nights recently. Both times after he'd killed. Silje Rolfsen first, now the dog. Did he really need that song? The only time he ever felt calm was after taking a life.

No, he thought. It's the fly inside my head planting these ideas. It tickled the inside of his skull. There it was, flitting around inside. He was scared that soon it would start buzzing again, and he knew that it wasn't the dreams he was waiting for. They couldn't save him from the waking nightmare of the daytime. The lullaby and the young girl's voice, he thought. Then he would finally have what he longed for.

He went into the living room and looked at the lullaby. It was years ago now that he'd first taken an interest in ballads. It was during that period when his slumber became more sporadic, but he was still able to sleep and to dream. Then he'd discovered the ballad called "The Golden Peace," tucked away in a box in the Gunnerus Library, and he'd read the promise contained on its title page. When he read the text, he realized that he believed in the promise it made. But a long time passed before he stole it and brought it home to understand how it could be used. That was after sleep had deserted him completely, and he realized what he would have to do, that he couldn't ask just anyone to sing the tune for him—not Anna, not anyone. He begged for it, just as he'd begged for sleep at night. Nothing comes to the one who begs.

Now the original text sat on the table in front of him. In secret he'd made a number of copies at work, long ago. For a while he'd been obsessed with finding out more about the ballad's history. But he didn't dare ask any questions after the first murder, so he'd contacted a genealogy specialist who had advertised her services online. He pretended to be an American searching for an ancestor. In reality he just wanted the genealogist to make inquiries about matters that he couldn't risk researching himself. But when she replied with a lot of intrusive follow-up questions, he'd finally understood what his dream about the man in the sky was trying to tell him. Stop searching. It didn't matter who Jon Blund was. The history of the ballad was of no consequence. The ballad meant sleep. It had to be sung properly, as if it were a matter of life and death, as if it were all that existed, as if it had no past. Good Lord! How he longed for sleep! *To sleep, perchance to dream.* Because when the song made him fall asleep, he could escape from this mortal sphere, and the dreams that came to him would finally give him peace.

He went into Anna's room and kissed her on the forehead.

"Isn't it cold in here?" he whispered, more to himself since he didn't want to wake her when she was sleeping so soundly. They no longer slept in the same room. She kept the temperature much too low for him. She slept with the window open all winter long and refused to turn up the heat. Suddenly, he had an impish impulse. He tiptoed over to the heater and turned it up full blast. Maybe he was being childish, but it was freezing in here, damn it! He left the window open.

Then he left the house. Outside he shoveled the driveway. He was meticulous about tossing all the snow up onto the big pile that he'd made in the yard behind the garage.

After the job was done, he drove back to the house in town.

To her.

27

Siri Holm woke up alone in the small basement room. She raised her head and looked around at the mess. This was Gunnar Berg's den far from home. She touched the lump on the back of her head and thought back to the previous evening.

She had regained consciousness a few minutes after hitting her head on the table. Gunnar leaned over her, holding a glass of water. He'd already splashed some of it on her face.

"You slipped on a tube of caviar," he explained. "It split open and it was really slippery. I tried to catch you. Maybe I should have warned you about the mess. It's only at work and at home that I'm the world's neatest man. This place is my dark secret. When I'm here, I don't have time to clean up."

"What on earth are you working on here?"

"I'm building a studio," he said. "I have some friends who play folk music, and I promised to build a real studio for them so they can record their songs. I studied electronics before I switched to history. It's a long-term project. I bought an old mixing console, which I'm trying to repair."

She now realized how much she'd misjudged him. He wasn't the awful stick-in-the-mud she'd always thought he was. She knew instantly that from now on she would like him. The old Siri, the one who wasn't pregnant, would have tried to seduce him. But lately, she'd put those sorts of ideas aside.

Instead, they'd sat and talked about ballads and Felicia's genealogy search and the fact that it seemed to have a lot to do with the two cases that had shocked the city. Finally Siri had asked him about the police log. Gunnar didn't know much about it, but that was when he'd made a suggestion. It was an excellent suggestion, and she'd been even more impressed by him. He'd brought his laptop along, so they had access to all the databases they needed.

They'd sat up half the night in that gloriously messy basement room of his, the partially built music studio. They'd eaten caviar sandwiches as they searched through the library's secrets. After she had fallen asleep on a threadbare couch, he'd gone home. So when she woke up, she had the place to herself. And she knew instantly what she had to do, so she took out her phone.

Singsaker was sitting in his car, trying to convince himself that the three shots of aquavit he'd had early that morning must have worn off long ago, so he could safely drive home. Then his phone rang.

"Hi, it's Siri." To his great surprise, he was happy to hear her voice. He didn't know what it was about Siri Holm, but it was impossible to stay mad at her.

"Hi," he replied.

"I've been trying to call Felicia," she said. "Her cell has been switched off for ages. It's not like her. But right now you're the one I want to talk to."

"Okay, let's hear it." He kept his tone curt, not sure he could handle anything else at the moment.

Then she told him about the missing police log.

He thought it fit the pattern.

"He steals historical sources connected to this Jon Blund, and at the same time he pretends to be a figure from Bellman's ballad universe. But we already knew that. In fact, we're more convinced than ever that Grälmakar Löfberg is our perpetrator," Singsaker said. He had an urge to tell Siri that he'd just received a tip about who this man might be, and now he was sitting in the car, about to pay him a visit.

"But that's exactly why I'm calling you. I know who Grälmakar Löfberg is," she said.

Singsaker tightened his grip on the phone.

"What did you say?"

"I found him."

"Why didn't you tell us this before?"

"We just found out."

"We?"

"Yes. My colleague and I were up researching all night."

"Explain."

"I was thinking that we really only knew two things about this Löfberg guy. First, that he's obsessed with Jon Blund. And second, that he seems to have free access to borrow books."

"Actually, he prefers to steal them."

"Right. Or he neglects to return them."

There were times when Singsaker felt like his brain was functioning better than ever before. This was one of those moments.

"He's borrowed other books, is that it?"

"What I'm telling you now, I'm technically not allowed to say. The laws about confidentiality, and all that."

"Don't tell me that librarians have those rules too," he joked, hoping it didn't sound like he was flirting.

"I've gone through all the lender files. Looking for books that weren't returned, and then filtering by various topics like the eighteenth century, ballads, Bellman, Jon Blund, and music boxes. Only one person has received overdue notices and letters demanding replacement fees for books within more than one of these subject areas."

"And who's that?"

"His name is Jonas Røed. I Googled him."

She told Singsaker a little about what she'd found out about Røed, who worked at the Ringve Museum. Significant factual details, although Google could tell them little about the man's mental state.

"Siri, you're amazing," he said, forgetting everything else. She was one of a kind, quite simply the sharpest knife in the drawer. It was impossible not to love her, at least a little bit.

He didn't tell her he'd already heard the same name from Jan Høybråten, or that he knew who Røed was, or that he'd actually spoken to the man when he'd had the music box appraised early on in the investigation.

Høybråten had told the police that he'd been at Ringve right after the letter was found, before it was sent on to the Gunnerus Library, and he happened to see Røed put the letter in his pocket. Unfortunately for Høybråten and the present investigation, during the previous year Røed, for his part, had seen the professor get a little too intimate with a girl after choir practice in Ringve. That was enough to make him keep his mouth shut.

But all Singsaker said to Siri Holm was, "Thanks."

"I do my best, you know," she said. "But there's one more thing."

"What's that?"

"What's going on with Felicia?"

"Let's talk about this later, okay?" he said, wondering what he would say if he tried to tell the truth.

28

Singsaker then called the Ringve Museum and was told that Jonas Røed had been on sick leave ever since Singsaker had gone out there, just after the murder. He asked for the man's address, which turned out to be in Heimdal. He wasn't pleased to hear where Røed lived, because the police had been working the assumption that the perpetrator lived somewhere near the murder scene. Yet Singsaker still had little doubt that Røed was their man. In addition to the reports from Høybråten and Siri Holm, there was the fact that they knew they were looking for a killer who had a good knowledge of music and music boxes. Singsaker sat in his car for a few minutes, pondering his conversation with Røed at Ringve. He played me, Singsaker thought. If Røed was the murderer, he might be insane, but he could probably also be extremely calculating and seem rational.

He punched in Brattberg's number and relayed his conversation with Siri and about the museum in Ringve.

"Does this Jonas Røed have gray or possibly red hair?" asked Brattberg.

"Red. Why?"

"Grongstad is here in the office with me. He says that the lab has analyzed the strand of hair found on the music box. It was in the process of turning gray, but there was enough pigment left that they could determine the original hair color. It was red. So that's a match with Røed. It may have been a single strand of gray in an otherwise-red head of hair, just as Grongstad mentioned. Go out to Heimdal right away. But you need to take someone with you," she told him.

"I'm down here in the garage," he said.

"Then I'll send Gran down," she said. "And see to it that you have a patrol car meet you out there. We don't want to take any chances. If Røed is our guy, we know what he's capable of."

Singsaker agreed. He ended the call and popped a lozenge in his mouth.

Then he leaned his head back and waited for Gran to join him.

Nothing looked particularly out of the ordinary about the small single-family house not far from the center of Heimdal. In fact, the property looked better maintained than many of the other yards on the street. That was probably due to the extensive shoveling that had been done to remove the snow. The driveway and the path up to the front door had both been meticulously cleared.

Singsaker followed Gran, who opened the gate. Both were in plainclothes. Gran had brought her service weapon, concealed under her down jacket. Two uniformed officers from the Heimdal police station had arrived in their own vehicle. One of them got out of the car and walked closely behind the two homicide detectives. They went up to the door and rang the bell. Singsaker studied the nameplate, which looked homemade—a weathered piece of driftwood with hand-drawn letters. It said JONAS AND ANNA. He looked at the writing and guessed that Anna must be the artist. The letters had a feminine air about them, filled with hopes and ambitions for a good home. The colors had faded, which meant the nameplate had probably been painted years ago.

No one came to the door.

Gran rang the bell again, while Singsaker considered their next move. He went back to the sidewalk, surveying the house. It wasn't very big; in fact, it was one of the smallest on the street. Yet the surrounding property was a good size, coming to an abrupt halt at the steep slope behind the house where all the snow had been piled in a huge heap. The house looked as if it could use a fresh coat of paint. He concluded that either Røed was a real neat freak or the couple had no children. There were no snowmen, push sleds, or snow-covered trampolines in the yard, nor any traces of kids having played in the snow in the areas that hadn't been shoveled. Røed was in his thirties, the age to get his first gray hairs, but also the age for having children. But at the moment, Singsaker was relieved to think that the man might not have any.

"Are you looking for Røed?" a voice someone suddenly said from behind him.

Singsaker turned around as he stuck another lozenge in his mouth. He saw a man of retirement age holding the leash of a little dog. Some sort of terrier was Singsaker's guess. He'd had an Irish soft-coated wheaten terrier early in his first marriage, a shaggy creature that they could never leave home alone because it would bark incessantly, tormenting their neighbor. Singsaker wasn't really a dog person, but he could recognize a terrier. He could also recognize a nosy neighbor when he saw one. As a detective, he had learned to set great value on the latter breed.

"Do you know the Røeds?" asked Singsaker.

"We're not friends, if that's what you mean. But I live there."

The man pointed at the house next door. It was almost twice the size of Røed's.

"It's impossible not to notice a thing or two when you live so close."

"It doesn't look like anyone's home," said Singsaker.

"We don't see much of them," said the man, casting a pensive glance at the house. "The wife is on sick leave and hasn't come outside in weeks. He leaves for town every morning."

"But I thought he was on sick leave too."

"Not as far as I know. He seems really involved in his museum job. He's not the type that's easy to get to know. But he sure can talk about music and musical instruments."

"What about his wife?"

"She's totally different. Much more social. Always willing to stop for a chat. At least she used to. But she hasn't seemed very happy the past few years."

"What do you mean by that?"

"I don't know. She stopped coming over for coffee like she used to before. And she doesn't smile anymore when we say hello. Things like that. And she started wearing sunglasses all the time," the neighbor explained.

"Do you know why she's on sick leave?"

"I've only talked to Jonas about it. I'm not really sure. He says it's her back. But what do I know? In some ways he seems perfectly harmless. A little like what we used to call a you know what, if you get my drift."

"What about his wife? Shouldn't she be at home if she's on sick leave?"

"Probably. But as I mentioned, we haven't seen her in a while. She could have moved away, for all we know."

"I see," said Singsaker, so deep in thought that he accidentally swallowed the lozenge whole.

"Has he done something illegal?" asked the elderly man all of a sudden. He stared at the police car, then shifted his gaze to Gran and the uniformed officer who were now coming toward them.

"No," said Singsaker.

"You're not here to turn off the electricity or anything like that, are you?"

"No, that's not exactly the job of the police," said Singsaker, wishing they were here for something as simple as that.

"He'll show up in the evening. But he usually gets home quite late," said the old man. Then he gently tugged on his dog's leash and continued down the street. His shoes squeaked as they pierced the hard-crusted snow that covered the sidewalk.

"No sign of life," said Gran, who was now standing next to Singsaker.

"That doesn't necessarily mean nobody's home," he said and headed back to the yard.

This time he diverged from the well-shoveled path that led to the front door. He plowed his way through the snowdrifts along the facade of the house. By the time he came to the first window, he'd sunk so deep into the snow that he had to stand on tiptoe in order to peer inside. By doing that he was able to gain the extra inch he needed to see through the window into what turned out to be the living room.

Empty and also extremely tidy.

Without much hope, Singsaker now moved on to the next window. Because of the slope of the property, at this point the foundation of the house was visible above the snow, and the window was higher up. Singsaker could see only that it was covered from the inside, possibly by a shade, and that the window was open slightly.

He stood there, rubbing the scar on his forehead from the surgery. The window was the type that swung outward. He reached up, grabbing the edge with his fingertips, and then tried to open it more. As he suspected, it had a brace that prevented it from opening any wider. With a sigh of resignation he let go and was just about to rejoin Gran. But then he caught sight of the flies.

"Shit!" he muttered. "In the middle of winter?"

A number of torpid flies had practically rolled out of the crack in the window. They made a few hopeless attempts to fly, but most of them tumbled down into the snow and lay there, looking like black snowflakes.

Singsaker bent down and picked one up by its wing. It was dead. Surprised, he flicked it away.

Again he reached up toward the window ledge and grabbed hold with both hands. Using all his strength, he managed to pull himself up so he could look inside. Only then did he see that the window was not covered with a shade, as he'd thought. It was covered with flies.

The entire inside of the window was swarming with a black layer of crawling and buzzing insects. In disbelief he pressed his face to the open crack. That was when he noticed the stench. And it was something he'd smelled before. The stink of death was one of his least favorite things about his job.

"We're going in," he said when he got back to the front door. He ordered the Heimdal police officer to get the necessary equipment from the cruiser.

The man came back with an ax.

Gran got out her gun and took up position on one side of the door. Singsaker stood on the other side while the Heimdal officer delivered two blows to the door to smash it open. Pulse quickening, Singsaker followed Gran into the house. The smell hit them as soon as they entered, the stench of a body that might have been there for days. The odor filled the whole house.

In that terrible pervasive smell, the tidy living room seemed grotesque. Now Singsaker noticed that this room was also filled with flies, buzzing languidly everywhere. He knew that the room with the partially open window was right next to this one.

They inspected the other rooms in the house first. The only thing that seemed unusual was the collection of half-empty bottles of sleeping pills in the bathroom.

After securing the rest of the house, the only room left was the one with the flies. Singsaker asked Gran to hand him her gun, a 9mm Heckler & Koch P30. Then he grabbed the door handle, opened the door, and went inside.

The air was black with flies. They swarmed at him the instant he opened the door. He was quickly covered with flies. They settled on his clothes and on his face. He wanted desperately to swat them away, but he couldn't let go of the gun, which he held out in front of him, gripping it with both hands. With each step he took into the room, the smell got worse.

Finally he found himself standing at the end of a bed, and then he saw her through the cloud of flies. She was lying on top of the duvet, fully clothed, and he caught a glimpse of the floral print of her summer dress underneath all the insects. Her face was already starting to decompose. Her hair was gathered in two thick braids that were draped over her shoulders.

Recently plaited, he thought. Someone had braided her hair after she died.

He gasped for air, but as a result, he inhaled a few of the flies. He turned on his heel and ran out, slamming the door behind him. He rushed to the kitchen and spat the flies into the sink.

Gran followed him, stopping in the doorway.

"Have you ever seen anything like that?" Singsaker asked when he noticed her.

"No," she said. "I've never seen flies like that, not in the middle of winter."

"What about the body? Did you look inside the room? She must have been there at least a week."

"At least we know now that Røed isn't here," said Gran."

"Right. So where is he?"

Singsaker turned again and spat what looked like insect wings into the sink. Then he phoned Brattberg to give her his report.

"Leave the Heimdal officers there," she said. "I'll send out Grongstad and his team."

"Didn't Grongstad study biology in college?" asked Singsaker. An idea had occurred to him.

"I think so. Why?"

"There's something I want to ask him."

Singsaker ended the call and then phoned the crime-scene tech.

"Do you know anything about flies?" he asked when Grongstad picked up.

"Not a lot. What do you want to know?"

"I thought they died in the wintertime."

"Not necessarily. Well, a lot of flies die from the cold, but plenty of them survive the winter in a semitorpid state in warm places, like cracks in a window, or the hollow of a tree."

"Do they ever pile up in huge swarms?" asked Singsaker.

"Maybe you're thinking of attic flies," Grongstad replied. "In rare instances they hibernate in large numbers. In the fall, the flies crawl into unheated rooms in cabins or houses. They'll settle in big holes in the wall or in cracks and crevices, especially in attics, hence the name. When warm weather returns, or if the space is heated in the winter, the flies emerge. When that happens, they're very lethargic and have a hard time flying. They mostly creep around. In extreme cases, they can fill up a whole room. I've even heard stories about people who have been suffocated by attic flies, but I don't know whether there's any truth to that. When the flies wake up, they seek out light and often gather around windows. Attic flies also have a tendency to show up in the same houses year after year. There's no real explanation for the phenomenon. Why do you ask?"

"I'll explain later," said Singsaker and ended the call.

He followed Mona Gran out of the house, filling her in on what Grongstad had said. On their way to the car he turned around and cast one last glance at the small house standing in all that snow, and at the carefully shoveled driveway. He turned on the radio the minute they got into the car. Right now, he needed music. He had no desire to talk. He was thinking about Felicia and how she, at least, hadn't been inside that house.

As they drove toward town, his cell rang.

It was Lars, his son who lived in Oslo. Feeling guilty, Singsaker let it go to voice mail. Then he thought about how he might become a father again. He hadn't done a very good job of it the first time around. So how was he going to handle it now?

The storage room she was now sitting in had no window and no bucket to pee in. It had nothing but two walls made of brick and two walls made of boards. The solid door was locked and wouldn't budge. It was almost pitch-black, and she could hardly see her own hands in front of her.

Maybe he hadn't tied her up this time because he knew that it would be impossible for her to escape. After he'd taken Bismarck away, he'd come in once to bring her something to drink, but she hadn't seen him since. Now and then she could hear him moving about upstairs, but for long periods he didn't seem to be in the house at all.

Once when she was sure that he was out, she'd tried screaming for help, hoping that her voice might reach through the foundation and out to the street. But she knew it was pointless. Her words bounced back to her as if they'd been pulverized against the brick wall.

What scared her most was that he no longer played the music box for her. Only now she did realize what solace it had given her, hearing that delicate melody. Each time she heard it, she felt like a veil of unreality was being spread over the whole situation. Part of her understood that it was a mistake to think that way, that she was just allowing herself to be taken in by the sick fantasies of the red-haired lunatic, and when that happened, she was feeling what he wanted her to feel. But she couldn't help it. She missed the tune. And it scared her to death that it had disappeared. What could that mean? Had he given up on her? Was he just waiting for the right time to beat her to death and slit her throat, as he'd apparently done to that other woman?

A few times, when she was positive that he wouldn't hear her, she had sung the song to herself. She'd had more than enough time to learn both the melody and the lyrics. Once, right after she'd sung the song, she had dozed off and dreamed of Bismarck.

Otherwise, she never slept.

And she imagined that the child inside her didn't either. They had landed in hell, and that was a place where no one ever slept.

PART IV

29

Trondheim, 1767

June nights in Trondheim never got as dark as the haunting thoughts that ran through Nils Bayer's mind. Aching after a long day on horseback, he dragged his enormous body the short distance from his lodgings to the hospital. On this summer night the bluish gray light seemed as heavy as it did in the middle of winter. His flask, which he'd filled in Ringve with wine simmered with sage, was already empty. Which was a shame, because the captain had assured Bayer that the drink would do wonders for his digestion, his state of mind, and his memory. He hadn't noticed any improvement in the first two, and the latter was not something he needed any help with—unfortunately.

Officer Torp had given him a detailed report. Yesterday two guards had transported the cadaver from the beach to the hospital. There the pastor of the hospital chapel had arranged for a simple coffin for the troubadour, and a sexton had prepared the body for burial. Then it had been placed in a room in the cellar. This morning the sexton had arrived to nail down the lid of the coffin, only to discover that the corpse was gone.

Nils Bayer met the pastor outside the huge wooden hospital building. The parish pastor was an educated Laplander who, in addition to being a cleric, was also an adjunct at the Seminarium Lapponicum. This was a school established to train missionaries, men who were dispatched to tame the free savages of northern Norway and turn them into devout Christians. With men like the hospital pastor in the lead, the heathens were to be drawn into the fold of the pious in the Lapps' own language. Apparently the pastor was still working on a catechism in this incomprehensible language

The parish pastor was a civilized man. He greeted Bayer, addressing him by his full name and title.

"One of the lunatics must be behind this," he said. "They live in the room above the cellar, where the coffin was placed. I can't even begin to imagine the monstrous treatment one of those demented idiots might have inflicted upon the cadaver. That poor troubadour's body may have been desecrated most atrociously. Oh, what a gruesome thought!"

The police chief looked at the pastor, whose face had paled beneath his dark hair.

"Isn't it true, Reverend, that the door to the lunatics' quarters is locked every evening from the outside with a most robust lock? A lock, I am told, that was imported from Germany and is said to be even stronger than the one used on the city gate at night."

"Yes, that's true. We use such a lock not only in the evening but also for most of the day. The town is right to protect itself from the insane."

"No doubt. But was this lock not in use last night for some reason?"

"Of course it was. No lock is used more diligently than this one. Of that I can assure you."

"And there was no sign that this lock on the door to the lunatics' quarters had been broken during the course of the night?"

"No, none at all."

"And the windows to this so-called loony bin are secured with bars?"

"The room has no windows. Only a slot in the wall up near the ceiling to let in a little light. But there are bars on both the inside and outside of the slot."

"I see. Could you then explain to me, Reverend, how one of these lunatics could have exited his quarters, gone down to the cellar, and stolen the body? And if he did manage to do this, where would he have taken it?"

"As you no doubt know, Chief, we have our own guard here."

"Yes, I know that. Mikkel Hanssen," said Bayer.

He knew this particular guard better by the name "Falling Down Mikkel." The man had a low tolerance for liquor, which made him unsteady on his feet after only a few glasses. This didn't mean he was any less keen on drinking than any other Trondheimer. Bayer enjoyed having a drink with him at the tavern, and until the man lost his footing and had to stagger home at an early hour, Falling Down Mikkel was always good company. This weakness of his had the advantage that he never got drunk enough to end up in a brawl, and Bayer had never had to arrest him. And in his opinion, that alone was a good enough testament to the man's character.

"I wouldn't want you to think we don't trust him completely. But what if he had a slight lapse in judgment? Even the most hard-hearted of us can occasionally feel pity for the lunatics and forget about the forces that underlie their insanity," said the parish pastor somberly.

"So your theory is as follows, Reverend," said Bayer, trying not to laugh. "Mikkel, the guard, allowed one or more of the lunatics out in the night so that they could steal the cadaver in the cellar and possibly take it with them back to their quarters or to some other dark cranny in our city. And there they did unspeakable things. And then?"

"I grant you that it may seem unlikely. But the idea that anyone in their right mind would make off with a dead body seems even less credible. Don't you agree?"

"I assume that no one has gone in to count the lunatics?"

"What do you mean?"

"If they're all in their quarters, then we can set your theory aside, Reverend, and focus on other possibilities."

"We wanted to wait to open the door to the lunatics' quarters until you were present in person, so we haven't counted them, no. But what if we're right? What if the body is in there? The mere sight of it would make me wish I were blind. The very thought! What a gruesome notion!"

"Where is Mikkel?" asked Bayer drily. "We need the key."

"I thought it best to take charge of the key myself until you arrived."

The parish pastor took out a big iron key from a pocket in his robes. "Kindly follow me," he said, now sounding calmer and with more of a Laplander's accent to his words.

Bayer walked behind the pastor, wondering if the man truly believed his own strange theories. Somewhere he'd heard that the Lapps believed people could leave their bodies to set off on a spiritual journey. Maybe this was what the pastor feared that the lunatics had done: moving in spirit form down to the cellar to make off with the corpse. That might be why the pastor came up with the implausible story about Falling Down Mikkel, in order to cover up his own beliefs. Bayer was glad he wasn't plagued by the delusions of religion. He had no patience for either the heathens or the Christians. For Bayer, the world was what he could see, and nothing more.

Inside the hospital, the pastor lit a lantern and handed it to Bayer along with the key. Then he pointed at the door, keeping a good distance away as the police chief stepped forward.

"How many are there?" Bayer asked before putting the key in the lock.

"Seven. There are seven lunatics," said the parish pastor, intoning his words so that they sounded almost biblical.

Bayer turned the key. The lock opened with a gurgle that sounded almost the same as when a man took the first swig from a bottle of imported aquavit. Falling Down Mikkel was apparently very meticulous about keeping his locks well oiled.

Then Bayer opened the door and peered into the darkness. He raised the lantern, holding it up in front of him, and saw the light reflected in the eyes of the insane. They were lying on bunks along the walls. One was sitting in the corner muttering to himself. He abruptly lifted his head to look at the lantern Bayer held, as if it might offer him salvation. Disappointed, he again lowered his gaze to the filthy plank floor, having seen Bayer's stout form, which bore no resemblance to that of an angel.

Here they sit, thought Bayer. Their only crime is believing in a world other than the one they're living in. He counted them. There were seven lunatics. They were all there. The room stank of sweat, rotting food, urine, and excrement, but nothing that smelled like a corpse. Bayer shut the door and once again locked away their lunacy.

"And you didn't notice anything out of the ordinary, Reverend, around the time the body disappeared?"

They were now outside again, standing between the main hospital building and the church. Both men faced the church, a beautiful octagonal building that the Dutchman Johan Christoffer Hempel had designed more than half a century earlier. Bayer had finally convinced the pastor to consider other possible suspects than the lunatics.

"Have any strangers visited lately?"

"No. At least no one who might have done something like this." The parish pastor gave him a determined look.

"Does that mean you have had strangers here?"

"You might say that. But I can assure you that this wasn't a plunderer of corpses by any means. There was a most distinguished gentleman here this morning. He said that he'd heard our hospital extolled highly. He praised our hospital and said he wished to make a generous donation. When he asked to be shown around, I saw no reason to refuse him. Truth be told, there was something I needed to tend to in the sacristy, so I allowed him to move about freely. He left very abruptly, but I assume he will return soon, and his donation will be much appreciated."

"And this visit was before the sexton went to the cellar to seal the lid of the coffin?"

"Yes, it must have been, because it was the sexton's shouts that interrupted me at my work inside the church. The poor man was greatly distressed when he found the body missing, and he ran shouting and screaming through the church."

"I can understand that. But tell me one thing: This distinguished gentleman, this generous supporter of the physician's art, did he happen to speak Swedish?"

"Now that you mention it, he did speak Swedish."

Nils Bayer bowed and thanked the pastor for his time. Then he hurried as fast as his stout body would carry him back to the police station. There he got out a pistol that he'd acquired when he was working in Copenhagen, although he'd never fired it. He loaded it and stuck it in a valise, along with a number of other essentials.

Then he went over to the stable, where he saddled his horse and tied the valise to the saddle. Before he left town, he rode over to the tavern where he'd tried to run into this Swedish gentleman. He was in luck and caught the innkeepers before they went to bed after a long summer night with many guests. There his suspicions were confirmed. The Swede had stopped by the tavern at dawn and in great haste had packed up his belongings. Then he bade the innkeepers farewell and rode off. The woman of the house noted that his horse was uncommonly handsome. Of more interest to Bayer was that he was planning to ride back to his homeland by way of the old road, the one used by pilgrims during Catholic times. He'd mentioned something to the innkeepers about a meeting at the border in two days' time, and that was why he had to depart so suddenly.

Nils Bayer cursed as he rode out of town. The Swede had a whole day's head start. His only consolation was that the other man was heavily laden, which would prevent him from maintaining any great speed. Besides, he'd have to stop occasionally and take detours so other travelers wouldn't see the cadaver on his horse. Still, Bayer would be forced to ride all night to have any chance of catching up with the man.

Of course, the story of a meeting at the border might be nothing but a lie, and the Swede could have taken any number of different routes back to his homeland. But it somehow fit with the picture that had begun to take shape in Bayer's mind. Besides, he had no other choice but to gamble everything on the toss of this particular coin.

Early the next morning he arrived at the river in Stjørdalen. From there he followed the trail on the north side of the valley, heading toward Sweden. He was more exhausted and achy than the horse he was riding, and he couldn't remember the last time he'd gone for so long with only water to drink. But he was determined not to give up or to allow his steed to rest until he had searched the whole of Stjørdalen, all the way up to the copper mines at Meråker.

He almost made it through the entire day without resting, and he was close to fainting when he reached a good-sized farm just before Meråker. He decided to stop and ask for a small glass of beer.

He was feeling both resigned and thirsty. He was near the border, and he feared that the Swede had slipped away with the corpse.

Perhaps he should ask for more than just a small glass. Bayer wished he could drown his sorrows, but he knew they were much too good swimmers for that.

"Beer is in short supply up here in the valley at this time of year," said the farmer. "You should come back in the fall, and we'll show you that our beer is just as good as any you can get in town. But if you're thirsty, we have something else to offer a traveler."

"And what might that be?" asked Bayer, hope in his voice.

The farmer went into the house and soon returned with two hefty glasses.

"Genuine Swedish herb aquavit," he said with a smile and handed one glass to Bayer. "We went to the market this past spring, and we've been saving this for our most distinguished visitors."

Bayer knew that up here in the valley his elegant Dano-Norwegian speech was enough to make him an honored guest in anyone's home. Especially when they heard that he had nothing to do with the mining operations. No one here knew about his meager circumstances back in town, and they paid no attention to the stains or mended patches on his vest. Here he was an educated man, a man of stature.

He thanked the farmer politely for the aquavit. He had an urge to down it in one gulp, but he restrained himself. The farmer expected Bayer to show a certain refinement in return for the hospitality, and he intended to comply, at least with the first glass.

They drank a toast and then took a polite swig of the liquor. It warmed Bayer's whole stomach, seeming to spread all the way out to his skin.

"Those Swedes indeed know how to grow herbs," he commented.

The farmer laughed heartily.

"You haven't by chance had any other visitors during the past day, have you?" asked Bayer feigning indifference.

"No. Weeks can go by in between visits from townsfolk," said the farmer. "And travelers to and from the mines never stop here."

"I understand," said Bayer. Then he offered another toast, and when he took another swig, which was bigger and less controlled than the first, he gave up all hope.

Four glasses later the farmer's hospitality had reached its limit, and Bayer had no more jovial anecdotes to tell. Besides, the bottle of strong Swedish aquavit was now empty, and the police chief had no intention of staying the night on the farm. So he offered his thanks and led Bucephalus out to the courtyard and into the woods on the other side.

After walking alongside his horse for a short distance, he attempted, with much huffing and puffing, to climb into the saddle. It was then that he noticed how strong the Swedes brewed their liquor. It took him several attempts to mount the horse. Only on the fourth try did he manage to fling his leg over the saddle, but no sooner was he seated than he suffered a violent fit of dizziness, which could just as well have been the result of a lack of solid food as a surfeit of drink. Suddenly, he slid off the saddle on the side of the path where the land sloped down to the river. He fell to the ground and began tumbling swiftly down through the forest until he struck a tree trunk and lay still, unconscious.

How long he lay there in that passed-out state, he didn't know. But when he came to, the twilight of the summer night had crept in. He could tell that he'd pissed his trousers and his face was covered with his own vomit. He was in miserable condition, and his only wish was that the night would swallow him whole. If it had been winter, he might have frozen to death there. He wondered whether that might have been an agreeable way to die and he cursed the summer. Doctor Fredrici had once told him that people who had nearly frozen to death said that, toward the end, the most pleasant sensation of warmth filled their body as the frost seemed to lose its grip. Yes, Bayer thought. That's how I'd like to die.

That was when he noticed the campfire. At first he thought it was hovering in the air. Then he realized that he was lying on his back with his head pointing down the slope, and that what he saw was down by the riverbank. He got to his feet as quickly as he could, given that he was starving, hungover, and exhausted. Then he once again studied the landscape. Someone was sitting down there next to the fire.

Filled with excitement, he made his way back up to the path where Bucephalus, to his great relief, was calmly grazing. He tied the reins to a tree, took his gun from the valise, and set off down the slope again.

He approached the camp as slowly and soundlessly as he could. The last part of the way he crouched down to creep through the vegetation.

Then he stopped.

A man was sitting near the fire, his back turned to Bayer. It looked like he was cleaning some fish he'd caught, preparing them for his meal. A short distance away stood the man's horse. And a little bit farther away was something lying on the stones. It was a big bundle wrapped in sailcloth. That had to be the body. Bayer had found his troubadour. With his right hand he pulled his gun from the pocket of his vest, taking a firm grip on it.

Then he slowly crept closer. As he was about to take his first step onto the riverbank, the sole of his shoe landed on a fallen branch, which made a crack loud enough to be heard over the rushing water. The man with the fish whirled around. But by now the police chief was near enough, and since he had a gun, he had the advantage.

"Kindly toss your knife into the river, my good man," he said with a wry smile.

The man had been using a knife to clean the fish. He had no other weapon within reach. The man studied the gun Bayer was holding.

Perhaps he was evaluating its quality and the likelihood that it might fail to fire if the gunpowder were damp, or the possibility that the gun might backfire and send the lead right into the pudgy face of its owner. Perhaps he also took note of Bayer's disheveled state and how his body was far from athletic. Most likely he was assessing whether Bayer's reflexes might be so sluggish that he could leap forward and knock the gun from his hand before Bayer even managed to pull the trigger. But after staring at him for several moments, the man apparently decided that in spite of everything the odds were in Bayer's favor, so he flung the fishing knife in a high arc into the rushing current.

"What can I help you with, sir," he asked drily. And Bayer knew at once that this was an adversary after his own heart.

Bayer looked at the Swede. His jacket was made from the finest velvet, and the collar of his silk shirt was cut according to the latest fashion. Even though his clothing had acquired a few stains after days of traveling, his appearance was still impressive.

"You serve a wealthy gentleman, as I understand it."

"Forgive me," said the Swede, clearly insulted. "But what do you know about me?"

"I know that a Swede who travels all the way to Trondheim to fetch a dead body would not do so just for his own amusement," replied Bayer. "It must be profitable for you in some way. For honor or money. Presumably both. And that also means that someone has sent you and is willing to pay for your services."

"So who are you?" asked the Swede, and now it was evident that he'd gained a certain respect for Bayer.

"Forgive me for not introducing myself. How tactless of me. My name is Nils Bayer, and I am Trondheim's police chief."

"Police chief. That means your duties include keeping order in town and checking the cargo that ships have on board upon arrival. Important work in the service of your king. But if I might inquire, what are you doing out here in the wilderness?"

"Allow me to be blunt with you. You seem like the sort of man who appreciates blunt speech."

The Swede nodded.

"I'm here to ensure that yon deceased troubadour is allowed to rest in peace."

"You certainly are blunt. And how to you plan to ensure that?"

"By obtaining an explanation for his mysterious death. You see, there is one thing that doesn't make sense in this whole strange story. *J'ai une mouche dans le casque,* you might say. I'm almost certain that you came to Norway for the purpose of killing the victim. His present status might bear witness to the fact that you've succeeded in your mission. But then I have to ask myself: If you really were the one who took his life and you need to prove his death by taking his body back to your employer—an employer who is so powerful that he does not dare cross the border for fear of the political implications this would have between our two countries—why didn't you take the body right away? Why go to the trouble of letting someone find him on the shore, only to steal his body back from the hospital? It seems rather . . . how shall I put it? Absurd."

The Swede studied Bayer in silence. Perhaps he was again considering how he might disarm the police chief. Bayer thought it was probably best to give the man time to think.

"So I've reached the conclusion that you did not kill him."

"Then why have you followed me here?"

"First," said Bayer, "because the king of Denmark and Norway, like your king, does not look kindly on grave robbers. On behalf of our highborn ruler I could have put a bullet in your forehead by now, and that would have been the end of it. But I had a different proposal to make. The primary reason for my presence here is that I would like to solve this case. I don't know what motivates you. But for my part, it is continuity, rationality, seeing that everything falls into place. That is what gives me peace in life."

"Thank you for this insight into your noble mind," said the Swede acidly.

"Let me remind you, sir, that I am the one holding a weapon and that you, as a grave robber in a foreign land, are not in a particularly favorable position. Therefore, I ask that you listen to my proposal. There are two parts."

"Let me hear it," said the Swede.

"First, I would like you to introduce yourself and tell me what you know about the troubadour's death. Second, if you are able to confirm the assumptions that I have already made, then you, sir, will help me bury the man here in Norwegian soil. You will not be allowed to mollify your employer by reporting deeds that you did not personally carry out."

The Swede stared longer at the gun than at Bayer. Then he sighed and said, "My name is Teodor Granqvist. I am Count Erik Gyllenhjärta's most trusted retainer. And to explain simply: I know this troubadour as Christian Wingmark, and he insulted my master in the most disgraceful manner. The count has every right to seek the revenge he desires. And as you have so shrewdly pointed out, he is waiting for me at the border."

"I see," said Bayer. "But you arrived too late to exact this revenge, didn't you? Our lutist had other talents besides his musical skills. He also knew how to acquire powerful enemies. Am I correct?"

"That appears to be so."

"You tracked him down to Trondheim. I can tell you are a man of great resources. Kindly tell me that you also know about the circumstances surrounding his death."

The Swede smiled.

"You're not entirely without resources yourself. Most importantly, perhaps, is that you don't give up very easily."

Then he began to recount what he knew, and Bayer listened with satisfaction. The tale he told was the missing piece in a puzzle that Bayer had tried so many times to complete in his mind. When the

Swede was done, Bayer was so elated that he almost forgot to keep his gun raised. But he quickly pulled himself together. Now all that remained was the part of the agreement with which Granqvist would not comply unless the threat of sudden death stood just a few feet away; his life was in the hands of a drunken and erratic police chief from Trondheim.

"I see that you have an excellent shovel tied onto your saddle," Bayer said, noticing how husky his voice sounded. "And I see a bottle there." He pointed to the liquor bottle lying next to the fish that had been prepared for the campfire. "You take the shovel, and I'll take the bottle," he said.

Granqvist got up and tossed the bottle to Bayer, who reacted faster than the Swede had anticipated, catching it in his left hand without losing his grip on the gun.

"The shovel," he said sternly. "And no more tricks, please."

The Swede did as he was told, and together the two men walked a short distance into the woods.

"Dig!" said Bayer. He sat down on a rock and pulled the cork from the bottle with his teeth.

Teodor Granqvist was a big man, and a powerfully built one. What Bayer possessed in sheer size, Granqvist had in muscle strength. He dug until he hit rock, and they both realized that the troubadour would have to be content with a shallow grave, no more than three feet deep.

"That will have to do," said Bayer. "Let's fetch the fiddler. I know he is longing to rest."

Granqvist led the way back to the riverbank. There he singlehandedly lifted the cadaver onto the horse and then led the magnificent steed over to the grave. Bayer, holding his gun, kept a good distance from him, not too far away and not too near. He watched as Granqvist set the bundle in the grave.

It turned out that the grave was not only shallow but also too short, and the corpse lay there with its legs sticking up in the air.

Granqvist grabbed the shovel and jumped down into the grave. "This won't take long," he said as he began hacking at the ground with the shovel to make the grave longer.

Bayer went over to inspect the work. That was when Granqvist saw his chance to attack. He filled the shovel with clay and then with lightning speed tossed the dirt up at Bayer, who was leaning over the grave.

The damp clay struck him like a heavy rag right in the face, filling his mouth and nostrils with soil. He took a step back, gasping for air as he clung to the gun. The Swede leaped out of the grave and lunged at the police chief. Bayer held the gun behind his back, making it difficult for the Swede to grab. Instead the Swede grabbed his left arm and yanked Bayer down into the grave on top of him. Both men landed on the corpse. But the Swede had failed to take Bayer's weight into consideration and when the police chief fell on him, even from such a modest height, it was enough to knock the wind out of a strong fellow like Teodor Granqvist.

Bayer felt the Swede go limp beneath him. For a moment Bayer lay still. Feeling bruised, he managed to pull himself up onto his knees.

The Swede was winded but not unconscious as he lay there on top of the corpse. Desperately, Bayer tried to crawl out of the grave, but his adversary had mustered his strength and once again reached out for him. This time the Swede got hold of the gun. He grabbed Bayer's wrist and pulled the pistol toward him. But Bayer was still holding on tight, and as the barrel swung toward the Swede's chest, the police chief pulled the trigger. It was not a deliberate action; it happened in the heat of battle, a reflexive movement. The gunpowder reacted to the striking of the hammer, exploding into the barrel and sending the bullet into Teodor Granqvist.

It killed the man instantly.

He fell back, and Bayer felt as though it happened so slowly that he seemed to hover in midair. Granqvist struck the sailcloth that was wrapped around the dead troubadour and then rolled down to rest beside him in the grave. Bayer was kneeling beside the legs of the two dead men, and there still wasn't enough room for the men's legs; they were stuck up past his shoulders.

Even though Bayer hadn't eaten a thing since the previous night, there was still something in his stomach that demanded to get out.

Then he sat there shivering for God only knew how long.

Finally, he crawled on all fours out of the grave and crept over to the liquor bottle that was lying near the rock where he'd been sitting only a short time ago. He grabbed it and emptied it in one gulp. Then he tossed the bottle aside with his left hand, which made him realize that he was still holding the gun in his right. Without thinking, he stuck the barrel into his mouth. The steel was still warm from being fired. He closed his lips around the metal.

And pulled the trigger.

Of course he hadn't reloaded the gun. This was merely an act. Something to cleanse himself.

Then he stood up and took off all his clothes. Slowly, like a sleepwalker, he went down to the river. He waded in until the water was up to his waist. Then he lowered his big, miserable body into the river. He ducked his head under, and for a moment he thought about staying there. But something inside of him wanted to keep on breathing. At last, he raised his head out of the water, gasping for air.

After he had given himself a good washing, he waded back to shore and put his filthy, foul-smelling clothes back on.

Then he did what he had to do. He made room for the men's legs and even said a few words before he shoveled earth over them. But from the lips of a heathen such as himself, his words were without solace. He buried the gun and Granqvist's possessions with the bodies. Then he cut the Swede's horse loose. He went back to Bucephalus and climbed into the saddle.

On his way back to town he gave a wide berth to the hospitable farmer's property. During the whole ride back he felt like an empty sack swaying on the back of the horse.

Nils Bayer had found the explanation he was seeking, but it had come at a price, and he never would have agreed to it if he'd known beforehand.

30

Singsaker *didn't often try* to hurry Dr. Kittelsen, the grouchy ME in the Department of Pathology and Medical Genetics at St. Olav Hospital. He knew it wouldn't do any good; it was even counter-productive. Kittelsen was a stubborn old man. But in this case, they were working against the clock, and Kittelsen had been helpful in similar cases in the past. Even though he worked only with the dead, he was capable of a certain empathy when a life was in the balance.

"We've had her on the table for less than three hours. This is science, not magic. If you want a neat solution, I suggest you take up reading crime novels," said Kittelsen in reply to the question he'd just been asked. But Singsaker wasn't satisfied with this answer, so he rephrased his question.

"So you haven't found the cause of death?"

"No," said the doctor, sounding resigned. "This individual has been dead a long time. We may not find a single cause of death; all we can do is rule out a number of possibilities."

"And can you do that at this stage?"

"You don't give up, do you, Singsaker?" said Kittelsen with a sigh. The detective realized that was a backhanded sort of compliment.

Then the doctor went on: "The larynx has not been removed, if that's what you're concerned about. In fact, there is little sign of violence. No skin punctures or any visible injuries to the skeleton or internal organs. The skull is intact, with no injuries. No external bleeding. And so far, no signs of internal bleeding either."

"So you're saying that she wasn't murdered?" Singsaker was putting words in the doctor's mouth, but he'd been in this business long enough to know that wasn't at all what Kittelsen had said.

"No, it's much too early to reach that conclusion. But she wasn't killed in any immediately observable way. And a preliminary examination of her airway indicates that she wasn't strangled. But given the state of the body, these are highly dubious deductions. We don't have a toxicology report yet, of course, but samples have been sent to the lab. She may have been poisoned. But I would guess that she died of natural causes. Most likely cardiac arrest."

"Cardiac arrest?"

"Norway's most common cause of death, Singsaker."

"Well, I'll be damned! At her age?"

"At her age, it's not as common, of course. But it's not unthinkable if she had high blood pressure, diabetes, or a heart defect."

"Can you estimate how long she may have been dead?"

"Hard to say. Maybe a week. It depends on the temperature in the room where she was found."

"We think that it was cold in there for a long time but that someone turned up the heat shortly before we found her," said Singsaker, thinking of Grongstad's theory that the flies had been awakened by a sudden change in temperature.

"In that case, she may have been dead for more than a week. But no more than two."

"I see," said Singsaker, concluding that she had most likely died about the time of the first murder. If that was true, if she was still alive when Røed captured his first victim, the question was how much she might have known.

"One more thing," he said. "Were there any maggots inside the body? I've heard that they can be used to determine the time of death quite accurately."

"Have you looked out the window lately, Singsaker?" said Kittelsen drily. "It's winter. Flies don't make larvae at this time of year."

"I know, I know. It's just that the body was swarming with thousands of flies when we found her."

"They must have been attic flies. The body is in an advanced stage of decomposition, but not because of any fly larvae."

Singsaker thanked Kittelsen for his help and put down the phone. Then he went over to Brattberg's office. Jensen was already there.

"So, what did Dr. Sunshine have to say?" asked Jensen as Singsaker sat down in the chair next to him.

"He was actually pretty helpful this time. But he expressed his usual reservations, of course. What was interesting was that he seemed fairly sure that Anna Røed died of natural causes."

"What does that tell us?" asked Brattberg.

"I don't know," said Singsaker. "She was alive during the first kidnapping. That much is certain. But he might have killed the first victim about the same time that she died. So it's possible that Anna Røed's death was the catalyst that pushed him to murder."

"But why would he leave his wife lying dead in bed for days, possibly weeks?" asked Brattberg.

"Maybe he loved her," said Jensen. "Maybe he didn't want to accept the fact that she was dead."

"Love, Jensen?" said Brattberg with a wry smile. "Røed doesn't exactly seem like the 'husband of the year.' But maybe they had a codependent relationship. Maybe she took care of him or played an important role in the facade that he presented to the world. Burying her would have drawn too much attention to him."

"It's even scarier if we consider the possibility that he didn't know she was dead," said Singsaker.

"An indication that he's a psychopath?" said Brattberg. "But let's disregard Røed's state of mind for the moment. Isn't it strange that his wife could lie there for close to a week, maybe even longer, and yet nobody missed her?"

"Yes, it's strange," said Jensen. "But we talked to her doctor, and he told us that she'd taken a two-week sick leave. She works as a home health-care nurse, and she told her colleagues that she was going to take another week off after her sick leave ended. They weren't expecting her back on the job until after the weekend. Maybe some of her friends or family realized they hadn't heard from her in a while, but it's also not uncommon for a week or two to pass without contact, even between good friends. Her doctor also told us that Anna Røed suffered from high blood pressure, which supports Kittelsen's preliminary theory. It must not have been easy for her to live with her husband. So she may have died from a heart attack or stroke, even though she wasn't very old, and even though such things are unusual in a woman her age."

"All right," said Brattberg, looking from Jensen to Singsaker and then back to Jensen. "So maybe he didn't kill his wife. But there's no question he's a killer. What have we got so far in terms of the motive for the kidnappings and murder?"

"Maybe he's the one who wants to sleep," said Jensen. "Maybe he kidnaps girls who can sing so they'll sing that lullaby to him. But when it doesn't work, he takes out their larynx. Maybe it's a form of punishment. Silje Rolfsen was his first attempt, a random victim. He may have acted on impulse. Maybe he heard her singing out on the street."

"You could be right," said Singsaker. "It seems like more planning was involved when he kidnapped Julie Edvardsen. He knew her slightly. He'd probably met her at Ringve, when she went out there to practice. Fredrik Alm said that someone kept staring at her during the practice session. I thought it was Høybråten, but it could just as well have been Røed. So he had her in his sights; he saw her as his perfect songbird."

"It sounds plausible, in a twisted sort of way. But how's it going with the Gmail lead from Felicia's Web site?" asked Jensen.

"We're working on the legalities," said Brattberg. "Google is reluctant to give out personal information. But hopefully we'll find out sometime today who set up that e-mail account. Most likely the sign-up info will be bogus, but if we get the IP address, we can trace it back to the list of subscribers from the service providers. They're probably going to balk at that too. These things take time. But I have no doubt that eventually it will lead us to Røed. But we need to focus on what we can do right now. He's on the loose, and we're hoping that Julie Edvardsen is still alive. I've just talked to Grongstad, and he says there's no indication that either of the victims was ever inside the house in Heimdal. There's no trace of Julie or her dog in any of the material that he's inspected from there and the place isn't really suitable for holding someone prisoner. The garage isn't locked. Only two bedrooms, one of which Røed was using. A bathroom, a kitchen, and an extremely tidy living room. No basement or attic. If we take this information, plus the fact that we found Silje Rolfsen in a different part of town, and that Røed's wife was alive during the first kidnapping, it must mean that he has another place."

"According to the neighbor, he leaves for town every day and is gone for long periods of time. The neighbor thought he was at work, but we know that Røed was on sick leave," said Singsaker.

"That gives us something," said Brattberg.

"I've assigned a team to go through the public records, but so far they haven't found anything indicating that he owns any other property," said Jensen.

"What about his family? His parents? Any siblings?" asked Singsaker.

"His father died in the eighties. Suicide. It was a nasty case. He was quite a famous pianist in his day. Weren't you and I the officers on duty at the time, Singsaker?"

"Oh, right. I remember now. A shotgun in his mouth. No suspicions of any foul play back then. His wife and son were home when he did it. I remember the boy. Wasn't he the one who had only three fingers on one hand?"

"And you complain about having a bad memory?" remarked Jensen.

"That means if Jonas Røed hasn't miraculously grown new fingers, his hand is still missing two of them."

Singsaker closed his eyes and tried to concentrate. All of a sudden he again saw quite clearly something that he'd glimpsed during his meeting with Røed out at Ringve. It was when Røed handed the music box back to him. Singsaker's eyes had noticed something that his brain hadn't properly registered. Something about the fingers of his hand. Prosthetics, he thought now. And then he understood what he'd seen in Røed's eyes: fear that he'd be caught out.

"Where did he live as a child?" Singsaker asked.

"Somewhere in the neighborhood," said Jensen.

But that was over thirty years ago and they couldn't quite remember.

"Well, his mother died years ago, so if he kept the house as part of his inheritance, the property would be registered in his name," said Jensen after some discussion back and forth.

"I still think we ought to look into this more closely," said Brattberg. "We need to find the deed to the house. If he sold it under his mother's name or his own sometime during the past few years, it should be relatively easy to find out the address."

Singsaker nodded, but at the same time he figured that if Røed had sold the house, he couldn't be using it as a hiding place. He stretched as he sat there next to Jensen. Suddenly he had one of the attacks of vertigo that he'd become accustomed to after the surgery. The doctor had said that he'd just have to learn to live with them. He was lost in his own thoughts as Brattberg began going over what they would say to the press.

Reporters had already gathered outside the cordoned-off area on C. J. Hambros Vei, and Vlado Taneski had written a story for the newpaper's Web site about the discovery of the body in Heimdal. The article had then been quoted and reprinted in most of the media sites on the Net. Brattberg was making arrangements for a press conference.

But Singsaker couldn't concentrate any of this. He was thinking about the little boy with two missing fingers—the boy he'd encountered at the very beginning of his career on the police force. He pictured the father's body, lying in bed, the back of his head blown away. He tried to recall exactly what the bed had looked like.

He got up as soon as Brattberg was finished, and almost lost his balance as he stood. He was dizzy, and his head was aching. As a man who had survived a brain tumor, he hated that feeling. Brattberg gave him a searching glance as he staggered out of her office. She may have noticed the beads of sweat on his forehead, because she looked worried. But the last thing he heard from her office was her voice as she picked up the phone and asked to be connected to police attorney Knutsen.

Singsaker ran downstairs and out to his car.

I can't keep this up much longer, he thought as he got in. When this case is over, I'm going to take a long break, get the doctor to put me on sick leave. Maybe I'll take a trip to the States. He noticed how this thought prompted a stabbing sensation in his ribs.

"Come on," he said out loud. "Try to remember." His head felt like it was going to explode. He could hear Dr. Nordraak saying, "Your problem is that you've got too many thoughts in your head all at once." Right now his mind was abuzz. He remembered the small conference room at Rosenborg School and the fact that he'd jotted down in his notebook Fredrik Alm's description of a house. Then he thought about the man with the missing fingers and something that the mother of Jonas Røed had told the police way back then about an accident in the garage. Images from the scene flitted past. Then he caught a glimpse of himself stumbling on the sidewalk on Bernhard Getz' Gate right near the crime scene. And at that instant, he realized that he'd stumbled over something. His foot had caught on something that was stuck to the gatepost. Wasn't that right? And suddenly he knew where Jonas Røed had lived as a child, and also where he most likely had been staying lately. Again he thought about what he'd written in his notebook in that small conference room at the school.

We could have caught that bastard two days ago if I'd followed up on the tip from Fredrik Alm, Singsaker thought as he turned the key in the ignition.

Jonas Røed was sitting in the kitchen cutting three thick slices of bread, but instead of eating them, he switched on his PC. He wanted to check the news, so he started with the *Adresseavisen* Web site. He didn't get past the first story:

"Macabre discovery of a body in Heimdal."

He laughed and lit a cigarette.

Isn't it always macabre when a dead body is found? Who the hell is this reporter? he asked himself. Then he studied the photo accompanying the article. In the picture he saw a house that he recognized.

"Good," he said. "Good. Good. That's very good."

Now the fly inside him was wide-awake. It was buzzing around wildly. It did that sometimes. Then it started hammering against one spot in his skull. Hammering and hammering, feverishly pressing against something. He got up and let it guide him across the kitchen floor. Right now all he could do was follow. It was carrying him along. His head was leading his body, until he ended up in the basement. Right outside her door.

Then he began to calm down. His breathing slowed. The buzzing inside his head subsided. He need to think clearly now. He stared at the door, and gradually he realized what he had to do. And it was a damned good idea. But he needed to be careful.

When he reached to open the door, he noticed that he had an erection and that he was still holding the bread knife in his hand.

When he opened the basement door at the top of the stairs, she was standing up. But she fell to her knees when she heard him coming down. And she stayed in that position, her face turned toward the door.

He moved quickly, but there was something off-kilter about his gait, something lurching, as if he wasn't in full control. For a long time he fumbled with the key, not managing to get it into the lock. Several times he dropped the key on the floor before he finally could insert it properly. When he turned the key she hoped that it had gotten stuck, because it took him a long time. But at last, he opened the door.

The first thing she saw was the knife dangling from his fingers as light from the bare bulb in the hall filled the storage room. He held it loosely, as if he hardly knew it was there. Then he slowly came toward her and crouched down. She felt his breath on her earlobe and caught a glimpse of his red hair out of the corner of her eye. She didn't want to turn her head.

Then he set the blade of the knife against her throat. She gasped, feeling how the cold blade almost pierced her skin as her throat expanded to let air pass through.

Breathe calmly, she told herself. Breathe calmly. But her chest refused to obey.

"I need to sleep now," he said.

He removed the knife and held it in front of her eyes. Only now did she dare to look at him. His gaze showed genuine bewilderment.

Then he laughed and tossed the knife out of the room.

"You didn't think I was going to kill you with a bread knife, did you?" he said, getting up. Then he went back out to the hall and closed the door without locking it.

He's losing his grip, she thought. He's slipping away. And that makes him more dangerous. But also more vulnerable.

She stayed where she was, wondering if she should take a chance and get up, open the door, and grab the knife that was lying right outside.

But no, he hadn't moved far enough away. Judging by what she could hear, he was over by the mattress at the end of the hall. It sounded like he was searching for something. Then the sounds stopped and he came back toward her.

When Singsaker arrived at the big brown house at the intersection of Ludvig Daaes Gate and Bernhard Getz' Gate, he noticed that the driveway had been meticulously cleared of snow.

He pulled over and parked. Then he got out and looked around.

Snow shoveling, he thought. I could have caught him on that alone. It was the same careful snow removal that they'd seen out in Heimdal and almost the exact same pile of snow behind the garage. The only difference was that a car was parked here, an old red Saab 9000. So at least he'd had that confirmed. Røed had a car, even though he wasn't sure it was in drivable condition.

Then Singsaker went over to the entrance. Tied to one of the gateposts was a frozen leather strap, almost entirely covered with snow. He took a closer look. It was a dog's leash, and whoever had taken it off the dog's collar had simply left it hanging there. That was what Singsaker had stumbled over. On that day the leash had lain under a layer of new snow. But why hadn't he looked more closely?

He got out his cell phone and called Brattberg, explaining to her what he'd found.

"Strictly speaking, we need to talk to the home owner before we can go inside. A dog's leash isn't sufficient probable cause."

"But everything fits. He's familiar with the place. It's his childhood home. Julie Edvardsen walked past here every night when she took a walk, and one evening Fredrik Alm saw her talking to someone who was shoveling snow. There's a leash tied to the gatepost, and right near here was where we found the body. He could have carried her there over his shoulder. That's why he didn't use a car. What more do we need?" asked Singsaker.

"Give me half an hour," said Brattberg. "Let me make some calls."

"Do you know what a perp like him could do in half an hour? He knows we're after him. He's desperate."

"Fifteen minutes," said Brattberg. "Don't go in alone. I'm sending backup."

Singsaker ended the call and walked toward the house. Even fifteen minutes seemed like an eternity. Maybe the killer had seen his car from the window and saw him get out. Singsaker didn't even want to think about what the man might do if he panicked. By the time he reached the front door, he'd made up his mind.

I'll just give the door a try, he thought. Reaching for the handle, he gave it a tug.

The door wasn't locked, and it swung open.

Julie was filled with a wild and irrational hope. He'll go past my door and back up the stairs, she thought. And he forgot to lock the door. She listened to his footsteps shuffling along the basement floor.

But suddenly he stopped and came back to her door. Slowly he opened it and again stepped inside.

"Come with me," he said in a flat voice.

He grabbed her by the hair and dragged her into the other storage room. There he let her go, and she sank to the floor, sobbing. At that moment she almost wished he would kill her. She didn't know if she could take any more. But then she saw the stun gun in his hand, and she realized that he planned to keep her alive a while longer.

When he spoke, there was an eerie calm in his voice.

"I need to sleep," he said. "But first we need to move."

He shifted the Taser to his left hand, closed his eyes for a second, and then aimed it at her.

That was when she heard it. Wasn't that a noise upstairs? Someone opening the door? Footsteps crossing the floor? Had someone come into the house? Or was she hallucinating? She wanted to scream. Maybe she could warn them.

But before she could do that, the shock hit her.

Chief Inspector Singsaker paused to look through the open door, thinking about what he'd found the last time he'd entered a room uninvited.

No flies here, he thought. That's something at least. Then he stepped inside and studied the entry hall. Someone had clearly fixed things up. The wardrobe, with its sliding door, and the newly painted whole walls made the place seem perfectly normal. But the living room in Heimdal had done the same thing. He sniffed at the air, drew it deep into his lungs. There was no stench of a corpse here, but he wasn't sure that the police dogs, who could smell death even weeks later, would have agreed. Then he moved farther into the house.

He quickly discovered that the remodeling hadn't made much progress. The kitchen cabinets were probably from the eighties or even older. The kitchen table was filled with clutter. Three freshly cut slices of bread had been left untouched. Next to them was an old laptop, and the monitor was on. If the computer had any screen savers, they hadn't yet appeared, which might indicate that the laptop had been in use only moments ago. He noticed that the *Adresseavisen* Web site was on the screen, displaying the article about Heimdal.

Beside the laptop was a glass containing a clear liquid. At the bottom hovered two pale membranes. Singsaker had an idea of what they might be, and he suddenly felt nauseated, almost like a young, inexperienced policeman looking at his first murder victim. There was something appalling and yet very sad about the two vocal cords, as if they wanted to tell him something about the meaningless deeds they had witnessed, and about the life that had been lost because of them. But they were no longer capable of uttering a sound.

The final things he saw on the table removed any doubt that he was right. A cell phone and a Visa card belonging to Silje Rolfsen. Singsaker quickly surveyed the rest of the room. He reluctantly had to admit to himself what he was doing. He was making sure that Felicia hadn't been here, that she had merely run away from him. Thankfully, he saw no sign of her.

He left everything where it was and went into the living room. There he found the same clutter. And the rest of the house was the same, but he found no indication that anyone was home.

Only the basement remained. He went downstairs without hearing a sound or seeing any other sign of life. When he opened the door to a storage room, he saw bloodstains on the floor. Then he opened the next door, and there he saw Julie Edvardsen. He had found her, but the girl didn't move. Was she dead?

Singsaker ran to her and frantically tried to find the pulse in her neck.

Suddenly it felt like an enormous beast had launched itself at the back of his neck. His whole body tensed into a huge knot of muscles as fifty thousand volts coursed through him.

Then he fell on top of her and lay still.

———

When he opened his eyes, Brattberg was leaning over him.

"They're gone. The man and the girl," said Singsaker. "You got here too late. Am I right?"

Brattberg nodded.

"I told you not to go in alone," she said, keeping her voice so low that the officers waiting outside the storage room couldn't hear.

Her words held no reproach. Singsaker wasn't stupid. He knew he had acted unprofessionally and that Brattberg had every reason to reprimand him. But he knew she wouldn't do that until the case was solved. Then he could expect a shower of criticism, but most likely he would not be suspended for insubordination. Besides, they both knew that no one could rebuke Singsaker better than he could himself. And no one other than Brattberg and Singsaker would ever know what they had said on the phone right before he entered the house. He was also sure about one other thing. Neither of them could have predicted the result of his actions. There was always the chance that he might have been able to rescue the girl. If things had turned out differently, his action would have been viewed as the only right thing to do.

He rubbed the back of his neck, which felt unusually soft and tender.

What he'd meant to say to Brattberg was not that his colleagues had arrived too late.

I was the one who got here too late, he thought. I could have stopped him two days ago if I'd followed up on what Fredrik Alm told me instead of going after Høybråten. Not that I could have guessed that shoveled snow would be so important to the case, but somebody should have checked out the tip. If it weren't for this miserable head of mine, Julie Edvardsen would now be safe.

31

So *they were back* to square one.

"He has nowhere else to hide," said Jensen, trying to be optimistic.

They were standing outside in the neatly shoveled driveway. It had started snowing again, and soon all of Jonas Røed's work would be in vain. Singsaker had given a brief report about his entry into the house and how he'd been assaulted by Røed, who had apparently been hiding behind the door, waiting for him. Now the police officers were considering how to proceed.

"No place to hide, and yet he's gone," said Singsaker.

"We'll find him," said Brattberg.

"But will we find the girl?"

"Let's hope so." Brattberg turned to look at the house.

"At least we've learned a few more things," Jensen interjected. "First of all, we've confirmed that he actually does own a car, an old red Saab 9000. The neighbor claimed that Røed rarely used it, but apparently he drove it into town this morning."

"I saw it. The car was parked here when I arrived," said Singsaker, and then he described what it looked like.

"Which means that he might have taken her with him, and theoretically they could be anywhere," said Brattberg. "We need to send out an APB to all police patrols in the whole district to be on the lookout for this car." She got out her cell.

"To think that he was right here all along. It's no more than fifty yards from where we found Silje Rolfsen. He's been right under our noses the whole time. He could have strolled across the street to the woods, carrying her over his shoulder, for God's sake," said Jensen. "No wonder there weren't any traces of a parked car."

While Jensen spoke, Brattberg called headquarters and swiftly issued orders.

Singsaker sighed heavily, lost in his own thoughts, as she ended the call.

"Grongstad has also found a number of interesting documents in Heimdal," she told her colleagues as she put away her phone. "One of them is an old broadsheet, apparently the original that was stolen from the Gunnerus Library. That might give us some insight into the way Røed thinks. Could you get your friend at the library to have a look at it so we can confirm that it's genuine? I've got it in the car."

Singsaker went with Brattberg, who gave him the broadsheet. Then he got into his own car. His head was pounding as if his brain, not his heart, was what pumped the blood through his body. He castigated himself. He should have known that Røed would be inside the house. He thought of the freshly sliced bread on the kitchen table, and the PC, which had been on.

But now the man had escaped. Once again they were one crucial step behind him. And the only hope they had now was that Julie Edvardsen wasn't dead. Singsaker hadn't felt a pulse, but he supposed she'd been struck by the stun gun, just as he'd been. Røed still had her, and Singsaker could only hope she was still alive.

But where was he? They'd found his two hiding places. Where would he go now? Singsaker stared blankly at the broadsheet that

Brattberg had given him. He could feel his pulse hammering in his temples. It was the pulse of a hunter. His deepest instincts told him that he should get out of the car and race through the streets on foot until he found Røed and could wrap his hands around the neck of that perverse curator from the Ringve Museum. Jonas Røed had tricked the police into thinking he was an innocent professional whose only obsession was music boxes. Røed had sent Singsaker on a wild-goose chase, hunting down Høybråten. And he had stood behind the door, waiting for Singsaker, who had assumed the house was empty. Singsaker felt like running until he tasted blood in his mouth, until his throat bled dry.

There was only one thought that calmed him down. Røed had more than enough to keep him busy with Julie. The theories that had made Singsaker believe that Felicia had somehow landed in the middle of this mess had turned out to be nothing but irrational worries. There'd been no trace of her in either of the places where Røed lived. Singsaker now had to accept that Felicia had simply left him. That was a fact. Still, it was hard for him to acknowledge that he'd turned the situation into something even more gruesome. Now he understood what else Dr. Nordraak had been trying to tell him. He was a police officer with a particularly strong character trait. He was actually able to think very clearly. As this dawned on him, he began to focus his attention on the broadsheet. I don't understand him, Singsaker thought, and I can't go running after him. Maybe that's what he wants. So I have to do what I'm good at. And then he realized that Brattberg was right: The broadsheet could be their key.

Felicia Stone opened her eyes and peered over the duvet. She looked around the apartment. It was good to be with family, she thought. She noticed that her headache was starting to subside, along with the dizziness. She'd been far away, but now she was finally home. Her head was clear, and she knew what she wanted to do.

She wondered whether she should phone Odd. Tell him where she was, what she'd been doing, and what she was thinking.

No. She wasn't ready for that. She got up unsteadily.

I wonder if there's any food in this house.

"It's a beautiful print," said Siri Holm, putting on a pair of white gloves before she picked up the broadsheet that Singsaker had brought her.

Singsaker hadn't thought of it that way, but now that she mentioned it, he could see that the broadsheet was truly one of a kind. He stood behind her and read over her shoulder. The title, "The Golden Peace," was printed in big Gothic letters and underneath were the words that made the greatest impression on him: "Dreams Re-create the World Each Night."

What if that's actually true? he wondered.

At the very bottom, the last line read: "I promise slumber and dreams to everyone who listens to me."

Were these the words that had become ingrained in the insane mind of Jonas Røed?

The background was a lovely picture showing a musician holding some sort of stringed instrument in his hands. He was surrounded by a group of people, all of whom were sleeping.

"Jon Blund," Singsaker said.

"One and the same," Siri Holm said with a laugh. "And look at the date."

Singsaker saw the date under the title. It said: 3 July 1767.

"What about it?" he asked.

"It's the same date as the first published issue of *Adresseavisen*. The Winding print shop must have been busy that day. This print would have been expensive. And I doubt whether the publisher earned much from it."

"Do you mean Jon Blund?" asked Singsaker.

"Yes, or whoever had it printed in Jon Blund's name."

"We still don't know who he was, do we?"

"No, but the answer must be in that police log or in the letter that was stolen. Has either of them turned up at the home of the killer?"

"I'm not sure. But I'll let you know if we find them."

"Odd," said Siri. She put the broadsheet down on the table and her face took on an usually serious expression. "You need to tell me where Felicia is. I haven't been able to reach her by phone."

Singsaker looked at her and at her belly under the pale sweater. Was she starting to show? Then he glanced around the room. He hadn't been inside the Gunnerus Library since last fall. He wasn't especially happy about being back here, but he could handle it.

He gathered his courage, and then told her everything. When he was finished, Siri gave him a look that was a mixture of gravity and astonishment.

"I certainly didn't see that coming," she said. "Did you really think you were the father?"

"I'm not?"

"No. Don't you think I would have told you if you were?"

Singsaker paused to consider. Then he said, "Well, I really did think I was." He knew that she was the sort of woman that took a lighthearted view of many things that others took seriously. But friendship was a different matter. "I know you would have told me. The truth is that I just couldn't keep this idiotic secret any longer, so I guess I decided to seize the opportunity to ease my guilty conscience when we figured out you were pregnant."

She smiled. "You would have been a good father," she said. "A little old, maybe, but a good dad."

"And here I thought you were such a good judge of character," he replied.

"I am." She put her hand on his shoulder. "The father is a university student majoring in literature in Bergen. He's coming to see me this weekend. It was stupid of me to tell Felicia that it was my father who was visiting. I should have told both of you the truth. It's just such a new thing for me."

Singsaker noticed something in her tone of voice.

"Don't tell me that you, of all people, have actually fallen in love."

"I wouldn't go that far. He plays the guitar, and I'm willing to give the relationship a chance. He's talking about continuing his studies in Trondheim instead of in Bergen. We'll see where it goes."

He smiled, wishing he were young again.

"But what's important right now is getting in touch with Felicia," she went on.

"She might be back in the States, for all I know."

"Have you tried to phone her?"

"Every free moment I've had. But without success, just like you."

"That's good. You can bet she's watching her incoming calls. So the more often you try, the better. She really needs to think you're desperate."

"That doesn't sound like very conventional advice. Shouldn't you be telling me that I need to give her time, or something like that?"

"Bullshit. I know Felicia. She wants you to be calling her every ten minutes. I'm sure of it."

Singsaker smiled, but he wasn't as convinced as Siri. Then he realized that he hadn't gleaned the information that he needed from their conversation. She was a shrewd woman, and she'd already helped him once before with this investigation.

"Jonas Røed," he said. "I've told you what we know about him, and you've seen the broadsheet. Does it tell you anything at all about him?"

"Not the print itself. But if I were you, instead I'd be asking myself, What is it that he wants most of all?

Singsaker thought about that for a moment.

"He wants her to sing the lullaby for him. He wants to sleep."

"Okay, let's say it's as simple as that. The next question is, What does he need in order to make that happen?

"Someplace where he can be left in peace, and a place to sleep," Singsaker replied.

32

"But *where the hell* would that be?"

Brattberg was talking louder than usual on the phone. Singsaker knew how much pressure she was under.

"It could be anywhere," he sighed as he turned onto Prinsens Gate and headed back to town.

Then she told him about the press conference and the flood of questions that had followed. A lot of them had to do with whether the police thought Jonas Røed was psychologically unstable and whether the police really had any idea how many mentally ill people were roaming the streets. Vlado Taneski, the reporter, seemed especially intent on making a big deal out of the issue.

Brattberg had little new information about the case. They hadn't managed to dig up any other address where Røed might have gone. He and his wife had lived an isolated life, with few friends and no contact with any family members. They didn't own a summer house or cabin. So far, no one on the investigative team had been in touch with anyone who knew of other places the couple might have stayed on vacation. Additional officers had been posted along the roads, and all vehicles leaving the city were being checked at several strategic points. But so far without result. Additional officers had also been sent to the Ringve Museum.

"And Grongstad's team is still up at the house on Bernhard Getz' Gate. He doesn't have anything specific to tell us yet. But we do have clear proof, including the dog's leash and evidence found in the storage rooms, that Julie Edvardsen was there. The blood in the second one is mostly old and probably came from Silje Rolfsen. But there are a few drops that are fresher, and they could have come from Julie or from Røed."

"Do you think he's already killed her? I had a strong feeling that she was still alive when I saw her."

"I'm choosing to believe she's still alive. He may have beaten her. But they haven't finished analyzing the blood yet. Her parents looked at the leash and confirmed that it belonged to their dog. Røed's computer mostly just contains research on music boxes and a bunch of stuff about various sleep techniques and dream analysis. There are also a lot of music files of Swedish ballads. But I don't think even a forensic psychologist would have guessed that the computer belonged to a dangerous criminal."

"What about Heimdal?"

"Mona Gran is the only one there at the moment. She's looking through various documents, hoping to find something. Even though Røed had a computer, he seems to have written out a lot of things by hand. I was thinking you could go out there and help her. But first you should take a break and get something to eat."

Singsaker looked at his watch. It always made him happy to hear his boss show some concern for him. And she was right. It was almost five o'clock and he hadn't eaten a thing since breakfast. But he wasn't really hungry.

He ended the call.

Without deciding where he was going, he put the key in the ignition. Then he happened to notice a special key on the key ring.

Slowly, he started driving. He knew what he had to do. Something told him that somewhere in that poor dug-up brain of his was the answer to the question about where Jonas Røed had gone. What he needed right now was to gather his thoughts. And in order to save time he had to take a detour.

A frosty mist hovered like a haze over the crust of ice. Beyond were the dark depths of the fjord. Singsaker knew that all he had to do was jump and he'd fall right through the fragile layer of ice and disappear down into the darkness.

Today he took his clothes off on the dock, since Jensen wasn't with him this time. Then he went down the three steps and leaped into the water before he could change his mind. The ice-cold water instantly enveloped his body. He rose up to the icy surface faster than usual. But instead of swimming back to the steps, as he normally did after surfacing, he splashed around, aware of the numbing cold. For some reason he started thinking about shoveling snow. There was something about that damned shoveling that was important, but he couldn't figure out what it might be.

He lay on his back, trying to float. That was something his ex-wife Anniken had been good at. She could float in the water for a long time, motionless probably for hours if she felt like it. Singsaker had never really mastered the ability to float. Anniken said it was because his body was never still. She was probably right.

It was definitely impossible to keep his body still in this ice-cold water. He felt the heels of his feet grow heavy and begin to sink. He began kicking his legs as he flung his arms out behind him and made his way through the water, swimming slowly back to the dock. He looked up at the dark winter sky. Night had started to descend and the first stars had emerged.

Suddenly he had an idea. He turned over and in two strokes

reached the stairs. There he climbed out, dried his hands on the towel, and dug his cell phone out of his jacket pocket.

"Hi, Singsaker," said a gentle voice.

"Hi, Gran," he replied. "Have you been at the house alone for very long?"

"The tech guys left about an hour ago. So it's just me now. I'm actually waiting for you to get here so I won't have to take the train back to town."

"Have you been inside the whole time?"

"Yes. Why?"

"And you haven't heard or seen anything out of the ordinary?"

"I've seen plenty of things that are out of the ordinary, let me tell you. I'm sitting here looking at a notebook filled with disconnected ramblings. This man is seriously sick. Listen to this: 'A night without dreams turns the daytime into a nightmare. What you thought was reality disappears and you're sucked into a long waking dream that you can never escape.'"

"A bit of a poet in him," said Singsaker.

"It's from what looks like a diary. But he doesn't seem to have written in it for a long time, not since long before the murder. It's too bad he decided to turn other people's lives into nightmares. His writings just get crazier and crazier."

"I see. But I also asked whether you'd *heard* anything out of the ordinary."

"Well, I've got *Satyricon* playing. Some people might say that's out of the ordinary, but that's their problem. So I haven't really heard much else."

"So in other words you haven't heard anything coming from outside the house?"

"No, not really. Why?"

"I want you to go out and take a look in the garage. But be careful. Don't go inside if you think anybody's there. And stay on the line so I can hear what happens."

"Okay, boss."

He heard her get up and walk across the room. A few moments later she opened a door, and then another. She was breathing harder when she got outside in the cold. And he could hear the snow creaking under her feet. He assumed that she'd made it halfway up Røed's driveway when she stopped abruptly.

"Singsaker," she whispered, "are you there?"

"I'm here," he said. "What do you see?"

"The garage door is open, like it was when I got here. Except that now there's a car parked inside."

"Go back in the house and call for backup. A full backup," he told her. "I'm on my way."

He got dressed without bothering to dry off properly. He almost toppled over when his pants got caught around his knees as he quickly tugged them on.

When at last he was fully dressed, he ran to his car without stopping to lock the door to the sea-bathing society, jumped in, and turned on the engine.

33

The ax was pointing at him. He reached for the handle. How was he going to make her sing now? He wiped the blood on his pants. Some of it he rubbed on his hair. Jonas Røed stood there, pale and red-haired, with blood all over his face. He was thinking. He was thinking the whole time.

Someone would come soon. He knew that. That was why he had to hurry with what he needed to do.

The fly was buzzing angrily now. Slamming against the wall of his skull. Then falling, dazed, back inside his head somewhere, only to start buzzing around again.

Singsaker's car skidded as he turned, but still he stomped on the gas pedal. It had stopped snowing, and the temperature had dropped. The plows hadn't yet made it through all the streets in the suburban neighborhood, and the snow was loosely packed under his tires. The car suddenly lost its grip on the road and went into a sharp skid. Desperately he yanked on the steering wheel, but instead of getting the car back on track, he drove it too far in the other direction, and the vehicle slid into a fence two houses away from Røed's property. The car broke through the fence, sending the planks of wood flying everywhere. Then it slid down a small slope and came to a halt in the snow in the middle of somebody's yard. The headlights lit up the snow in front of the bumper, and Singsaker could hear the front wheels polishing the snow crystals underneath into shiny lumps of ice.

Feeling dazed, he turned off the engine and climbed out to stagger through the snow. He was heading for the road when someone came out of the house behind him.

"What the hell do you think you're doing?" shouted a furious voice.

Singsaker turned to face the man, who had come out in his slippers. He recognized the neighbor that he'd talked to earlier in the day. Standing behind the man was the little terrier, barking excitedly. Apparently the only thing big about the dog was his bark.

Singsaker held up his ID.

"Police," he said so brusquely that the man stopped. "Of course you'll be compensated for the damage. Now I suggest that you get back inside your house, lock the door, and stay there."

The man stared at Singsaker, who was standing out there in the snow with his gray hair sticking out all over, melted snow dripping down his face. He glowered at the man, who turned around and did as he was told.

Taking long strides, Singsaker made his way out of the yard and over toward Røed's house.

Once there, he jogged over to the garage, where he saw an old red Saab. Røed's car. It wasn't locked.

He opened a door. The interior was very neat. A crocheted blanket covered the backseat. Anna Røed's handiwork, he guessed. Singsaker shuddered at the thought that Julie Edvardsen, her hands and feet bound, might have lain on this blanket that had once been so lovingly created. He thought of the stink of urine in the basement at Bernhard Getz' Gate.

It's a strange form of concern this guy shows, Singsaker thought angrily.

Then he jogged over to the house. He looked around, then stopped to listen. No sign that backup was on its way. That was odd. Gran was supposed to have phoned in the alarm. Why hadn't anyone else arrived?

With a premonition of dread, he opened the door, which still showed the damage it had sustained when the officer had used an ax to open it earlier that day. That was why it no longer closed properly.

Then he went inside.

The distinct smell still hung in the air. He moved cautiously. If Røed was here, Singsaker at least wanted to have the element of surprise on his side.

Slowly, he pushed on the door to the living room. It opened with a creak that he hadn't expected.

But Røed was not who he found inside. Mona Gran was sitting on a sofa with her back to him. With an ax embedded in the back of her skull.

He took three steps closer.

Over the shoulder of his dead colleague, he could see that she was holding her cell phone in her hand, as if still trying to tap in the number to headquarters.

Singsaker fell to his knees. The whole room felt as if it were spinning, as if it had come loose from the rest of the world, released from the pull of gravity to swirl alone in a universe without mercy.

A jumble of scattered fragments rushed through his mind, bits and pieces of conversations he'd had with Gran at the beginning of this investigation. He remembered her telling him about the doctor's appointment she'd had, and her attempts to get pregnant with her boyfriend. Only days later, her life and all her dreams had come to an end here, on this sofa.

Everything had ended here.

In an hour, one of his poor colleagues would be standing outside in the snow as Mona Gran's boyfriend opened the door. And this colleague would know that his presence there was about to destroy the man's life.

Singsaker stood up, feeling faint, and left the house. Out on the front steps, which were now covered with new snow, he again fell to his knees, without thinking about how vulnerable this made him to another attack from Røed.

He stayed there as he tapped in Brattberg's number.

"He's here. He's out here in Heimdal, and he killed Mona." That was all Singsaker managed to say.

It occurred to him that this was the first time he'd ever used only her first name.

Brattberg was shocked. She wanted Singsaker to tell her more. Wanted him to explain. He couldn't just say that a colleague was dead without any other explanation.

He simply replied, "Come right away."

Then he lay down, and everything inside him went black.

There was no police car parked outside. He'd had the ax in the garage, and it had felt natural to take it along.

The cracking sound it made as it struck the back of her head had sent him in unexpected directions. He'd gone back out to Julie, and when she'd seen the blood on his hands, she'd given him that half-dead look that he'd seen in Anna's eyes and his mother's. As if he were evil through and through. Then she'd closed her eyes and stopped shaking. How was he going to get her to sing for him now?

Then he went back and saw the policeman go inside. It was one of the two officers from his childhood. The one who had come out to Ringve and talked to him. The one who had almost seen through him. Now he watched the policeman from the crack in the bedroom door. The man knelt down, as if the dead policewoman were some sort of altar. Then he just stood up and left.

When the officer was gone, Røed cautiously entered the living room and pulled the ax out of the dead woman's head, which made a sinister sucking sound. Then he paused, wondering whether he'd ever sleep again.

He wiped the blade of the ax on the sofa and left the room.

Singsaker rubbed snow on his face in an attempt to pull himself together. He was consumed with rage. He got up and stamped his feet. He wanted to go back to get the ax and look for Røed. Instead, he started pounding on the walls of the house with his bare fists. He hammered on the walls next to the front door. But this did more damage to his hand than to the house. His knuckles began to bleed, and drops of blood fell on the white snow. That was when he noticed it.

A trail of blood led away from the door and around the corner of the house. It wasn't his blood. He switched on the flashlight on his cell phone and followed the trail. From the house it continued in an uneven line toward the yard behind the garage. At that point the thoughts he'd had during his icy swim came back to him. Something about the shoveled snow. There was something striking about the two heaps of snow that Røed had made at both houses.

Singsaker moved slowly now, trying not to make the slightest sound as he moved through the deep snow. When he reached the back of the snow heap, which was a good distance down the slope behind the garage, he saw it. An opening had been dug into it, and this opening led down a dark passageway. He leaned down to shine the light inside. That was when he heard the creak of the snow behind him. He turned abruptly and saw the ax coming toward him.

Julie Edvardsen blinked her eyes, exhausted. A short time ago she'd felt completely frozen as he dragged her over here from the car, pulling her by the hair. But that feeling had begun to fade. The cold was slowly losing its grip, to be replaced by an almost pleasant sensation of numbness, and with it an overwhelming urge to sleep. Again her eyes started to close.

But I mustn't fall asleep, she thought. *I mustn't, because then he'll take me. He'll put the knife to my throat or he'll kick me to death, the way he did with Bismarck.*

All of a sudden she regretted not eating any of the food he'd brought her. It would have given her the strength to stay awake. Now her body temperature was dropping, and she was starving. But she had to fight back.

Then she heard sounds outside. Someone was walking through the snow.

He's coming back, she thought. Now I have to sing for him. I have to sing or this time he'll kill me. She tried to gather her strength. Tried to see if she had any energy left. When Julie was little, her mother had always liked telling her stories about people in crisis who discovered they had strength they never knew they possessed. But she didn't know whether that was true of her; maybe it only happened in stories. Then she started thinking again.

Who am I? What am I fighting for?

Again she heard sounds outside.

Someone was fighting. She heard deep, grunting male voices and heavy breathing. Then suddenly a scream, from some violent pain. And a laugh.

She knew that laughter. It belonged to him. But somebody else was out there too. And that gave her hope.

The other, unknown person screamed again. Then she heard a sound that reminded her of when he'd kicked Bismarck in the basement. A gasp from the unknown man, and then silence. She shut her eyes and stayed still, listening. A lifeless body was dragged inside the snow cave next to her. She heard something being tied up, tight.

Still she refused to look.

Only when he had crawled back outside did she dare open her eyes.

She was staring at a lifeless shadow. It was too dark for her to get a good look at him, but she felt a strange closeness to this man who might have been trying to rescue them—her and the baby. And she thought that if she ended up dying in here, she was glad that at least she wasn't alone.

Then he came back.

"So? Are you going to sing?" he asked, his voice strangely gentle as he pointed at her with something that could be a knife.

She stared at him. Felt how tired she was. She had decided to sing for him now. She was hoping this was her chance to escape. Maybe she could even save this man who was lying beside her in the dark.

And so she surprised herself when she said weakly, "No."

Not until she uttered that word did she understand why. If I sing, she thought, he'll kill us anyway. But if I refuse, I'm not sure what he'll do. Not knowing was a form of hope.

She could feel him looking at her in the dark. She remembered those sad eyes that she'd seen outside his house on Ludvig Daaes Gate; it was his gaze that had lured her into this nightmare.

Then he started singing.

He didn't hit the right notes, but that just made his song all the more bewitching, rawer and more heartrending, as if it contained all of his insanity. He sang the whole ballad, right to the very end. He sang about dreams, about the cruelty of the world and the great liberating slumber, and when he was finished, she was so tired that she didn't think she could keep her eyes open much longer.

In the dark, she couldn't tell what was happening. She heard him move his arms very quickly a couple of times. Then came the lonesome sound of something breaking. After that he fell down next to her and lay still.

In the distance she heard the sound of sirens.

34

Trondheim, 1767

Nils Bayer *rode back* toward Trondheim early in the morning.
He headed across Småbergan near the fortress and saw the city
spread below him in the dawn light.

It was a small town. After the years he'd spent in Copenhagen,
he would always think of Trondheim as small, and he was afraid
that would be his downfall, in one way or another. But at daybreak,
he couldn't help but like what he saw of Trondheim: its rickety
wooden buildings with thatched roofs, its streets and alleyways, its
coachmen, fiddlers, scholars, fishwives, men of rank and men of
drunken stupors, its whores and lunatics. He felt a certain affection
for this strange little country where he'd ended up. An inexplicable
faith in the future reigned among Norwegians. Meanwhile, he came
from an old country, a land that had enough to do just holding on
to what it had. But in Trondheim, in small, poor Norway, there was
good business to be done. A man could obtain the newest books from
Europe. Research was being conducted. People were investigating
new ideas. This was a new time for Norway.

Bayer remembered, on a damp evening when he'd been invited

to Søren Engel's home, Bishop Gunnerus, perhaps the wisest and most learned of all the Norwegians he'd met, had confided something to him.

"Norway is a country that will soon be reborn," the bishop had said "That's why people here are looking forward to the times to come."

These thoughts should have made Bayer feel more optimistic, but they didn't. They could do nothing to fend off the nightmarish images from the night before. He saw them over and over again in his mind. The light glinting off the muzzle of the gun. The Swede falling, dead, a patch of blood spreading across his white shirt. The legs sticking out of the grave. The river streaming past with its enticing offer of eternal oblivion. Nils Bayer had become a murderer since the last time he'd seen Trondheim. And it was as a murderer that he would live out the rest of his days in this city.

He clucked to the horse and set off for the ferry landing. Once he had reached the other side, he rode straight home and slept the rest of the day.

He was wakened in the middle of the night by a dream that he was back at the river. The two Swedes had risen from the grave and were staring at him, as if they felt sorry for him. Then the flies had come and settled over them. The insects came from all directions and gradually both corpses were covered with flies until they became buzzing shadows in the night. He raised the gun and fired a shot into the dark. Then the flies took off and disappeared, leaving nothing behind. The two bodies had vanished.

Bayer tossed and turned in bed, then reached for his flask, which he'd set on the night table. It was empty. There was nothing to drink except for a jug of water from Ilabekken that had been left standing too long. He greedily downed the water, noticing that he was shaking all over. His nightshirt was drenched with sweat. He tore it off and got dressed. Then he went out to fetch his horse and rode off into the night.

In Brattøra he woke the ferryman, paying him three times the usual fee to cross the river. Then he rode over toward the Ringve estate, arriving a few hours past midnight. Everyone was asleep, which was for the best, since he hadn't come here to make a social call. He left his horse in the woods outside the estate and walked the rest of the way. Instead of taking the road to the courtyard, he headed through the tall grass and walked around the house to the backyard. There he found the flower beds that had been planted by the mistress, and he began to dig.

He dug with his bare hands, getting dirt under his nails. It was hard work, but he was driven by a dreamlike obsession. His memories of recent events, the lack of anything to drink, the bright night under the stars—all of this filled him with an intensity that made him forget the limitations of his stout, heavy body. After a while he found what he was looking for. He pulled it out of the damp soil and wiped it with the palms of his hands. Then he smiled for the first time in days. He took what he'd found and put it in the saddlebag on his horse.

He rode back to town. When he arrived, there were still a few hours of night left. This time, he slept soundly, and when he awoke, he finally felt rested.

He went over to his office. There he found Officer Torp, who jumped to his feet when the police chief came in.

"People have been worried," Torp said, tilting his head to one side. "Where have you been?"

"I've been chasing a ghost," said Bayer. Then he told Torp about his hunt for the Swede. But in this telling, the Swede managed to get away somewhere beyond Meråker and then disappeared into enemy country with the body of the dead man.

"We need to put this case behind us now," he concluded.

"That would indeed be a good thing," said Torp. "There is so much we have neglected these past few days. We've received so many complaints about watered-down beer, about Eriksen the baker selling moldy bread, and about selling in the marketplace without a permit. We have enough on our hands."

"Yes, we certainly do have enough on our hands," replied Bayer absentmindedly.

Then he sat, leafing through the notebook on his desk. It was the notebook that had belonged to the lutist Jon Blund, and after a moment he found a ballad that he liked. It was called "The Golden Peace." He read the text, which had to do with deep slumber and sweet dreams, the kind of sleep that he wished for more than anything else. He noticed that this song was the last one in the notebook. After it, a page had been torn out, and the rest of the pages were blank. He tore out the ballad, then went over to the stove and placed the notebook amid the kindling on the floor. It would be put to good use in the fall. He turned to Torp, who was sitting at the other desk, seemingly engrossed in some important documents.

"There's one more thing I have to do before I can devote all my attention to restoring order to the streets of Trondheim," he said. "In the meantime, you'll have to deal with the chaos as best you can, my dear Officer Torp. I suggest that you start with the moldy bread. It sounds like a serious matter that might bring in a sizable fine for the town treasury."

Then Bayer folded up the pages containing the words of the lullaby, stuck them in his waistcoat pocket, and left.

"And you want only three copies?" asked Mr. Winding, holding the text in the air as if he could read it better from afar.

"That's all a poor police chief can afford, I'm afraid," said Bayer with an apologetic smile.

"You could order a less expensive printing. It's not that we can't produce the engraving that you want for the front. I have excellent craftsmen in my workshop, some of the best in the realm, if I may say so myself. But it will take time and cost money to create that sort of image."

"But that's what I want," said Bayer firmly.

"The price will be charged accordingly, as I said. I won't be able to get this done until . . . let me see. On the morning of the third of July, I will be delivering the first issue of this gazette's reports. I can have your prints done a little later that day."

"Good. The same day as Nissen's publication. I'll have the same date on the front, as a reminder."

"Fine. So you want this image you've described? Slumbering people, the title 'The Golden Peace,' the date, and the name Jon Blund printed on the cover, along with the text that comes before the song? And on the three following pages, the text and melody. This may turn out to be one of my finest prints," said Winding, sounding pleased. "But I'll have to ask you to pay in advance."

Bayer took out his wallet and emptied it on the printer's counter. Then he took his leave and went back to his lodgings. In the bedroom, he knelt down and pulled something out from under the bed. It was the big, heavy metal object he'd found buried in the yard on the Ringve estate. Taking it with him, he set off for Søren Engel's mansion.

It was the servant with the dark complexion who once again opened the door. They exchanged a few jokes, and then the servant, just as he'd done last time, ushered Bayer into the brightly lit library.

"Pardon me, but would you like me to take this . . . this . . . item for you?" asked the servant, motioning discreetly at what Bayer was carrying.

"No, thank you. I'm planning to consult your master about this," replied Bayer.

Søren Engel kept him waiting nearly half an hour. Bayer didn't mind, because wine had been set on the table as soon as he'd arrived. And he took an entertaining book from the shelves behind him. It was a copy of the play *La Vida es sueño*, by the Spanish playwright Pedro Calderón de la Barca. With this book to read, the time passed quickly.

"Forgive me," said Mr. Engel. "But I'm a busy man. If you'd given me some advance warning, it would have been easier for me to make time for you."

"Oh, I'm fine with waiting a bit, when there's plenty of sweet wine and reading material," said Bayer cheerfully, setting the book down on the table next to him.

Engel smiled broadly.

"Do you know what defenestration means, my good Søren Engel?" Bayer asked abruptly.

"Of course I do," he replied. "Who hasn't heard about the monstrous events that took place in Prague during the last century? But why do you ask, Police Chief Bayer?"

"Let's come back to that in a moment, if you don't mind."

"Certainly," said Engel, smiling uneasily.

His face turned stony when Bayer took out the metallic object he'd hidden under his chair. It was a beautifully cast figure. Anyone who was familiar with such things would have recognized it as a weather vane.

"Do you happen to recognize this?" asked Bayer softly, holding it up for Engel to see. The merchant turned pale.

"Where did you get that?" he asked curtly.

"I found it buried in the yard at Ringve. Don't you think that's strange?"

Engel just glared at the police chief.

"Let me tell you a story," said Bayer. "Let's call it a little dream that I had."

JØRGEN BREKKE

Engel still didn't speak. He leaned forward and poured the last of the wine from the carafe into his glass. He drank it all before saying, "I hope this won't take up too much of my time."

"No, it's a very precise dream. And it's not particularly long," Bayer told him. Then he began his tale.

"Once upon a time, there was a man who possessed a fortune greater than anyone else's in the town where he lived. He also had two beautiful daughters, but no male heir who could take over the flourishing family businesses and carry on the family name.

"As you can imagine, such a man would be very particular about whom he would allow his daughters to spend time with. Whoever won their hearts would become the son he lacked and the future administrator of his dazzling fortune. One day this merchant traveled on holiday with his wife and two daughters to visit some other highborn friends who lived in the country. There they planned to take part in the springtime festivities. It was a costly affair, and musicians had been hired to elevate the mood. After a while, things grew so merry and lively that the wealthy gentleman forgot to be as vigilant as usual when it came to watching his daughters. The elder girl happened to strike up a conversation with one of the musicians, a poor but charming foreigner who was most handsome. The two of them left the celebration to stroll among the flower-filled meadows that surrounded the estate. There she gave him a blossom.

"The next day the gentleman and his family went back to town, unaware that a new member of the family had begun to grow in the elder daughter's womb."

Here, Bayer paused as he looked at Søren Engel. His face was pale, his eyes very dark. His hand was clutching the stem of the wineglass so tightly that his knuckles had turned red. Bayer realized that he needed to finish his story quickly, before Engel exploded and threw him out.

"Only, a few months later the truth became apparent. The elder daughter was forced to confess her sin, and it was quickly decided that she should be sent away to give birth to her child in secret. But that was not enough for the poor patriarch. The thought that the filthy and impoverished troubadour was the father to his only grandchild was too much for the man to bear. And so he conspired with his friend who lived in the country. Together they invited the lutist out to the friend's estate with promises of a new engagement. When he arrived, they invited him up to the dining room, which is on the second floor, and from there they threw him out of the window. That is called defenestration. An execution that employs a window.

"The poor lutist struck a weather vane that was fastened to the entrance gate below and was skewered on the metal spire. The weather vane bore an astonishing resemblance to the one I found buried in the garden of the Ringve estate. The weather vane created a huge entry wound in his abdomen, but only a small exit wound where the tip of the spire stuck out of his back. And there the lutist was left hanging, bleeding until he was drained of blood. At some point the weather vane broke off, and the man fell into the courtyard, where the two gentlemen stood waiting.

"In my mind, I picture this happening late one night after all the workers on the estate had gone to bed. The two murderers decided to transport the body as far away as possible from the scene of the crime. And so they took the deceased down to Ringve Bay, where the owner's new boat was moored, and then they sailed with the corpse to the other end of town. There they carried the body ashore, not leaving any trace behind. It wasn't long until daybreak, and only a few hours since the last tide. They counted on the body being carried away on the waves, so that it would be unrecognizable before anyone found it. To make the job of the salt water even easier, they removed the dead man's clothes and threw them into the sea on their way back to the estate. They might also have done this to humiliate this tramp even further, this man who had been so bold as to lay hands on the daughter of the town's richest and most powerful man."

Bayer stopped and drank the rest of his wine. He knew it would be a long time before he would taste wine of this quality again.

"What are you trying to tell me with this story of yours?" asked Søren Engel, his voice ominous.

"Nothing. I'm not trying to tell you anything. I just felt it was important to tell this story to someone who would listen," he replied.

"Is it money you want?"

"No, not at all. Justice is all that a police chief strives for as reward for his efforts."

"And how did you plan to achieve justice in this matter?" asked Engel. "You know that although I may treat you as a friend, I am more powerful than you could ever imagine in those twisted dreams of yours."

"There are many different ways to achieve justice," said Bayer. "And sometimes a person has to wait a very long time. But I am equally as patient as you are rich and powerful."

"Then you will have to go somewhere else to wait. You have no proof, nothing that would hold up against my word and the witnesses whom I can produce to speak on my behalf."

"I never said that this matter would come before a judge. I said that justice comes to those who have the patience to wait for it," replied Bayer. He said nothing about his own witness, the Swedish gentleman who had followed the lutist out to Ringve on that evening and had seen the whole thing from the meadow near the estate. He was a witness who would never enter a courtroom on this side of the grave, and so he might as well never have existed.

Bayer stood up and bowed. He could feel his heart pounding in his chest, and his head spun, but he forced himself to meet the gaze of Søren Engel one last time.

He didn't yet know what sort of justice awaited this enormously wealthy murderer. He knew that the only punishment he could mete out lay in the words he had spoken and this last look. No matter how much money Engel had, he would have to live with his deeds, sleep with them every night, and dream about them while he slept.

"I must ask you never to set foot in my house again," said Engel as the police chief left the room.

Feeling surprisingly lighthearted, Nils Bayer made his way across town until he reached the pub. There he dug deep into his pockets to find a few pennies. *Enough to help me through the rest of the day,* he thought.

Ingrid came over to fill his glass. They smiled at each other like old friends, and she could tell he didn't feel like talking at the moment. She let him sit there in peace all afternoon, and when evening came, she brought over a plate of dried meat and sat down across from him at the small table in the corner.

"You need to eat some solid food, my dear police chief," she said gently, putting her hand on his shoulder.

He gave her a wan smile.

"I'll eat something if you'll marry me," he said. Both of them knew that it was said in jest. But both of them knew that he meant what he'd said.

This time she gave him a look that he'd never seen before.

"I'll marry you the day you put away the bottle. I grew up with a father who was lost in the grip of alcohol. It was liquor that set fire to my home and robbed me of my family. I'll never marry you as long as you keep drinking. Show me that you can stay sober until Christmas, and then I'll give your proposal serious consideration," she said. Then she leaned forward and kissed him on the cheek. "Now eat," she told him, and left.

———

When Bayer staggered home that night, he was feeling ebullient and self-confident. He was lost in his own thoughts, which were unusually simple for a change.

"Six months without a dram. I can do that. Neptune, the god of the sea himself, knows that I can do it. I'll keep myself afloat."

When he reached Kalvskinnet, he decided to stop by his childhood home, but his mother refused to let him in, telling him to come back when he was sober. Then he reeled home to his own bed and dreamed happy dreams about Ingrid Smeddatter without any clothes on.

Three days later, he went to see Winding to pick up his prints. He hadn't had a drop of anything but boiled water in those three days, which caused him to shake and sweat. But he was feeling better now. A little better each day.

Bayer studied the three prints with satisfaction. He tucked them under his arm and went back to the office, where he found Torp, who was in a splendid mood.

"A messenger from the prefect is waiting for you," he said, beaming from ear to ear.

"You don't say," replied Bayer in measured tones as he glanced at the man sitting on a chair at the back of the office.

"I'll leave you to talk in peace," said Torp, going out to the stairwell.

Bayer greeted the messenger, who told him the purpose of his visit.

"After much consideration, our honorable prefect has reached the conclusion that for a long time the police chief of Trondheim has not been properly appreciated, as befits the important position that he holds. For that reason, the prefect wishes to elevate our city's police chief to the same level as police chiefs in other parts of our country. He has decided to grant to you, Nils Bayer, the right to keep half a skilling for every barrel on which duty is paid upon delivery to our city. You will find all of the details described in this letter."

At this, the messenger bowed and handed Bayer a piece of paper sealed with wax that was imprinted with the prefect's coat of arms.

"I understand," said Bayer, tossing the document on the desk. "I understand all too well. Please convey my best greetings to the prefect and his house."

Bayer ushered the messenger to the door. As he bade the man farewell, Torp come back in.

"What fabulous news," he said.

"That depends on how you look at it," replied Bayer. "Everything in life has its price."

Torp gave him a confused look.

"But something good may come of this after all," he added. "And we soon may be able to increase your wages ever so slightly."

"Only if the police chief sees fit to do so," said Torp with a bow.

"Now go out there and keep order in Trondheim. That's what I'm paying you for, isn't it?"

Torp bowed again and went out the door with a smile on his face. Evidently he had long since stopped trying to make any sense out of the police chief.

Nils Bayer set down two of the broadsheets that he was still holding, then took the third with him. He went over to the Hoppa. There he found Ingrid Smeddatter sitting alone in the empty dining room.

"Quiet morning?" he asked, smiling.

"Quiet and peaceful until you arrived," she said, laughing.

"I have a present for you," said Bayer.

She took the broadsheet that he handed her and studied it.

"How lovely it is," she said. "But why would you give me a present?"

"Because we're three days closer to Christmas," he told her.

35

The sound of sirens grew louder. At the same time, she grew weaker. Life was slowly seeping out of her.

It was pitch-black and very quiet inside the snow cave. No one was singing anymore, and the only sound was the faint breathing of another person.

In the silence she thought she could hear her own pulse.

Thud, thud, thud.

It was getting slower. Even though he hadn't stabbed her, she wasn't going to last much longer in the freezing cold.

She imagined that she could also hear the heartbeat of the man who had tried to save her. But she knew that she was hallucinating in between those moments of clarity when she understood what was happening to her.

I'm going to freeze to death. That's why I feel so warm. I read about that somewhere. Dreams, hallucinations, warmth.

That is how we leave this life.

———

Thorvald Jensen thought mostly about Odd Singsaker.

Why was Odd always the first one to arrive and then bear the brunt of the situation? And yet he was the weakest of them all. He was the one who could least afford the stress. For a long time now, Jensen had thought that his colleague might have returned to work too soon after his illness, that maybe he ought to have been given other assignments instead of working on an active investigation. He suspected that Singsaker had been more affected by his health issues than he was willing to let on; instead he tried to cover up and trivialize what he'd been through. Jensen had never said anything to him about his concerns. He wasn't sure if that made him a good or a bad friend. At the moment, none of that mattered. Right now the important thing was to get him to safety. He hoped that nothing serious had happened after Singsaker phoned. He hoped he was still alive.

They had assembled outside in the street. Six police vehicles, two ambulances, and a fire truck with axes and ladders and other equipment that might prove necessary. They had blocked off the entire street and started evacuating the neighbors. One of them had immediately filed a complaint that Singsaker's car had burst through onto his property and smashed the fence. The police had wasted a lot of time trying to calm the man down, but they weren't taking any chances in such a risky situation. The closest neighbors had to be moved to a safe area.

Jensen was in charge of the operation, and no one could tell how uneasy he actually was. He ordered the officers into position. There was no indication that Røed had a gun, which should make things easier. It was dark now, and they could use that to their advantage. He'd spoken to the chief of the firefighters and asked whether they could shut off the power in the area. They happened to have an electrician with them. Strange, thought Jensen. The firemen always seem to have someone who's an electrician. Jensen watched as the firefighter went over to a junction box a few yards down the street, carrying a tool. Everyone waited in silence until they saw the light over the front door of Røed's house go out. A few seconds later, all the streetlights in the area switched off.

Jensen was pleased to have darkness settle over them. It allowed him to think more clearly, although his feeling of dread was increasing. With every task they carried out, every routine move they made, and with every minute that passed, it became more and more evident that something was very wrong. It was too quiet.

Jensen slowly became convinced that the house was empty, or that at least there was no one alive inside.

"We're sending in a team!" he shouted, pointing. "We're going in the front door!"

A group of nine men from the SWAT team moved like soundless shadows, splitting up to take positions on either side of the door. Then they disappeared inside, stomping loudly and shouting.

Going for the shock effect, thought Jensen. These guys know what they're doing.

Fifteen minutes later he was standing inside looking at the body of Mona Gran. The SWAT team had secured the house but hadn't found Singsaker, Julie Edvardsen, or Jonas Røed.

Several other officers stood next to Jensen, and some of them had removed their caps. Jensen had been on the force for almost thirty-five years. It had been a long time since he'd lost a colleague in the line of duty. Why did this have to happen now? Why did she have to be so much younger than he was, her whole life ahead of her?

He couldn't bear to stay in the room for long. Grongstad would have to handle things here.

Back outside, he paused to think, staring at the ground. Damn it, Odd, where are you?

Then he saw the trail of blood on the snow.

He used his flashlight to follow the blood through the yard and around the huge mound of snow. There he saw the opening.

He shuddered when he found the ax lying in the snow outside, blood on the blade. His pulse racing, he crouched down, then crawled along the narrow passageway, which was just big enough for him to fit through.

He aimed his flashlight straight ahead and saw a big space dug out of the snow. He could almost stand upright in it, and there was enough room for three people to lie side by side. He looked at the three lifeless bodies. In the middle was the man they'd been hunting, with a knife sticking out of his throat. Strangely enough, Jensen was fairly certain that the man had done that himself, but Grongstad and Kittelsen would have to confirm it. Blood ran from the wound, and the blood that had already landed on the snow had begun to congeal into an icy crust.

To the left of the man lay Julie Edvardsen, her eyes closed as if she were asleep.

Singsaker was lying on his stomach, his face turned away. He had a deep wound in his thigh.

Jensen leaned forward to touch Singsaker's neck and feel for his pulse. He held his fingers there for a moment, then moved them slightly, and finally he felt it. It was weak. Weak as a fly grazing his fingertips. He pulled out his radio and quickly shouted orders to his colleagues. Then he moved over to the girl and touched her neck. Here too he felt a pulse. Very weak, but it was there.

But Jonas Røed was dead.

36

E*lise had read the page* at least five times, but it was in English, so she didn't understand all of it. Foreign languages had never been her strong suit. Julie had inherited Ivar's talent with languages and could read English easily. Elise tried over and over to make some sense of this page, searching for some explanation, as if it might tell her where Julie had been taken. *Sandman*. It seemed to be about dreams and sleep. That much she had figured out.

She put it down and sighed.

Then the phone rang. She picked up and listened for several moments without saying a word. Then she hung up. Her hands were shaking. But this was a different kind of shaking from what she'd experienced over the past few days. She ran to the bedroom where Ivar was sleeping and threw herself onto the bed.

"Good Lord, Elise, calm down," said her husband, putting his arms around her. He thought she needed to be consoled again.

She looked at him in the light that streamed through the open bedroom door. He was still in pain, but now she could set his mind at rest.

First she needed to take a deep breath. Then a few more. She wanted to be totally calm when she said the words.

"They've found her," she told him at last. "Julie is being taken to the hospital right now. They say she is suffering from hypothermia. But she's going to be all right."

He turned over so he could switch on the light.

Then they sat there, staring at each other. Her hands were still shaking.

We're going to get her back, she thought.

Nothing will be the same as before.

Odd Singsaker woke up in a hospital bed when his phone rang.

It was his son, Lars.

This time he needed to take the call. He couldn't spare him from everything. No doubt Lars had read the news reports about the recent events and was worried.

"Hi," Singsaker merely said.

"Hi, Pappa. How are you doing?"

"Well, all these stitches hurt like hell. But I'll survive."

"You're tough for an old guy."

Singsaker was relieved. This was a new tone of voice from his son. Or rather, it was the new way they'd started communicating after the christening in the fall, when his second grandchild was baptized. At the time, he'd been staying with his son's family in their cramped apartment in Torshov with Felicia. For the first time in his life he'd discovered that his son had a sense of humor. At least that's one thing I've taught him, he thought. But then he'd realized that Felicia was the one who'd done it—she'd brought father and son closer without either of them noticing.

"I've been trying to call you for a while," said Lars.

"I've been really busy with this damned case."

"But not so busy on the home front?"

Singsaker gave a start. How did Lars know? Whom had he been talking to?

"What do you mean by that?" he asked. Now he heard a voice in the background: "Did you get hold of him? Is he okay?"

Then Lars said, "There's somebody here who wants to talk to you."

Singsaker sat up in bed, silently holding the phone to his ear. Had he heard correctly? Was it really her voice he'd just heard?

"Odd, how are you?" she said then.

"Felicia? Are you at Lars's place?"

"I didn't know where else to go. There aren't really a lot of places for me to stay in this country."

"I thought you went back to the States."

"I almost did," she told him.

"What are you going to do now?"

"I want to come home," she said.

"Do you mean here, to Trondheim?"

"Yes."

Singsaker closed his eyes. There was a faint rushing sound in his head.

"Then I guess it's your turn to visit me in the hospital," he said, thinking about the week he'd kept vigil over Felicia in the fall. Her injuries had been far more serious than his. If he was lucky, this time they'd let him go home in a few days.

"I'll come and see you every day until you're well," she said.

"So you're not mad at me anymore?" he asked.

"No," she said. "I was never mad at you."

A few seconds after he put down the phone, it rang again. It was Lars, and he spoke in a low voice.

"Did you forget something?" asked Singsaker.

"I wanted to say something when Felicia wasn't in the room," he replied.

"What's that?"

"She was in really bad shape when she got here. She just lay on the sofa for almost twenty-four hours before she managed to pull herself together. You need to take care of her, Pappa."

"Thanks," he said. "I will."

Then he turned off his phone and went to sleep.

He was lying on his back when Felicia came into the room. A nurse who bore a striking resemblance to Siri Holm had just tended to his wound, this time leaving off the bandages.

The stitches were red and itchy.

Felicia came over to him. He noticed the sweet smell of alcohol and sweat as she leaned over to kiss his forehead. Neither of them said a word. She bent down and kissed the first stitch, letting her lips linger there for a while. She was breathing slowly, easily. When she raised her lips, the stitch was gone and the edges of the top part of the wound had grown together.

She did the same thing with the next stitch.

Without a word, she worked her way down until they had all disappeared, along with the wound on his thigh. Then she straightened up and looked at him with that wise and melancholy expression that she had occasionally. It was a look that could sometimes, briefly, convince him that melancholia was the only healthy approach to life.

"Sleep well, my dear," she said, kissing him on the forehead once more.

Then he woke from the dream.

He was alone. Felicia wasn't there. He looked at his watch and saw that it was a little past ten in the morning. A whole day and night had passed since they'd last spoken. This was the first time he'd slept soundly since that phone call.

He'd been waiting. Three times he'd talked to Lars on the phone. His son told him that Felicia had booked herself a ticket on the three o'clock plane yesterday afternoon. So why hadn't she come to the hospital yet?

He decided to call Siri.

"Hi, Odd. Happy birthday!" she said. "I thought you'd give me the chance to call you. That's usually how it works on someone's birthday, you know."

"Shit. Is today my birthday?" he said, suddenly confused.

"Must be your memory playing tricks on you again." She laughed. "Isn't Felicia there with you?"

He'd spoken to Siri last night and told her that Felicia was coming back.

"That's why I'm calling," he said. "I haven't seen her, and she's not answering her phone. I was wondering if you could drop by the apartment and see if she's there."

Siri assured him that she'd be happy to do that during her lunch hour.

At 11:55 she called him from outside his apartment on Kirkegata. The door was locked, the windows were dark, and there was no sign of Felicia Stone.

He sighed.

"I'm sure she'll turn up," said Siri. "She probably decided to spend an extra day in Oslo."

They both knew that sounded very unlikely.

He thanked Siri for her help.

After he put down the phone, someone knocked on the door and a nurse came into his room.

"There's a young man here who'd like to speak with you," she said.

Behind her, Singsaker could see Fredrik Alm in the doorway. The nurse left as the boy came into the room. For a moment he stood there, not sure what to do. Then he reached into his pocket and took out a black notebook. Singsaker recognized it at once.

"Where did you get that?" he asked as Fredrik handed it to him.

"At school. It was in the Lost and Found box, and when I saw your name on it, I thought I should bring it over. I guess you must have left it behind when you came to talk to us. I also wanted to thank you—for rescuing Julie."

Singsaker felt a pang of guilt.

We should have caught the guy sooner, he thought. It was my fault.

"How's she doing?" Singsaker asked.

"Not so good. She's glad to be alive, of course. But she says that she can't sleep at night."

"What about the baby?"

"We don't know yet," said Fredrik. "She doesn't want to talk about it. She says she needs time to think things over."

"Tell her I said hello. And you take care of yourself."

Fredrik Alm nodded, turned around, and headed for the door.

"And Fredrik," said Singsaker before the boy left. "Thanks for the notebook. I was really wondering what happened to it."

After Fredrik left, he paged through his notes. He felt sorry for the boy. How could he give Julie what she needed? Could anyone do that? And then there was the baby. Difficult decisions had to be made, and Fredrik would have very little say about them. No matter what the outcome, he was going to have a tough time of it. He was much too young to be a father, but who could stand to lose a child, no matter what age he was?

Singsaker kept looking through his notebook. The last pages contained his notes from the interviews at school. He tormented himself by reading the very precise description that Fredrik had given him of the house where Julie had talked to a man who was shoveling snow—the house that turned out to belong to the murderer, the place where he had held both Silje Rolfsen and Julie captive. Again he told himself that there'd been no reason to believe that the man shoveling snow was of any importance to the case. It was just a tip. Something that had to be checked out when they had time. But no one had done that. There was no getting around the fact that he was the one who had forgotten all about it.

Finally Singsaker turned back to the page where he'd written some passages about Felicia and himself. It was from the night before this whole horrible case had begun, which felt like ages ago, or like something he'd imagined in some awful dream. They'd eaten dinner and then made love twice. Something told him that it might have been the last time he could demonstrate that sort of prowess. At his age it was quickly becoming a physiological impossibility.

He chuckled to himself and lay back on the pillows.

One day passed and then another. Felicia didn't show up. Finally he had to accept that she wasn't coming. Several times he picked up the phone, thinking that he'd call her father in Virginia. But he didn't. He wasn't ready to confirm what he feared and perhaps already knew. He didn't think he was strong enough to handle the truth.

On Singsaker's last day in the hospital, Dr. Nordraak unexpectedly came in to remind him that he'd missed his follow-up appointment, which was understandable, given the recent events. So they scheduled a new appointment. As Nordraak was about to leave, Singsaker decided to ask him something.

"I'm sure you've read about the case I was working on when all this happened, right?"

"Of course. Everybody's heard about it."

"What's your professional opinion, as a psychiatrist? What goes on in the mind of a murderer like Røed?"

Nordraak looked at him as he straightened his silk tie. The tie had a pattern of little blue elephants, but strangely enough it looked quite stylish on him.

"My professional opinion?" he said, hesitating. "It's not really much different from what was reported in all the newspapers. And you, as an experienced police officer, have probably reached the same conclusion as I have. Røed was most likely suffering from a severe personality disorder. That's a constant and, many would say, incurable mental defect. We're talking about a lack of empathy, grandiose ideas, no sense of boundaries in terms of his behavior, and the inability to control his impulses. But it also seems likely that at some point he entered a psychotic state that not only reinforced his difficult personality but also made his thoughts bizarre and incomprehensible. As a doctor, I would say that he was probably always a difficult person, with a potential for violent and criminal behavior, but that it was only during a brief period that he was actually ill in a pathological sense."

"But how would you explain how, after he kidnapped his first victim, Røed continued to function at his job? When I talked to him right after the murder, he seemed perfectly lucid. He was extraordinarily cunning in the way he led me toward Høybråten, who he knew had his own dark secrets. And he dropped a few remarks that diverted attention away from himself, such as the fact that the music box had been modified by an amateur. The man was a professional curator, after all."

"It's impossible to say anything for sure about Røed's state of mind now that he's dead and we're unable to observe him. But it's not uncommon for psychoses to come and go. That's what happens with so-called bipolar patients, for example. But as I said, we can't really speculate."

"Could the absence of dreams lead to psychosis?"

"Yes, in a sense. It's not necessarily the lack of dreams but rather long periods without sleep that can lead to serious psychotic states.

As far as Røed is concerned, it's really a question of which came first—the chicken or the egg? Insomnia could just as well have been a symptom of his condition, rather than the root cause of it. Many psychotic patients struggle with sleep. If he seemed lucid when you talked to him, he may have slept well the night before and was experiencing a milder form of his illness."

"But not many insomniacs kill innocent people," remarked Singsaker drily.

Nordraak paused for a few moments before answering.

"You're right about that, Singsaker. You're right. But you asked me for my professional assessment of Røed, not my personal opinion."

"And what's your personal opinion?"

"I think that what it said in the newspapers about the lullaby and the fact that he might have kidnapped the women to help him sleep is only part of the picture. I think he cut out Silje Rolfsen's larynx because to his ears it wasn't functioning the way it should. He enjoyed killing. That's my theory, Singsaker. Violence was the only way he could quiet the turmoil inside of him. Murderers like Røed kill primarily because they personally gain something from the violence and because of the sense of power it gives them. The man was an evil bastard. And we're never going to find any scientific explanation for evil."

"A monster?" said Singsaker.

Nordraak thought for a moment.

"No, a human being. Unfortunately, a human being."

Then he wrote down the new appointment time for Singsaker and left the room.

Several hours later, Singsaker was discharged from the hospital.

"Felicia vanished. Can anyone say how? Like the bird from its cage, like the ice in the spring, like love when it's wounded, like a trip without return."

Luckily Singsaker hadn't noticed the music playing as he sat in the restaurant the following day. Siri Holm sat across from him, and she couldn't help hearing the tune. What an awful coincidence, she thought.

It was cold outside, and a draft was coming in the windows. Singsaker was wearing a wool sweater, but he was still freezing. He'd been to Mona Gran's funeral earlier in the day. Her partner had wanted a civilian funeral with no police uniforms, but there was still a huge crowd. All the pews in the church had been filled.

That's how it always is when young people die, thought Singsaker.

Again he felt the weight of the guilt that he couldn't rationalize away. If his memory had been functioning the way it should, she might still be alive. It was because of such thoughts that he couldn't concentrate on what Siri was saying. But he could tell she was trying to cheer him up.

"This police log makes for really exciting reading," she said. "It was written by a police chief named Nils Bayer, who worked in Trondheim for a number of years, starting in 1762. This particular entry was written in 1767, about Jon Blund, and it's almost like reading fiction. It turns out that this Jon Blund was a Swedish ballad singer who arrived in Trondheim and was then killed. After Blund's death, Bayer found his notebook, and one of the ballads included was 'The Golden Peace.' It doesn't say anything specific, but I'm guessing Bayer was the one who went to Winding to have it printed."

"Does that mean that Nils Bayer is the closest we're going to get to this ancestor that Felicia was looking for?"

"Yes, although I imagine that Røed made up the part about the ancestor. But this Bayer was a really odd guy. I've gone through the archives and discovered that he actually emigrated from Trondheim to America in 1776, almost ten years after the ballad was printed."

"So you've solved the case for Felicia," said Singsaker.

"The case that wasn't a case," Siri replied, correcting him. They both knew now that the e-mail address that was used to contact Felicia had been opened in the name of Grälmakar Löfberg and could be traced back to Jonas Røed's PC at the Ringve Museum. But no one had been able to figure out why Røed had contacted her about doing this genealogical search. It was assumed that he'd been obsessed with everything that had to do with the pseudonym Jon Blund and that he'd seized the opportunity to find out more information about him.

"It'll still take a lot of digging to find out more about Bayer," Siri went on. "The only thing I know is that he was Danish and he'd worked as a police officer in Copenhagen. I was thinking of reading through the entire police logbook. Bayer really seems to have had his finger in a lot of different pies during his time in Trondheim, and it looks like he associated with plenty of powerful people. There's enough material for several crime novels here."

"Maybe you should write them," said Singsaker, smiling for the first time since they'd started talking. "You're so interested in mysteries, after all."

"No, I'm a reader, not an author," she said. "By the way, I'm excited that the police made public the letter that was in the wall at Ringve. Can you give me a hint as to what it says? Who was this Jon Blund exactly? Does it mention anything about him in the letter, like the rumors say?"

"I haven't read it," he said.

Then their food arrived. Fish soup. Neither of them had ordered wine.

Singsaker waited until they'd finished eating. Then he told her what he'd decided.

"I'm going to ask for a leave of absence."

Siri looked at him, but she didn't seem the least bit surprised.

"I can't take it anymore. And I'm not functioning the way I should."

"You're planning to go and find her, aren't you?"

"The thought did cross my mind."

"And do you realize that you might not like what you find?"

"I still need to look for her. We had something going, the two of us."

"I know you did."

"It can't just end this way."

"How long are you going to be on sick leave?"

"With this thigh wound? A few weeks. With this head? At least a year if I talk to the right doctors. But I'm not going to take sick leave. I've already talked to Brattberg. She's giving me time off without pay. I have money. And to be honest, I'm tired of being sick."

Afterward, he went home and straight to bed. He knew that if he just lay there long enough and wrestled with his thoughts hard enough, he'd be able to handle it. And when that happened, when sleep finally took him, he knew what he was going to dream about: her.

They had to meet again. Anything else seemed impossible.

Elise Edvardsen was awakened by a door slamming. She went out to the front hall and looked outside. Had Julie gone out in the middle of the night and left the door open to slam in the wind?

No, there were no footprints in the snow outside.

She closed the door and turned to go back to bed. But outside the bedroom she stopped, aware of the anxiety that hadn't left her even after their daughter returned home. In fact, it almost seemed worse now.

Then she moved down the hallway just as she'd done on that first terrible morning when her whole world had been turned upside down. She opened the door to her daughter's room with the same paralyzing feeling that she'd had on that day.

But now she saw Julie's head resting on her pillow. Maybe she was asleep. Maybe she was just pretending to be asleep.

Elise Edvardsen breathed a sigh of relief, even though she knew the reprieve was only temporary. Her worries would come back as soon as she crawled into her own bed and lay down next to her husband. That was how her nights were now, after Julie had come back to them. She would lie awake more than she slept. She had the worst thoughts about what her daughter must have endured, and it would take her most of each morning to put these images out of her mind.

Strangely enough, she thought all this worrying might have made her stronger. Better able to tackle the difficulties that lay ahead. But she wasn't sure. She wasn't sure about anything.

37

A country manor outside of Copenhagen, July 1767

Cowslip, almond flowers, cat's foot, blue violets."

She recited the names of the flowers she'd gathered on her way in. When she reached the house, she put all of them in a small vase and took it over to the desk. She had made up her mind. She would write to her father, Søren Engel, and tell him who her chosen one really was. It didn't matter that her betrothed had forbidden her to reveal his identity. Or that he said he was happy with his life as Christian Wingmark, as a lutist and troubadour, and that he would never demand his rightful place.

Before she began to write the letter, she sat and daydreamed about the last time she'd seen him.

He had come to seek her out at Ringve, where her father had sent her before she was to continue on to Copenhagen. They slipped out into the meadow together and did the same thing they'd done when they'd met there in March. Then they lay still, and he told her. He was seven years old when he was aboard a ship that went down during a storm. They hadn't been far from land, and he'd grabbed hold of a mast that was floating in the waves. After he drifted ashore somewhere along the Swedish coast, he'd simply started walking.

That may have been the greatest mistake of his life. If he'd stayed on the shore, someone would have found him and realized he'd come from the sunken ship. Instead he'd walked inland.

He remembered everything now. All the years in the hospital.

If only he'd remembered back then. Something had struck him on the head when the ship sank, and it took years before he could recall who he was, and by then he was no longer a rich man's son from Trondheim, heir to the Ringve estate, son of her father's best friend. He was the boy who didn't know who he was. A fool. A solitary soul without hope.

He'd arrived in Stockholm as a poor young man. But he could play musical instruments and compose songs. It was his mother who had taught him to play the lute when he was a small boy. At the hospital, he had borrowed an instrument from the pastor who came every week to teach him his letters. Even though he may have forgotten everything else, he hadn't forgotten the music. And it was how he was able to earn his living for years. Until at last fate had brought him back to Trondheim and the Ringve estate and to her. When he arrived at the estate in March, everything had come back to him.

And then he knew who he was.

But no one had recognized him. How could they? They had spent almost twenty years trying to reconcile themselves to his death.

I will tell them now, she thought to herself. *If they know the truth, then we can get married.* Her father couldn't possibly imagine a better husband for her than the heir to Ringve, the estate they had visited so often. Then she wouldn't have to stay here in Denmark, far away from him, and he could live the life that had been intended for him. Everything would be good. And besides, she was worried. She didn't know what her father might do as long as he was ignorant of her sweetheart's true origins. He had been so furious to learn about the child she was carrying, and about their first meeting in March. There was no alternative. They had to be told.

And so she began writing the letter.

Trondheim, July 1767

Søren Engel read the letter from his daughter in silence. Then he got up and gave orders for his horse to be saddled and brought from the stable. He rode at once to Ringve Manor, where the captain received him. Engel handed him the letter and watched as he read it.

"Can this be true?" asked Engel.

"I thought there was something familiar about his face," said the captain, visibly shaken. "I thought there was something about his face when he fell."

Engel stood there without uttering another word. He couldn't help thinking about the last thing Nils Bayer had said to him: "There are many different ways to achieve justice."

Had the police chief somehow known about this? His thoughts were abruptly cut short by the captain.

"What have we done?" he cried. "What have I done?"

"I think we have killed more than just the father of my daughter's unborn child," said Engel. "I fear that we have also killed your son."

Before Søren Engel rode back to town, he allowed Wessel to keep the letter, as if it might offer him some consolation. The captain then summoned one of the carpenters who was working on the estate at that time. They were busy putting in new paneling in the drawing room.

"Take this letter," he said, "and put it inside the wall. I don't want to see it ever again."

"But if you don't want to see it, wouldn't it be better to burn it?"

"It's impossible for a person to burn away his sins," said the captain. "He has to live with them, no matter how dreadful they might be."

The carpenter cast a frightened look at the man, wondering whether the lord of the manor had gone mad. Then he took the letter and left.

AFTERWORD: A FEW WORDS ABOUT THE NOVEL AND THE HISTORY OF TRONDHEIM

The story about Nils Bayer in eighteenth-century Trondheim is, of course, just as much fiction as the story about Odd Singsaker's hunt for Julie Edvardsen's kidnapper. Most of the people described in the novel's sections set in 1767 are pure fabrication. But what's true is that back then Trondheim was a small town of barely five thousand inhabitants, and the upper class consisted of very few people, many of whom are still well known today. These individuals had an enormous influence on the history of the city; it's nearly impossible to imagine a Trondheim of 1767 without them, and for that reason they could not be entirely excluded from this novel. In *Death Song*, I've chosen to approach this challenge in two ways.

First, even though all the key players in the story are fictional, they do possess some traits that I've borrowed from real people. Trondheim was the first town in Norway to have a police chief, and that occurred as early as 1686. In 1767, Trondheim's police chief was Søren Madsen Næbell (who lived until 1780). Like Nils Bayer, he paid far too much for this official post, and subsequently had constant money woes. He was also a quarrelsome man who clashed with many of the other public authorities in town. But unlike Bayer, there are no indications that he had any sort of drinking problem. On the contrary, he was a highly enterprising and moral police officer who did much to shape and elevate the status of the police force in Trondheim.

The wealthy gentleman Søren Engel was not closely modeled after a real person, unlike Nils Bayer, although his name bears a similarity to that of the far from impoverished Thomas Angell (1692–1767). Angell was somewhat older than Engel, and in reality he died in Trondheim the same year in which the story takes place. He is still known today for having willed his entire fortune to the city's poor.

I should also mention that in 1767, Trondheim had a town physician by the name of Robertus Stephanus Henrici (1715–1781). He had very little in common with the novel's Dr. Fredrici except for the fact that during certain periods he had financial problems, and he was very generous about giving medicine to those who needed it in town. The pastor at the hospital church was a Sami man named Andreas Porsanger (1735–1780). The Wessel family did own the Ringve estate, but in 1767 there was no Preben Wessel whose son had gone missing.

I also included a number of historical figures in the background of my story. For instance, the founders of the Royal Norwegian Scientific Society were Bishop Johan Ernst Gunnerus (1718–1773), Chancellor Gerhard Schøning (1722–1780), and State Councilor Peter Frederik Suhm (1728–1798). In addition, the founder of the newspaper *Adresseavisen* was Martinus Nissen (1744–1795).

The geography of eighteenth-century Trondheim is documented in several excellent maps. And so the town in which Nils Bayer finds himself is quite similar to the one that actually existed in 1767. However, back then there was no tavern called the Hoppa in Ila. At that time, Ila was a quite new and not very developed suburb. But toward the turn of the century and well into the 1800s, that part of town grew rapidly and gradually became known for its hostelries. One of the taverns that Nils Bayer visits does have its roots in real life. The inn at Brattøra was established in 1739 and during its first years was the ferryman's residence. Much later, the building was moved to the Trøndelag Folk Museum in Sverresborg, where it continues to serve as a pub under the name of the Tavern.

As far as the town's police chief is concerned, he did not live in the same place as Nils Bayer, nor was his office located in the same place as in the novel. And if Søren Engel had actually built a mansion in Midtbyen in 1767, he would have been the first to own one of the huge wooden mansions that today characterize the old section of Trondheim. The building known as Stiftsgården was finished in 1778, while Hornemannsgården was constructed a few years later.

I should also mention that in the eighteenth century no one spoke—much less wrote—the way they do in my story. If I had attempted to imitate speech patterns from the 1700s, the modern reader would have found the novel very hard to comprehend. Nevertheless, I've tried to include a few archaisms where appropriate. Bayer's free use of Latin and French phrases was originally inspired by what is perhaps one of the world's very first crime fiction stories—Maurits Christopher Hansen's novella *Mordet på Maskinbygger Roolfsen* (*The Murder of Machinist Roolfsen,* 1840), in which Latin and other foreign words abound. But it's also in keeping with the zeitgeist of the eighteenth century, which was an era when a learned man had to master three or four languages simply to keep up with the times.

WHERE EVIL LIES
Jørgen Brekke

*A story of obsession and murder that
transcends time – and place*

1528. A young Franciscan monk travels to Norway to collect
a set of scalpels from a barber surgeon with whom he shares a
dark obsession: the dissection of human corpses. The monk's
deadly legacy is a mysterious manuscript, the Book of John –
bound in human skin.

Nearly five hundred years later, it seems that the shocking
and ancient practice of flaying is experiencing a revival . . .

2010. Trondheim, Norway. Inspector Odd Singsaker is
leading the investigation into the death of Gunn Brita Dahle,
a university librarian who was brutally flayed – and the theft of
the priceless Book of John. The prime suspect is a security guard
at the library, who was once an academic high-flyer but now lives
an isolated existence following the unexplained disappearance
of his wife and son some years back.

2010. Richmond, Virginia. When the curator of the
Edgar Allan Poe museum suffers the same fate as Dahle,
US Detective Felicia Stone flies to Norway to join Singsaker
in the hunt for a serial killer. The more they delve into the
past, the more sinister their discoveries become . . .

The key to the psychopath's next move is held within
the manuscript. But can they track it down and work out
the clues before another person has to die?